MY STARS SHINE DARKLY

BOOK 1 OF THE SATORI CHRONICLES

AMY SUNDBERG

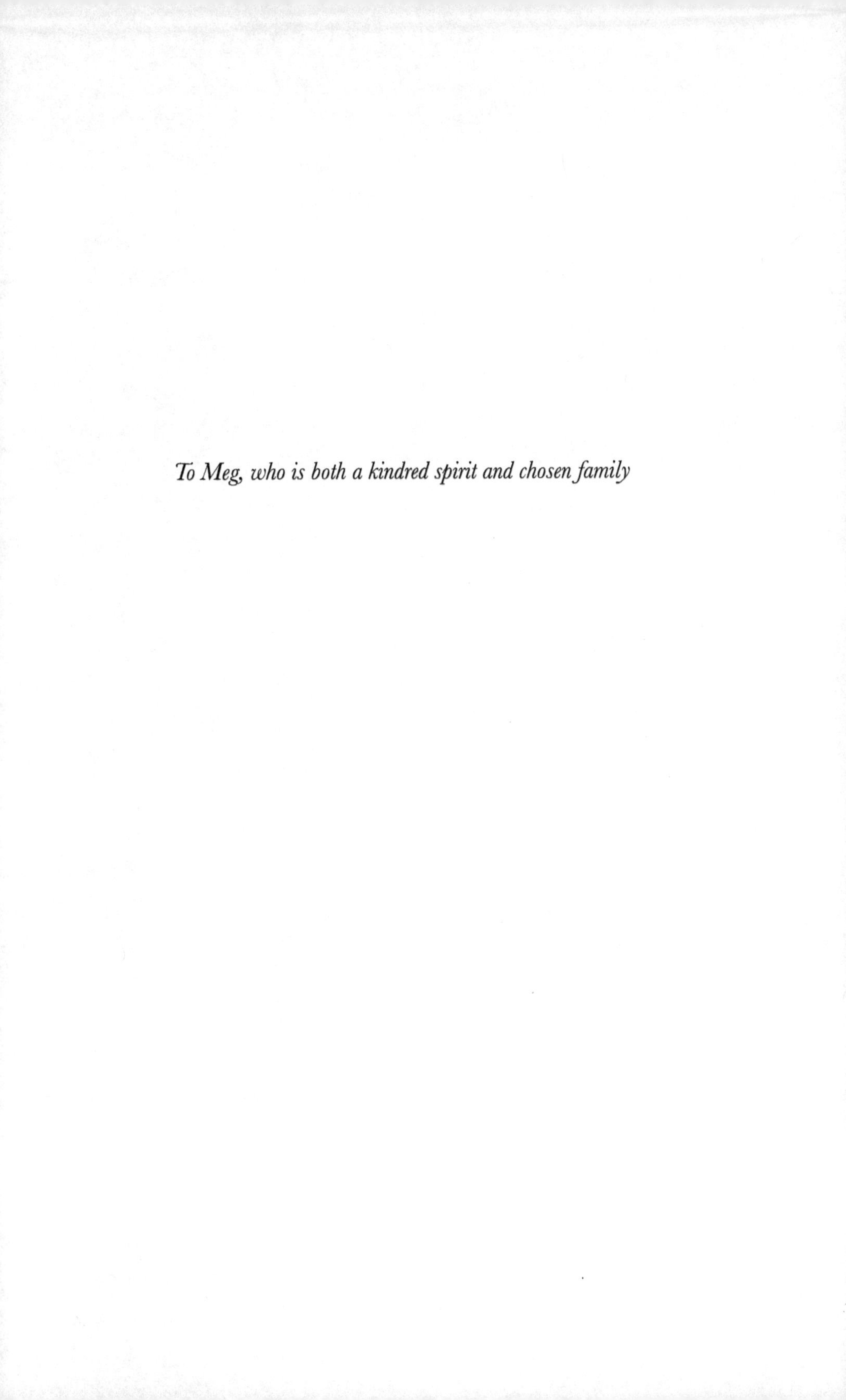

To Meg, who is both a kindred spirit and chosen family

"But I hate to hear you talking so, like a fine gentleman and as if women were all fine ladies, instead of rational creatures. We none of us expect to be in smooth water all our days."
	—Jane Austen, *Persuasion*

"My stars shine darkly over me."
	—William Shakespeare, *Twelfth Night*

CHAPTER 1

*P*roper young ladies don't go to the races.

But I love speeder bike racing, and I want to see my brother Leo when he finally crosses the finish line in first place.

I always say *when* in his hearing, but I really mean *if.* Leo isn't great at racing. He's too conservative when he should push harder, and then he's too reckless to make up the difference. In our practice races at home, I beat him almost every time. But if proper young ladies don't go to the races, they definitely can't race themselves. Even the fact I know how is a closely guarded secret.

Some days this secret chafes against me, but today is Race Day, and due to a particularly devious plan of mine, this proper young lady is right in the thick of things, running an entirely admirable charity booth, the first and only at Race Day. We started it just this season, and so far it's been a surprise success. We've raised consider-able funds for charity, and I get to sneak away and watch Leo race. Everybody wins.

I direct the hired young men to hang the red and white bunting and the new sign I stayed up late last night crafting. Tantalizing smells drift from adjacent booths, selling all different kinds of pasta smothered in red or white or cheese sauce, fresh bread sticks with olive oil, little cakes coated with generous amounts of pastel frosting. And wine, everywhere wine of every variety imaginable: red, white, sparkling, frozen, some mixed with water, some mixed with something stronger for the grown men to drink.

Gianna Costa, my partner at the booth, fusses over her qualpad, making sure it's connected to the net and ready to accept customer payments. The Doge of Neopolitan's model eldest daughter, she used to be my best friend. Our families had been neighbors out in the country, our fathers so close I grew up calling her father Zio Roberto. But those days are long over, and it's easy to forget we used to like each other.

Nevertheless, she agreed to my plan without much fuss, which makes me wonder if she secretly feels as stifled as I do in San Marco. I can't deny its beauty: the graceful arching bridges over its network of canals, its gorgeously manicured public parks, and its rich tradition of skillful artisans. But it's also a city replete with rigid hierarchies, judgmental media, and rules and limitations in every direction. As far as I can tell, there's no real escape from that anywhere on the planet of Sanctum.

Whatever Gianna's reasons, I would never have been able to convince our parents to allow us to do this without her, so I have to be grateful, even if it sticks in my throat. The city version of Gianna is prim and proper and popular and perfect: all the things I'm not. I hate owing her anything.

The crowds swell as we finish setting up, and as soon as we open for business, a long line forms at our window. Gianna gives a fixed smile to a male customer as she hands over a bright red rosette. The ruffles on her dark gray dress cover even more neck than mine does, and when she doesn't think anyone is looking, she obsessively strokes her black gloves as if assuring herself her perfect skin will never be touched. She must be as hot as I am, but not a single bead of sweat betrays her discomfort. I have to wipe my own damp neck every few minutes with a clean handkerchief.

We're doing particularly brisk business today due to the new innovation—my idea, of course—of selling homemade baked goods as well as the multi-colored rosettes. People are hungry on Race Day, and even if I started this endeavor with ulterior motives, I still want it to be successful. All the proceeds go to the poor children of San Marco, for shoes and clothes and better nutrition and education. And the money always runs out long before growing children's need for bigger shoes.

I actually baked some of these treats myself, the muffins and the sweet breads, under the direction of our cook, but I would never admit such a thing. Not in polite company. Proper young ladies don't spend time in their kitchens.

Our new treats have proven to be a huge draw to our booth. I've been able to talk several customers, stopping for a delicious scone, into buying a rosette as well. A quick look at the numbers shows we've increased our sales over the last race day by thirty-six percent. Not bad for our first foray into a new market sector.

I turn a dazzling smile onto my next customer, whom I recognize as the man who runs the iced cakes booth a few spots down. We haven't actually been introduced, but I've made a point to learn all my neighbors' names. "Signor Alfonsi, isn't it a fine day? What can I get for you? We have two flavors of scones today, lemon currant and wild blueberry. Or we have some particularly delicious strawberry sea salt muffins, if that tempts you?"

He doesn't look like he agrees with me about the fineness of the day, and at my mention of the baked goods, his scowl deepens, emphasizing his jowls. "You don't have a permit for selling food," he grinds out. He knows who I am, and he doesn't quite meet my eyes. "I ought to turn you into the authorities."

I nod as if he's made a valid point. "I understand your concern, Signor Alfonsi, but if you read our permit, I think you'll find it covers both our souvenirs *and* our refreshments." I'd made sure of that before selling Gianna on the idea.

He ignores what I said. "It isn't proper, you young signorinas being here on a Race Day with no supervision."

I feel my smile becoming stiffer. "We're here representing the San Marcos chapter of the Ladies' Aid Society. Everyone in the community is familiar with our good works. And Signorina Costa's respected nurse is with us, as you can see." I nod to where the old woman is drowsing at the back of the booth.

"It isn't proper," he repeats. He looks around as if to get outside approval, but no one is paying attention to our little altercation. Not yet.

Except Gianna. She has an uncanny ability to sense anything that threatens her reputation. It's part of why she's no longer any fun. She digs an elbow into my ribs. "See?" she hisses. "I told you. Why make trouble when we have a system that works?"

"I'll take care of it," I whisper back.

"We can't afford a scene." She jabs me in the ribs again. "Our baked goods are competition for him. Just give him what he wants."

Signor Alfonsi stands back with his arms folded, smirking. He might not be able to hear Gianna, but he can guess the gist of what she's saying. I point at the screen. "Thirty-six percent. That's the increase in today's sales. And he doesn't have a legitimate grievance against us."

She sighs. "No one minds the rosettes. They're pretty and patriotic. What good is an increase in profits if our parents make us shut down the booth?"

I hate her both because she's right and because she's better at playing the game than I am. I come up with new ideas like selling baked goods that shouldn't cause problems but inevitably do. Gianna, on the other hand, has an unerring instinct for doing exactly what she can get away with and not a pinch more. She looks so innocent with her wide blue eyes and honey-colored hair, usually woven into an elaborate up-do. But she's much smarter than most people give her credit for.

She plays up her angelic appearance now, pushing me aside to deal with Signor Alfonsi personally. I can't bear to listen to the tripe she'll spout to satisfy him. We still have half the baked goods we've brought to sell, and now we'll take them all home with us to rot in our overflowing pantries. No, I'll bring them to the Aids' main office to be delivered to needy families. But even so, I feel beaten. Every innovation I introduce either fails or gets shot down before we even try.

The booth feels claustrophobic. Another trickle of sweat slides down my back. Gianna doesn't need my help selling a few more rosettes. She already has Signor Alfonsi smiling and nodding, and in a horrifying development, she's handing him free baked goods. I can't take it anymore. I yank my apron over my head and ball it up, throwing it into a corner before I slip out the back exit. Gianna doesn't even glance my way as I make my escape.

I pull a hood over my elaborately coiffed hair in spite of the heat and sink into the anonymity of the masses. Many of the people around me are young and poor, but there are plenty of older people here too, and some are even men of property. The finest families of Neopolitan have their young bucks racing this afternoon in between the professional races. A few of them might even go pro someday on a lark. Proper young gentlemen are allowed a lot more leeway than proper young ladies.

I see a few people I know, colleagues of Father's in the Senate, but I fade into the groups of revelers around me to avoid being seen. I push through the throngs to the stands around the track. The race before Leo's is still in progress, and everyone is standing, cheering their favorite racers and booing their rivals. Plastic cups of wine slap together in good luck toasts, sloshing their fragrant liquid onto the ground. Most of the men I might know are down in the boxes in front; up here cheerful celebration prevails. Some of the women yell along with the men. A group of bearded men right behind me launch into a popular drinking song, and I find myself humming along.

If my parents saw me right now, they'd drop dead in horror, but this moment is all mine. I press my body against the railing and look down at the oval track with its high barrier walls. The opalescent sheen of the safety force field shimmers in the sun.

A group of four speeder bikes leads the pack, looking like they're engaged in a choreographed dance. They bob up and down like apples at one of the fall festivals, trying to prevent their opponents from passing them while keeping to the tightest possible curve. Sometimes they lean so far to the left it's a wonder the riders can stay on their bikes. The screams increase in volume as the race moves to its conclusion. I know no one is looking at me, so for once I can yell as loud as I want. No one meeting me in Mother's drawing room would guess I am capable of such things.

Just as the bikes round the final corner, one bike shoots beneath the frontrunner, crossing the finish line a hair's breadth before him. The crowd's cheers become so loud I can feel them vibrating through my body, and I scream right along with them. The replay flashes on the huge screens above us, its repetition not removing an iota of excitement from the moment.

My hood falls back, letting the sun beat onto my unprotected face, but I don't care. I shove my fist into the air in rhythm with the other spectators, singing the victory chant for the winner.

If only my father hadn't been elected Senator nine years ago—the same time that Zio Roberto became Doge—and moved us all to the city with him, things would never have gotten so desperate. I wouldn't be here now, screaming my lungs out in an effort to carve out a little piece of life for myself. It's becoming more and more difficult to remember who I am.

EVENTUALLY THE CROWD CALMS DOWN, and the young woman next to me offers me a swig of red wine. As I wipe my mouth afterwards, I notice her staring at my hair, white ribbons laced through the thick dark strands, symbolizing my purity. I pull the hood back over my head with a jerk and move further down the stands, away from the question in her eyes.

I see my brother near the starting line, even from this distance. The sun reflects off his flashy golden suit. He's known as *Ragazzo d'Oro*, and everyone jokes he's trying to blind his opponents to get an edge. He always laughs at this sally, his straight white teeth flashing against his olive skin, even though I know he secretly hates it. He has to get attention somehow, for the family's sake, but Leo would rather be in his workroom creating the masks he loves. For a while it seemed like he might love racing too: he used to practice with me every day, but lately he simply shrugs and makes excuses. His heart isn't in it, even as he smiles up at the crowd.

I have the same smile, the same dimple on my right cheek. We are twins. He's my little brother by twenty-one minutes, a fact I never let him forget. It's all I have to flaunt; he gets everything else I want. We bear an uncanny resemblance to each other for fraternal twins, enough to make Mother uncomfortable. She frets that a boy and a girl shouldn't look so much alike. Leo should be taller than me, and broader. I should have more curves. Everything about me should be soft, and everything about Leo should be hard. But the truth is more ambiguous.

Mother does her best, but we would have exactly the same smile if I hadn't learned how to control mine so finely. Where Leo's is unreserved, mine is restrained. Where his is bold, mine must be demure. Where he shows all his beautiful teeth, I have to keep mine hidden or be admonished by my mother. "Sienna," she'll say in a voice of long suffering, "why are you baring your teeth like a wild animal? You'll be the death of me yet." It sounds like a joke, but given the actual state of her health, it isn't funny.

My brother holds his helmet under his arm and waves, pretending to enjoy his moment in the spotlight. The spectators love him even though he never wins, and his nickname punctuates their dull roar. I can tell he hears it because his smile stretches even wider, his eyes scanning the stands. Then he turns away to put on his helmet, tests its fastenings like I always remind him to do, and shuts the visor.

He has a mediocre spot in the line-up, a few rows back and in the middle. Last time he'd been closer to the inside, but he's dealt with worse positions. He sits astride his bike, fussing with his gloves, revving his motor, distracting himself from his terrible nerves. I'm the only one who knows he used to throw up after every race. That was last year though; he seems to have moved past his post-race nerves, just like I told him he would.

The lights above the racers start to flash: red, yellow, then *green*, and the racers kick up off the ground and shoot forward, jockeying for position. Leo spends the first few laps gradually improving on his starting place, creeping closer to the inside. He passes one bike, two, then a third. He's solidly in the middle but unlikely to do better.

I look away from him to watch the frontrunners. Stefano and Antonio lead the pack as usual, but they're trailing behind a bike I don't recognize. A new racer? I wonder why I haven't heard about him. He's all in black, uniform and bike, and his helmet has a single yellow insignia on the back. He's an exceptional rider, moving with his bike as if it's an extension of his own body, smooth and controlled. He doesn't seem affected by the normal stunts these amateur racers pull. Antonio shifts his engine up to an ear-splitting buzz, a trick I've seen him use to disarm new opponents before, but the rider continues to calmly execute his skillful turns, just enough acceleration to keep a bike's length between him and his opponents, not enough to cause him to lose control or move further out in the turn. He has enough of a lead he doesn't have to defend on the vertical: unless he screws up, he's got this race in the bag.

But with so many laps to go, the odds are he will screw up, and everyone—his fellow racers and the fans up in the stands—knows it.

A few moments later, he laps Leo, and the screens show the rude gesture he makes as he maneuvers by for the whole world to see.

I groan out loud. Leo is so easy to rattle. And why'd this new guy have to taunt him anyway? It's not as if Leo is a threat to him. Maybe it's because of his ostentatious golden suit. Maybe this guy has heard of *Ragazzo d'Oro* and wants to make an example of him.

Maybe he's just a *stronzo*.

Now Leo is trying to catch him. It's tight maneuvering with Antonio and Stefano right on the rude racer's tail, and I can imagine how furious they must be that Leo, with no chance whatsoever of winning, is getting in their way. But he's only half a bike's distance behind the mystery rider, and he's slowly closing that gap. If only he weren't accomplishing that by driving recklessly. But I know Leo, and I can see him cutting his corners awfully close.

I get caught up in the drama of the moment in spite of myself, rooting for my brother under my breath. "Come on, Leo, just wait, look for your opening and wait for it." I want him to show this newcomer he can't waltz in here and mock a Tascioni like that.

And then the new racer makes a critical error: he accelerates too much into one of the turns and has to go slightly wide. Leo pumps on his overdrive to take the inside spot, and for a moment it looks like he has it. "Yes!" I'm yelling now. "You show him!"

But Leo's accelerating too fast into the curve and he loses control of the bike. I see the critical moment when the bike tilts that extra degree too far and smashes into the track's wall. The bike, with my brother glued onto it, ricochets off the wall and onto the ground, a long skid that almost entangles Stefano, who I know will have words with Leo after the race. The bike slides all the way to the outside wall. I'm not worried for my brother's health—the track's force fields will protect him from the worst of the impact—but I am worried for his spirits. He's inured himself to losing, but he hates not finishing.

I turn my attention back to the leader of the race. He's used Leo's wreck to pull even further ahead and easily beats the others across the finish line. He stands up and puts both arms in the air in a victory pose as his bike coasts to a stop. His name thunders over the track: "Signor Enoch Royse, winner!" His face fills the screen above our heads: his skin is extremely pale, as though he's never been out in the sun, and his hair is so blond it's almost white, flowing down past his shoulders. He's baring his teeth in a manly grimace.

I don't know who Enoch Royse is, but I already know I don't like him one bit.

CHAPTER 2

By the time I return home, Leo has been back for hours. After the race I'd hurried back to the booth, only to watch our sales plummet to their former levels without the boost from the baked goods. I'll never buy another iced cake from Signor Alfonsi, no matter how tasty they are. Then, after returning with Gianna to the Doge's Mansion, a great stone edifice on the Grand Canal, I took my own family's amphicar to bring the remaining baked goods to the Aid Society on the other side of the city for distribution. When I walk into the spacious grand foyer of our house, I am cranky, tired, and sticky from my time in the stifling booth.

I peel off my gloves with relief as I run lightly up the main marble steps and up the second flight of stairs to the nursery wing where my brother and I sleep. My heart always gets a little lighter when I enter the designated playroom, its walls decorated with colorful murals of the handmade masks San Marco is famous for. A large version of our family tree is painted on one long wall, tracing our lineage back to the Founders who first immigrated to Sanctum from Earth. My old tea set still sits on a small table in the large side alcove along with Leo's rocking horse Champ, who I'd always ridden more in spite of the large collection of dolls I was supposed to care for. Doors lead to each of our bedrooms, the VR rec room, and the small supply closet Leo has turned into his workshop.

Leo lounges with a bag of ice on his face, feet up on the ottoman, watching replays of the race. His right pointer finger is in a blue plastic splint, and his short curly hair is particularly messy. "Don't wallow," I say. Then to the projection, "End program." Leo could bring it right back up, of course, but instead he groans and leans back on the plush sofa.

I sink into my favorite wing chair and begin unlacing my boots. "You all right?"

"I'll live." He moves the ice so I can see the dark swelling around his left eye. "That Enoch character left me with quite a prize." He frowns at his finger. "Doctor says the splint stays for at least three weeks. What a disaster."

"Or a well-deserved break?" Leo is obsessed with making masks. I still remember the first time we made masks together when we were six years old. Mine collapsed into a soggy mess; Leo's fit him perfectly and he spent an entire week painting and perfecting it. As soon as he finished, he began making a new one, and he's never stopped since.

He grimaces. "It means I'm stuck with the masks I've already completed for the Mask Maker's Festival. I was planning on crafting at least five more."

"Good thing you don't need the funds." I kick off my unlaced boot with relief and start on the other one. Both my feet ache from standing so long. "Who was that other racer, anyway?"

Leo shrugs. "I didn't stick around to meet him."

"You let him rattle you."

"Yeah, well, he's an arrogant *cazzo*. I don't have to meet him to know that. Stefano says he's the son of the new ambassador from Providence." He makes a face like he's tasted something bad. No one on Sanctum likes the Providentials; they arrived a generation after the rest of the original settlers, they're the only nation that speaks a different language, and everyone agrees they can't be trusted.

"All the more reason to beat him." My other foot is free. I

unbutton my high collar, then reach around awkwardly to unzip my dress and slip out of it altogether, leaving it in a puddle on the floor. Still clad in camisole and pantaloons, I lean back with a sigh. It's nice to be able to move more freely.

If our parents walked in, they would be shocked by what they saw. They have no problems with Leo wearing his comfortable brown trousers and an undershirt inside the house. They won't even scold about his black eye. They approve of his racing, certainly more than they'd approve of his mask-making habit, something a scion of the Tascionis should never stoop to master. But for me, modesty trumps comfort every time.

Leo replaces the ice on his eye. "My head hurts," he complains. "Entering the racing league this season was a mistake."

I pop back to an upright position. "You love racing."

He gives a dry laugh. "No, Sienna, *you* love racing. I'm just along for the ride."

I scoff. "Don't be ridiculous. Besides, the guys would give you so much *merda* if you gave it up now."

"Why do you think I keep showing up at the track? And don't let Mother hear you talk like that."

He's falling into his melancholy like he always does after a race. It's my job to jar him out of it. "Oh really? Are you her spy now?" I pounce onto the sofa next to him, reaching out to tickle his sensitive underarms.

Usually he attacks me in return until we both dissolve into giggles, but this time he swats me with his ice, holding his injured finger carefully away from me. "Not now, Sienna. I'm serious, I'm not in the mood."

This can't just be about losing the race. "What's the problem? Spill."

He moans. "It's nothing."

"I don't believe you."

A pause, and then he whispers, "Don't tell Father."

I'm shocked he has to ask. "Twin pact, remember?"

Our loyalty to each other had always been understood, but our twin pact had become formalized the summer we were seven. One day Father caught a glimpse of me running into the forest wearing a pair of Leo's pants when Leo and I were supposed to be memorizing a psalm. He waited until that evening, then accused me at the dinner table, his usually remote face flushed with anger. I'd known he was going to spank me to get his point across, and the force with which he'd let those hits fall…I quailed at the thought. But Leo lied and said it had been him in the forest. I thought he'd be spanked instead since skipping psalm practice was quite an infraction, but Father just laughed. "Boys will be boys," he told Mother.

That night Leo had crawled into my bed and held my hand. "I won't let anyone hurt you," he whispered fiercely. "Twin pact." Mother and Father didn't know a quarter of the things we got up to after that. We'd lie for one another without a second thought.

"Yeah, yeah." His body relaxes, and I snuggle into his heat, being careful to avoid his injured finger. "It's just…I have this big oral test in civics. If I fail, I could flunk out. You've got to help me, Si. Can you imagine what Father would say if that happened?"

It doesn't bear thinking about. I'd known Leo was slacking, but I hadn't realized it was this bad. And while Father might go easy on Leo, flunking out would be completely unacceptable for his only son. "When is it?" We'd have to start an intensive study program immediately.

"Tuesday."

"Oh." Only a few days to correct course. "Well, I'm sure you can learn the basics by then. Your civics class isn't very advanced, if you don't mind me saying so. How far into the textbook have you read?" He makes an indistinct mumble. "Have you read *any* of it?"

"No. I was busy making masks for the festival, and then…." He shrugs.

I can't help being irritated at how cavalier he is about his education, something I would die to have. "Leo! You knew this would catch up with you eventually."

He puts his head in his hands, wincing when he touches his tender eye. "I've been copying from Stefano Palermo's tests all year. I didn't know there'd be an oral exam: Professor Buccho and I alone in a room together, talking about civics." He makes a gagging sound. "He makes it sound like a casual little chat, but it won't take him long to figure out how little I know."

I try to calm him down. "You can probably fake it, right? You know a lot about our government just from growing up around Father."

He shakes his head. "No, *you* do, but I filter it out as much as possible. You know how much I hate that stuff."

I look at him in genuine shock. "But you're going to have to follow in Father's footsteps one day."

He moans again. "And I'm going to be absolutely hopeless at it. All I want is to win an apprenticeship with one of the mask maker masters."

"Father will never allow it, and you know it." A Tascioni becoming a lowly artisan? Our parents would rather see us die than shame the family name like that.

He hangs his head. "You think I don't know that? That's why every second is so precious. I don't have time to study, I have to use my time to make as many masks as possible before the inevitable."

His words bruise my heart. We're both trapped in our own ways. "If only I could take the test for you," I joke.

Leo laughs the way I knew he would. "I wish you could. You'd probably get full marks without even trying." He hits the back of his head against the couch. "Why am I so stupid? I don't know what I was thinking, falling so far behind."

We both know he'd been busy dreaming about his masks. "Start reading, Leo. And read fast."

But instead he glares at me from underneath his ice pack.

I DRESS FOR DINNER. Another gown, this one light pink because Mother says light colors highlight my youth. I enter the dining room first, right after the gong rings, and stand by my chair, careful to hold shoulders down and chin up. The massive table, handcrafted from a wood so dark it's almost black, dominates the long, narrow room. A large chandelier crafted locally from purple and clear glass draws the eye, and our elaborate table service is laid out in its full glory. Lizabetta has told me the servants measure the placement of each piece with a ruler to ensure the proper perfection.

Mother arrives a moment later, clad in the heavier and darker evening gown her age and station require. She gives me a small nod of approval and stands by her own chair. We wait in silence, glow balls of white and yellow circling above us to add a dignified ambiance. The table is set with precision: two goblets at my father's place at the head, one goblet everywhere else, golden linen folded into crisp triangles, simple white china with golden rims, crystalline cutlery that is all the rage.

My father strides into the room, cravat folded neatly, beard carefully trimmed and waxed, his aquiline nose dominating his thin face. He's wearing a new coat tailored to showcase his powerful shoulders. Two servants follow him to pull out Mother's and my chairs. Father surveys the table and his family for a long moment before sitting. We follow his lead. A servant pours wine into his goblet just as Leo hurries into the room, his cravat askew, his eye looking even angrier and more swollen than before. He stands erect next to his chair at my father's right hand. "I apologize for my tardiness."

There is a tense pause before Father chuckles. "Sit down, sit down, and tell us the story behind that eye."

I bridle in spite of myself. When I'm late to dinner, I remain standing by my chair. I do not eat, I do not drink, and I cannot snack later. If I complain to Mother, she tells me fasting is good for both my character and my figure, and that's the end of it.

The servants bring out the soup course as my brother tells the story of his aborted race while awkwardly using his spoon with his injured hand. He makes himself sound like a good-natured underdog, beloved by the people. But when he mentions the name of his rude opponent, Father stops him.

"Enoch Royse? The new Providential ambassador's oldest son?

Oh, that's very interesting." He puts down his spoon. "You didn't antagonize the boy, did you, Leo?"

Leo presses his lips together. "Of course not, Father. *He* antagonized *me*. He was unsportsmanlike."

Father shrugs off the criticism. "Any citizen of Neopolitan would know that, but we can't expect the same behavior from foreigners."

Mother pats her lips with her napkin. "I'm calling on his mother the day after tomorrow. Sienna will accompany me, of course."

"I didn't realize there was a new Providential ambassador," I say. "Wasn't the last one only stationed here for a year and a half?"

Mother raises a discrete eyebrow at me for daring to volunteer an observation, but Father doesn't seem to notice. "That's very astute of you, Sienna. In light of the big news, Providence decided to recall their ambassador and send someone in higher favor with their Supreme Leader. His cousin, I believe. They grew up together and are very close."

Mother gives the tiniest shake of her head in my direction, but Leo is busy gulping down his soup and I can't resist. "What big news?"

"Sienna, do we need to review conversational etiquette for young ladies?" Mother asks. She has set her spoon in its finished position even though her bowl is almost full.

But Father intervenes. "No, no, Sophia, a little curiosity is natural." Mother bows her head, but her lips are pursed. She thinks Father overindulges me. "In the privacy of the home, of course," Father adds, giving me a sharp look.

I know better than to push for more. "Of course," I agree.

"We're announcing it to the press tomorrow," he continues. "It's the Satori."

I smooth my face into an expression of bland interest. I'm fascinated by everything having to do with the Satori, but it wouldn't do for my parents to know that. Leo raises his good eyebrow at me. He's gotten an earful of my speculations ever since the Satori came into orbit around our planet six months ago. And when Father accompanied Zio Roberto to Fidelium, the planetary capitol, to engage in a series of diplomatic meetings with them last month, it was all I could do to restrain myself from peppering Father with questions upon his return.

The Satori arrived in a pair of far-ranging starships, having travelled thirty-one years from their home planet New Honshu in an adjoining solar system. They'd chosen Sanctum as their first stop and had asked permission to send down a diplomatic mission. The press seemed unclear about what they wanted, repeating the reassuring statement they were a peaceful exploratory space-faring race. Father undoubtedly knows more, but he's been keeping his mouth shut.

But I'd finally broken Gianna down into a giggled admission. "The women wear pants, just like the men," she'd whispered, shocked by her own audacity in even admitting this was possible. "They're a strange, decadent race. Their technology far surpasses ours, and I heard some of them have bio-engineered enhancements. Like"—she licked her lips—"unnatural beauty, strange eye colors, and stuff like that. Maybe even tails!"

I share her shock, but mine is tinged by curiosity. Bio-engineering is strictly forbidden by both the law and the Church, a rigid prescription no nation on Sanctum dares to flaunt. It was part of the international treaty under which human society on Sanctum had been formed so many generations ago. And when the founders of Providence had shown up a few generations late, all parties had allegedly been deeply relieved at their agreement on this point. It was crucial, Father likes to say, for all nations to agree on certain deeply held beliefs. It's why, in spite of occasional differences of opinion, we've never been dodged by war and chaos here the way our ancestors had been back on Earth.

And now here come the Satori, waltzing in to shake everything up. But I've seen photos of the Chief Diplomat and his wife, and they look just like us. Well, almost. The wife's skin tone is a deeper brown than most of the citizens of Neopolitan, but certainly not unusual on our world as a whole. And they are extremely good-looking. Media star good-looking. But in the photo the wife isn't wearing pants, there are no tails in evidence, and the speech of greeting their ambassador gave had been in fluent Gallo, expressing general positive sentiments with which everyone could agree.

"They have asked our permission to open an embassy in Neopolitan," Father continues after a pregnant pause. "This will be their first regional embassy."

He doesn't have to say more. It's a huge honor for the Satori to have asked us first, hence the new, more prestigious ambassador from Providence.

And maybe I'll finally get to meet a Satori myself.

"The Satori ambassador was very impressed by your father during their visit last month." Mother beams at Father. "It's a credit to him that they wish to have a presence here." She turns her laser focus on me. "And Sienna, I want you on your best behavior. I heard about your charity booth debacle today."

Oh no. "What debacle?" I try to replicate Gianna's innocent look, but it feels all wrong.

"What's this, Sophia?" Father frowns.

"Sienna decided to sell food at her charity booth along with the usual rosettes, and she vexed the local tradesmen."

"One local tradesman," I correct. "And our profits increased thirty-six percent before we were forced to cease sales."

Father shakes his head. "Sienna, you know when we agreed to this project of yours, we didn't mean for it to be a commercial endeavor. Charity work is all well and good in its place, but it's about piety and humility, not innovation. You know very well you don't have the temperament for responsibilities outside the domestic sphere."

I do! I want to scream. *I am capable of so much more than you can imagine. If you would only give me a chance!* But we've had this argument before. It never ends well, and we haven't even made it to the pasta course yet. Leo and I exchange a look, and I find myself wishing for the millionth time I had his opportunities. I can't trust myself to say anything, so I only nod and stare at my empty soup bowl.

"We'll need to make a superior impression on the Satori representatives," Mother continues. "Promise me you'll be especially careful of your conduct, Sienna, and speak to me if you have any doubts whatsoever about the proper thing to do. You've always been a bit... high-spirited."

She has called me far worse things. I nod and stay dutifully silent. Luckily the servants choose this moment to clear the soup course and bring in the gnocchi.

That's how I am forced to ensure my place in this family. By keeping my mouth shut.

CHAPTER 3

Mother gives Lizabetta special instructions regarding my clothing and hair for our visit to the new Providential ambassador's wife. I spend seventy minutes sitting ramrod straight in front of my vanity in my white frilly underclothes, Lizabetta curling and braiding and attaching small sparkling jewels to my hair, her white gloves folded neatly on the edge of the table. Her hair is thicker and curlier than mine, but she gets to tame it in a simple bun. It's one of the only simple things about her life, between meeting Mother's meticulous standards and sending most of her wages home to support four younger brothers and sisters.

Whenever I tell Lizabetta how pretty she is, with her rosy cheeks, long eyelashes, and neat ankles, she laughs and tells me I'm being absurd, but I can tell she likes the compliments. She doesn't get many of them in our household, and I know she can't afford to get married, not with so many hungry mouths already at home. She also can't afford to go to nursing school, a closely held dream she confessed to me once late at night.

When Lizabetta is finished, my head feels heavier than usual. If Mother has her way, I will be sculpted into perfection. I do my own makeup, snapping open my large mirrored case with relief. My newest day gown, baby blue with lots of handmade white lace at the collar and cuffs, makes me look like an infant at its christening. White boots and white gloves I'll struggle to keep clean finish the ensemble.

Ninety minutes for me to transform into a china doll. Meanwhile, Leo has been at school this entire time. I'd give my right pinkie for the chance to attend his classes, but I still read all his assigned texts. I remember my off-hand offer to take his looming oral exam in his place and imagine how I would make brilliant answers in the face of Professor Buccho's Socratic questioning. But Leo will do all right. He has to.

But when I emerge from my room into the playroom, the drapes are drawn across the entire long wall of windows and Leo is lounging on the couch watching a soap opera. "Classes canceled?" I ask.

He doesn't look at me. "Not feeling well," he mumbles. When I yank open one of the curtains, he winces, his face pale and sweaty. "Close it," he yelps. "Seriously, Sienna, I have the worst headache."

I do as he asks and then put my hand against his forehead. He is cool to the touch. "Are you sure you aren't faking?" I tease.

He pushes me away and shoves his head under a pillow. "Do you have to talk so loud? Go away and be fancy somewhere else."

I feel a pang of conscience. "Do you want anything? Tea? Bread with olive oil?"

"I can't work on my masks, my brains feel like they're being squeezed out of my head, and I'm going to flunk out tomorrow. So no, I don't want any tea."

I try not to take offense at his grumpiness, but I'm worried about him. He should be studying for tomorrow, not lounging around and complaining.

Mother is waiting for me in the grand foyer, a diminutive figure between two of the white marble columns, her foot tapping impatiently against the matching floor. A huge painting of a blindfolded lady Justice holding a scale is displayed in state behind her, greeting all our guests the moment they enter the house. The servants have to clean the white floor three times a day to keep it spotless.

Mother holds me at arm's length and reviews my appearance. "Next time you should use a lighter lip shade," she finally says. That's as close to approval as I'm likely to get. She hands me a light wrap and a ridiculous hat with plumes that add at least twenty centimeters to my height. "I expect you to be on your best behavior today." She gives this reminder every time we leave the house. As if I could ever forget.

We walk out into the bright sunlight and down the short flight of stairs to the house's private dock on the canal, where our luxury amphicar already waits next to the gondola we keep for festival days. I look back at the sandstone edifice of our house, hulking and golden, the windows glaring in the sunlight. The stern and impenetrable rectangle reminds me of a prison. There is nothing remotely soft about it.

As the amphicar pilots itself through the narrow canals of the city, Mother briefs me on the ambassador's wife. I've been learning English, the official language of Providence, but the entire Royse family speaks Gallo fluently, which is a relief. After a while I tune Mother out, nodding at appropriate intervals, and watch the city pass, drenched in the late morning sun. The amphicar buzzes gently through the water, the old buildings towering over us on either side of the canal. San Marco has a faded look during the day, painted the same pastel colors as Signor Alfonsi's iced cakes, green plants spilling from our signature glass planters on almost every windowsill and balcony, their vines weaving around wrought iron fixtures.

We navigate between other private amphicars, the public water-buses, and the occasional gondola, traveling underneath a series of bridges connecting the islands of our city, some low and heavy and iron, others pedestrian bridges that look like they're hung with strands of gold. And people everywhere: walking by the side of the canal, biking across the bridges, sitting on the decks and patios, children hanging from cheap open motorboats, fingers trailing in the water.

The new ambassador's residence is in an older fashionable neighborhood not far from ours. A good location, right on a canal so we don't have to take to surface streets or, worse still, walk through the tight warrens of alleyways that make up the heart of many of the larger islands. Our amphicar attaches to their dock, and as we disembark, a camerafly zooms next to us, buzzing in my ears until Mother stops it with a practiced swat. "Newsies," she says in disgust. "They don't understand the meaning of common decency." She gives a firm nod at her own wisdom as we prepare to make our entrance.

Ten minutes into the visit, everything is going exactly as I expected. A servant showed us into a typical San Marco sitting room: a window obscured by wispy curtains overlooks the front canal, and petite and delicately carved furniture suitable for females is pleasingly arranged, three embroidery frames at the ready. Two predictable needlework examples are displayed over the mantle: "Silence is golden" and "Blessed are the meek, for they shall inherit the earth."

Signora Royse is like the few other Providential women I've met: soft-spoken, dowdier than Neopolitans, skin so pale I wonder if she's ever been outside, and secure in her subtle superiority over Mother and myself. The strangest thing about her is the way she breaks off in the middle of a sentence to speak English in a high voice to her little dog, who is beribboned within an inch of her life. Mother humors Signora Royse with good grace; she's too important to insult. If there's an undercurrent to the conversation, I attribute it the usual ebb and flow of politics, nothing more.

Until Enoch strides into the room, and we all stand to greet him. He's big and tall, so bulky I'm surprised he races as well as he does. His almost colorless hair is pulled back in a half braid I've never seen on a man, and his hand completely encloses my own when we shake, a quaint Providential custom that still discomfits me. I have to subdue the instinct to wipe my gloved palm on my skirt after reclaiming it.

Having a male relative intrude during an introductory visit is unusual. But when he actually sits down next to me, I know with a jolt we've moved beyond eccentricity or difference of customs into ambush territory. I should have seen this coming.

I look over at Mother, who gives me a tiny smile that means she had a hand in arranging this whole thing. Which means…I look back to Enoch, his strange pale eyes and his insincere smile that doesn't reach them, and I clench both fists. I thought I had more time, but with both our mothers placidly watching our meeting unfold, there can only be one explanation: they are considering a match between us.

And both Leo and myself think my new suitor is a first-rate *testa di cazzo* before we've even exchanged three sentences. How typical.

Aware of Mother's eyes on me as she and Signora Royse murmur together softly, I do my best to maintain a polite pretense. "How are you finding our city?" I ask Enoch.

He gives me a pitying look. "It's charming, I'm sure." His tone of voice indicates he finds it anything but. "And so old-fashioned. A city constructed on an archipelago! How impractical. The traffic is intolerable to someone used to more modern infrastructure."

I do my best not to react to the insult to my city. "The founders of Neopolitan wanted our capital to be a place of beauty and culture." I hate how pompous I sound, how after one simple question on my part, all my conversational choices have become poor ones. "They wanted something unique and memorable, which is why they decided to incorporate canals as well as roads. They modeled it on an Italian city back on Earth that stood for centuries before flooding rendered it uninhabitable."

Enoch laughs. It isn't a friendly sound. "Well, I'll certainly remember it. But we shouldn't let the past hold us back from progress."

I change the subject. "I heard you won your speeder bike race a few days ago."

He puffs out his chest. "It wasn't much of a challenge. We don't have formal races back home, but the way you Neopolitans drive, I felt I had an unfair advantage all the same."

"My brother competed in that race."

He looks at me blankly before laughing. He obviously hasn't bothered to look up the name of the racer who crashed because of him. "In that case I'm sure he experienced a rude awakening." And then he waits, all ease and relaxation, leaning back in his chair as if it's a throne, for me to bring forward a different topic, another chance for him to mock me, my family, and my home.

Enough. My parents might have some ill-advised ideas of a personal familial alliance with Providence, but I'm not their bait.

They can wait and have Leo marry one of this nightmare's little sisters if they want it so badly. I meet his colorless eyes with a coolness I do not feel. I refuse to introduce another topic, and I refuse to look away.

He doesn't take quite as long as I expect to cave. Of course, he's received his own orders to make nice from his parents. I'm not the only one at a disadvantage here. "Your hair is becoming, the way it's arranged with all those jewels."

A compliment no less, even if it is a nod to my family's wealth more than anything else. I look down at my lap, my gloved fingers intertwined with one another, and fake extreme embarrassment. "Oh Signore," I gasp out, channeling Gianna with every syllable, "you shouldn't say such things to me. It simply isn't proper."

I'm given the satisfaction of hearing him stammer. "I d-d-didn't mean anything by it."

I wonder if tears would be too much? Probably. I err on the side of caution and give a few delicate sniffs instead. "Of course not, Signore. I'm sure things are done differently in Providence." I raise a fluttering hand to my breast. Enoch's open dismay would be comical when I relay this story to Leo later.

My little performance has garnered the attention of our mothers across the room. "Why, Sienna, whatever is the matter?" Mother asks, her voice stiff with warning.

I pause, and Enoch jumps in, just as I thought he would. Boys like that can't bear to follow the "Silence is golden" aphorism, and it isn't meant for them anyway. "I must apologize." He stands and moves away from me, and it almost looks like he's hanging his head. "I didn't realize the extent of a gently bred Neopolitan female's modesty. It was entirely my error." I can't believe he's actually fallen for my act. He might be a superior racer, but intellect is obviously not his strong suit.

His mother titters. "Oh, you rascal, what have you said now?" She turns to Mother. "Enoch is always getting into some mischief or another. Naturally high spirits, you know how it is, your boy must be the same."

Mother doesn't mention it's me she called high-spirited just two days ago. Instead she laughs too. "Isn't that always the way?"

"You are to be congratulated on such a virtuous young daughter," his mother continues. She's looking me over openly now, and with a sinking heart I realize I've managed to further endear her to the match. "I'd heard rumors the young ladies of San Marco were fast, and I'm relieved beyond measure to find them false. I have my own daughters to think of, you know." She turns to Enoch. "Run along now, we womenfolk have taken up enough of your time." He gives a brief bow before making his escape, and his mother looks after him with pride. "He'll be starting his studies here in a few days, but I wanted to give him some time to acclimate first."

"I am happy to recommend the school my son attends," Mother says, unbending slightly. "The *Alexander Academy for Young Men* is the most exclusive prep school in the city."

Signora Royse sighs and clucks her tongue. "I can already tell I'm going to depend on your counsel."

"Any way I can be of service." Mother gently extricates her hand from her new best friend's and I laugh on the inside. "And now we really should be going and allow you time to settle into your new home properly."

After several more minutes of pleasantries and compliments, we make our exit, and Mother grabs my arm, her fingers sinking into my flesh as we walk to the amphicar. "You've never been stunned by embarrassment in your life," she hisses, a smile still plastered to her lips in case anyone is watching.

"He was rude." My own smile doesn't falter even a little.

"You barely spoke to him."

"I'm a good judge of character."

Once we're in the safety of the vehicle, she sags back against the cushions. "Do you want to be the death of me? Because if you do, you've chosen a good way to go about it."

I forget the recent sitting room drama. "How are you feeling? Are you sick again?"

She sighs. "You know how it is, I'll be fine. But Sienna, think what it would mean to me to see you well settled."

Mother has been sick for years. Sometimes she has better periods, and other times she's terribly ill, scarcely leaving her bed. Her worst spell had been right in the middle of Father's campaign for Senator; his opponents hadn't been able to attack him as viciously as they otherwise might have due to her poor health. *Think of the silver lining*, Mother had insisted. But I couldn't, not when I was sick to my stomach every night in bed, worrying she wouldn't wake up in the morning.

She knows how it affected me, and she has no qualms about using that against me. I stare out the window, but I don't see any of the scenery we pass. "I'm too young to marry," I finally say.

"I was married at eighteen. If you have a normal engagement period, you'll be following in my footsteps."

"He's not a Neopolitan."

"I didn't raise you to be parochial."

Then why have I never traveled beyond the borders of our little country? But I know Mother isn't going to bend to these petty arguments. The truth is…"I don't like him."

"Don't be naïve, Sienna. He'll be a powerful man someday. He'll provide for you in the manner to which you're accustomed. And you'll be rendering a service to both your family and your country. These are the things that are important."

I feel smaller at her words, but I shake my head. "Leo doesn't like him either."

Mother scoffs. "Leo's not the one getting married. You depend on your brother entirely too much. Remember: your first duty will be to your husband and your second to your father."

I give her a pleading look. "What about my duty to my heart?" I can barely get the words out.

"Claptrap and rubbish. Has Gianna been lending you those romance novels of hers again? Reading them is her only flaw."

I can recite a whole list of Gianna's flaws, but I restrain myself and focus on the matter at hand. "I don't have romantic ideas, Mother. But you're the one who taught me how important the domestic partnership is. I shouldn't marry him. We aren't suited."

I want her to prolong the conversation, to express concern, to tell me she wants my happiness. But she does none of those things. Instead she tightens her lips and looks out the window. "We'll see what your father has to say about it."

And that's it. She's done speaking with me. We spend the rest of the trip in uneasy silence.

CHAPTER 4

*L*eo is still collapsed on the couch when I return, and I can tell he's been crying. My brain whirs at a rapid pace as I try to figure out how I can fulfill our twin pact and save him from himself. It's a tricky problem, but I don't let that stop me. I begin to formulate my most audacious plan yet. I look at my brother, eyes squeezed shut, bruise blooming across one eye and cheek like a ludicrous flower. Is it worth the risk? Can I really pull my scheme off?

But even as I hesitate, I know the truth. I'm dying to impersonate Leo and go to the Academy in his place, I'm dying to express my opinions, and I'm dying to show people what I can really do. Even if that means pretending to be somebody else.

"All right, I'll do it." Leo's eyes snap open at my voice. "I'll take the exam for you."

Leo stares at me. "You can't be serious." But I can see the hope in his eyes. "I'm taller than you, and your hair…."

I lean towards him. "You know that's not true. You're only a few centimeters taller than me. If that." He puts his hand to his chest in mock pain. "And nobody will be expecting it. They'd never guess in a million years we'd do something like this."

"Because it's a terrible idea."

I lower my voice, trying to imitate him. "Because it's a terrible idea." Not bad. "Except maybe it isn't. It's not like I'd have to pretend for very long, and you're so surly, if I refuse to talk much people won't even think it's suspicious."

He still looks skeptical. "Do you think you could pass the exam?"

"Are you kidding? I'd destroy it. How much money do you have?"

He mock punches my shoulder. "What? You going to charge me money to pass my test?"

"Would that stop you?" We both know the answer is no. "I'll need it to buy Lizabetta's help." Leo looks confused. "She wants to go to nursing school, but she can't afford it. A nice contribution to her school fund should win her to our side. And you know Mother and Father never give *me* any money. But you, brother mine, are a different story. Besides, you've been selling more and more of your masks." He's organized an anonymous arrangement with one of our favorite mask shops.

"She wants to go to *nursing school*? How do you even know that?"

"Because I spend ninety minutes minimum with her every day while she helps me get ready? You think we spend all that time together in silence?"

"I don't think about it at all, to be honest."

Sometimes my brother can be supremely irritating. "Well, we don't. We talk about all kinds of things. And I can't ask her to lie and steal for me unless I give her a safety net. Something worth risking her position for." I name a figure.

Leo's mouth falls open. "You want me to give that amount of money to a maid?"

I stand up. "I don't know, how much is it worth to you to pass this course? Maybe you're right. Maybe we should forget the whole thing."

He grabs my arm. "No, wait. Okay, okay, I can get the money."

I smirk at him. "That's what I thought. Now excuse me, I have some hair to shave off."

I DON'T REALLY SHAVE my head. But Leo keeps his hair short, and there's no way I can fake that.

I explain my plan to Lizabetta, including the money for her tuition. She shakes her head at me. "You're always up to something, aren't you? You can't leave well enough alone. What would your mother say?"

"She'd probably disown me." Mother must have been born good. She acts like my worst impulses are completely foreign, like no other woman in the history of time has behaved as I do. And maybe she's right, but…honestly, I get bored. I hate sitting around doing nothing when I could be doing something, especially something that might fix a problem or accomplish something in a more efficient way. I hate waiting. I hate hoping someone else is going to fix things, only to have nobody step forward. I don't know how all the women in my acquaintance stand it. "Will you help me?"

Lizabetta is only four years older than me, but she always seems so much more. "For tuition for my schooling? How could I not? My grandmamma says the only constant in a woman's life is a good education." She gives me the mischievous grin Mother never gets to see. "It's an awful idea, but it's your funeral."

"And you can get one of Mother's wigs?" Mother has a collection of wigs from when she was particularly ill.

Lizabetta nods. "I packed those wigs up myself. I know right where they are." She reaches out and fingers my hair, up in the elaborate style she did this morning. "But are you sure? You know what they say. Your beauty is your hair."

I swallow. In my case this is particularly true. I'm scrawny, short, and boyish, with barely any curves to speak of. My thick dark hair is my only claim to beauty; Mother has repeated this truth so often I wonder what I will be without it. "It will grow back soon enough." I say it airily, as if I don't really care, even though I feel a little sick to my stomach.

Lizabetta gives me a look to let me know she's aware I'm faking, and then she gestures to my vanity table. "No time like the present. I'll fetch the wig and the appropriate tools, and then you can tell me if you've changed your mind."

"I'm not going to change my mind." I say it through gritted teeth. I'm telling the truth. I'm too stubborn to back down now. At least that's what I tell myself as I remove my dress so it won't get completely covered by hair.

Twenty minutes later Lizabetta is back, and I watch in the mirror as she cuts huge chunks from my hair, which until a minute ago had reached all the way down my back. As she cuts it shorter, I can't look away. Lizabetta pauses when it's still long enough to salvage. "Last chance." Lizabetta meets my eyes in the mirror. "You sure you want to do this?"

My face already looks strange framed by wild curls. "Absolutely."

She cuts my hair closer still. It would almost feel soothing if I weren't aware of what I'm losing. When she's finished, short, awkward curls stick out all over my head. Just like Leo's.

Lizabetta turns away to put away her shears, and I continue to stare. My brown eyes look bigger, my eyebrows harsher. I don't look like a boy, not exactly, but I don't look as much like a girl either. I look in the middle, like I could be either one. My head feels so much lighter, I have to shake it several times to get used to it.

Then I grab my makeup kit and go to work. I remove all the makeup I'm already wearing, and when I'm done, I already look more like Leo, freckles and all. I go to town on my plucked eyebrows with a brush and a pencil, making them wider but not as dark as I usually wear them. I use some foundation to make my lower lip look slightly less full. Luckily our smiles already look the same, complete with the one dimple. I use a sponge to mimic just the tiniest bit of stubble on my jawline.

Last comes the piece de resistance: the black eye. It doesn't have to look exactly like Leo's black eye since no one but my parents have seen him since the accident. But I do want it to grab everyone's attention. If people are staring at my gruesome eye, they're much less likely to notice anything else out of the ordinary, like, say, the fact I'm a girl instead of a boy.

I spend an hour working on it. I have to remove everything and begin again twice. But even though I've never done a black eye before, I've spent a huge amount of time with my makeup kit. It's one of the few things I'm supposed to be interested in that I actually enjoy.

Finally I turn my head to check out all the different angles before sitting back on my bench with a sigh. Lizabetta has been experimenting with the long black wig, trying styles to see what will look the most natural. "You're going to be wearing this wig for a long time," she says, fussing with some stray hairs. "I hope you know what you're —oh!" She has looked up and seen my reflection in the mirror. "Oh my."

I lower my voice to match Leo's register. "Pretty good, don't you think?" I stand up and practice walking with a swagger. It feels wrong, like I might trip and fall.

Lizabetta laughs. "Take bigger steps," she suggests. "And stick your chest out more."

"I don't want to call attention to my chest," I protest. "What little I have is still too much."

Lizabetta tosses me some stretchy fabric. "You're going to have to bind yourself. Wrap that around your chest as tightly as you can manage. You're small, it should work well enough for one outing." I stare at the cloth with interest, wondering how Lizabetta thought of it. But before I can ask, she cocks her head. "It *is* only going to be for one outing, isn't it?"

"Of course." I try to make my feet feel heavier as I walk back and forth.

Lizabetta wrinkles her forehead as she scrutinizes me. "Your hands don't look right," she finally says. "But I don't know what we can do about that. Leo's clothing has pockets, so maybe keep them in your pockets as much as possible." My pantaloons don't have pockets, so I can't practice Leo's slouchy hands-in-pockets way of walking.

My qualpad chimes. "Thirty minutes until your scheduled embroidery session with Mother," it intones. I read somewhere its voice is supposed to be soothing, but given how many hateful reminders it gives me every day, more often than not I want to slam it against a hard surface.

"We'll have to hurry." Lizabetta hands me a tight cap with a velvet band around the edge to fit onto my head. It's a little tight but not unpleasant. She slips the wig on over it and begins fussing while I remove all my Leo makeup and reapply my normal colors. We finish right as my qualpad chimes its five-minute warning.

I shake my head, making sure the wig won't slide off. My temples feel blessedly relaxed. "Maybe I'll wear a wig from here on out," I tease, wiggling back into my gown. "Then you can style it without me. Think of all the time I'll save." I catch her hurt look in the mirror before her face recovers its usual pleasant expression. "I'm kidding, Lizabetta." I reach out and touch her shoulder. "You know I enjoy our time together."

"What you really mean is that you hate embroidery." She gives me a wink. "Go on down, you're going to be late." I gather my skirts so I can run. "And don't forget these!" She hands me a fresh pair of white gloves, and I hurry downstairs. It doesn't do to keep Mother waiting.

Particularly when I don't want her to have a single whiff of what I'm plotting.

CHAPTER 5

I feel naked without my hair and skirts. It's disconcerting to see the outline of my legs through pants as I walk San Marco's streets to get to Leo's school.

And that's another strange thing. I am walking alone. And I'm not afraid. Mother says it's not safe for a young lady to walk alone in the city, and it certainly isn't proper. If I tried it looking like myself, someone would be sure to see me and I'd be the subject of gossip for weeks. But here and now, no one cares. It's as if I'm invisible.

I've never been happier.

I race up and down the pedestrian bridges, tapping my fake finger splint on the railings. I don't have to slow down. I don't have to place my feet daintily or keep my posture perfect. In fact, I can't. Leo's shoes are too big for me, and even with wads of paper stuffed into them, they flop as I walk, changing my gait. My new haircut is covered by a smart cap that makes me feel like I'm on an adventure, and in these boys' clothes I'm not overheating even a little bit. Even the tight wrap around my chest feels supportive rather than constricting.

On top of everything it's a beautiful spring day, the cherry trees in blossom and the vines that crawl over so much of San Marco beginning to bloom with their droopy white flowers, their sweet odor concealing the worst of the rancid smell from the water. I nod at the men I pass, meeting their eyes, and they nod back. I can feel myself puffing out my chest naturally, just like Lizabetta suggested. I wend through the Artisans' District, narrow cobblestone streets devoid of amphicars, enjoying seeing all the talent of Neopolitan on display: hand-made lace, glass work, jewelry, furniture, and even the occasional mask shop for the people who can't make it out to Paraval Island, San Marco's mask-making center.

I cross one last bridge to stand in front of the Academy in the Sapphire, one of the oldest districts in the city. Most of the buildings look as if they're built to last a thousand years, constructed from the distinctive blue-black stone quarried nearby. The streets here are wider than many other parts of the city, easily able to accommodate several lanes of amphicar traffic, and the sunlight reflects off the stone, making it appear even bluer. The Academy is important enough to take up an entire building in a place of honor next to the most prominent law firm in the city. I stare up at its crenellated façade several stories up, impressed in spite of myself. All the best families' sons are educated here. I've never been inside.

I'm still staring up like a *coglione* when someone checks me with their shoulder. I recognize Leo's friend Dante looking at me with amusement. "Hey Leo, you coming or what?"

Thank goodness Leo has the reputation of being quiet. It will stand me in good stead today. I follow Dante through the sliding doors, through the gleaming lobby with its immaculately dressed men standing behind tall glass tables, murmuring into headsets, and to the elevator bay. "You ready for the test?" he asks, slouching against the wall while we wait.

I copy Leo's shrug. I'm afraid to actually say anything. What if my lowered voice sounds fake? What if everyone figures out who I really am? My hands start to tremble, and I shove them in my pockets, hoping Dante doesn't notice.

"Yeah, me neither." He yawns hugely, showing me the entire back of his mouth. "I was up all night cramming, and now I'm so tired I can't remember my own name." He looks closer at me. "You don't look tired though. You look *excited*." His tone is accusatory. "What's wrong with you, man?"

I shrug again, trying to play it cool. "Excited to get it over with."

There's a pause long enough for me to think, *he knows, he definitely knows, how can I convince him not to tell anyone?* And then he bursts out laughing. "That's my man." He shoulder-checks me again. "Your mother make you stay home on account of that eye?"

I'm beginning to understand the utility of Leo's shrug. "You know mothers."

"Do I ever." The elevator dings as the doors slide open. "Level three," Dante tells it. "So you know that *stronzo* Providential who gave you that shiner? Enoch what's-his-name? He's in our class now." Which means I'll have to see him again. Great. "Turns out he's just as big a *testa di cazzo* when you talk to him as when you race him."

"I'm shocked," I say. Then, because I can't help my curiosity, "Is he smart?"

Now it's Dante's turn to shrug. "Eh. Who can say. He doesn't know anything about our country, that's for sure. He goes on and on about Providence as if it's the second coming. If he loves it so much, why doesn't he go back there? That's what I want to know."

The elevator dings again on our floor, and I follow Dante to the classroom, relieved I won't have the opportunity to screw up Leo's directions. When we walk through the door, my eyes are instantly drawn to Enoch, who looks bigger and blonder than ever. He's holding court in the section of chairs furthest from the door, and furthest from the huge projection of a diagram of the Neopolitan system of government that covers the entire front wall. Otherwise, it's a completely ordinary classroom, nothing like the hall of wisdom I'd imagined from home.

I sit with Dante on the other side of the room, but I keep looking over, so I see when one of the guys whispers in Enoch's ear and he looks directly at me.

He stands up. Oh no. I want to keep a low profile. I showed up with only a few minutes to spare on purpose. The last thing I want is the attention of the entire room.

But as he saunters over, I forget about that. I'm Leo now, not

Sienna. I don't have to pretend to be overcome by embarrassment. This is my one chance to say what I really think.

I stay seated. He towers over me, but he'll do that even if I stand, and if I stay sitting, it looks like I'm not afraid. And I'm not. What's he going to do, beat me up in a classroom full of Leo's friends? I doubt it, not unless he has some severe anger management issues. I have to assume as an important diplomat's son he's been taught how to behave. As a statesman's daughter, I've certainly never been allowed to show any anger.

"You're Leonardo." His voice is low, surprisingly mellifluous. It's the only thing about him that I like. "Sienna's brother."

"That's right." I look away from him as if I'm bored.

"I plan to court her, you know." His vowels are strange and pinched-sounding, but otherwise his Gallo is perfect. I continue to ignore him.

"Tell me...." A big smirk creases his face. "Is she as uptight and mousy in private as she is in public? Or does she warm up once you get to know her, if you know what I mean?" He gives a lewd wink. "I have a personal interest."

The insult sinks into me with almost physical force. I stand up so fast, I knock over my chair. Maybe I don't have as much of a handle on my anger as I think. "She's a *human being*," I hiss. "You stay away from my sister. She's way too good for the likes of you."

He reddens, looks over his shoulder at all the eyes watching. I'm in trouble now. I try to remember whether I'm supposed to put my thumb inside or outside my fist if I need to punch him. Meanwhile, Enoch seems to be swelling to an even bigger size, and he moves to grab me. "Why, you little..."

But he's interrupted by the entrance of Professor Buccho. All the other students scramble to their seats. Enoch freezes over me for a moment, having visible trouble reining himself in. "Boys." The professor's voice is stern, brooking no nonsense. "What's all this then?"

Enoch turns, both hands clenched into fists. "Nothing, Professor."

Professor Buccho looks at me. I've never met him before, only heard Leo complain about how strict he is. He stands less than a head taller than me, his brown beard and nails carefully manicured, his belly straining at his waistcoat, which is missing one button. "Nothing, Professor."

"Very good then. Signor Royse, given how recently you've joined us, you are excused from this examination. Signor Tascioni, you seem quick on your feet"—I'm still standing—"so I'll begin with you. These exams will take the entire class period. Once you have spoken with me, you may leave. Questions?" He gives a perfunctory pause. "Excellent. I suggest you don't interrupt this process with any undue rowdiness or your grades will be affected. Am I clear?"

"Yes, Professor Buccho," we all drone.

I follow him into his tiny nook of an office, just big enough for a desk and two chairs. So many empty takeout boxes and bags clutter the desk I can't even see the projection inputs for his screen. A map of Neopolitan covers one wall, and a list of the Senators and Assemblymen, including their committee assignments, covers another. "Sit, Signor Tascioni." He nods at my eye. "That blow to your head wake you up?"

"I don't know what you mean, sir." This is the most dangerous time. If I'm going to be caught, it's now.

Professor Buccho raises his bushy eyebrows at me. "I am referring to your propensity to sleep through my lectures."

Oh God. What would Leo say to that? I freeze, trying to come up with the right response.

"Are you aware how much your parents pay for you to attend this hallowed institution, Signor Tascioni? Thirty thousand marks per annum. Thirty thousand marks for the privilege of getting a crick in your neck from sleeping in my classroom."

I swallow. "I apologize, sir."

"Is that so? Unfortunately, Signor Tascioni, it's my job to make sure you get the superior education your parents are paying for. Shall we begin?"

"Yes, sir."

"Explain to me the structure of our national government." A pause. "In broad terms." He leans back and taps his fingers together.

I can tell he expects me to fail. Does Leo really not know something so basic?

"Neopolitan is a republic, sir. Power is shared between the Senate, the Assembly, and the Doge and carefully balanced between the three."

"And what determines the makeup of the Senate and the Assembly?"

Another insultingly easy question. "The Assembly consists of one hundred assemblymen who are elected by the people every two years. The Senate consists of twenty-five senators who are elected every five years."

"And when you say the people, you mean?"

"Registered landowners." Women can't vote by default since women aren't allowed to own property, but I don't think Professor Buccho cares about that particular detail.

"And how else are the Assembly and the Senate different?"

"Senators draw no annual salary for their service and are traditionally members of one of the founding families. They can serve as many terms as the people see fit to give them. Most laws and amendments are introduced and debated in the Senate before moving onto the Assembly. Assemblymen, on the other hand, are paid for their service and can serve a maximum of three terms."

"And the Doge?"

"The Doge is elected in a formal procedure by the Senate and Assembly. Once in office, he also serves for five years. He can serve a maximum of three terms, although the last three Doges have only served two each. The current Doge has about a year remaining of his second term."

Professor Buccho continues to drill me on basic civics questions. I'm shocked at the ease of the test: could Leo really not pass this himself or did he vastly overestimate the difficulty of the material being covered?

Finally the professor sags back in his chair. "Very well. I'm pleased you seem to have a decent grasp of the fundamentals. But make a greater effort to stay awake in class, do I make myself clear, Signor Tascioni?"

"Yes, sir."

He stands up. "And don't get into a fight with the new Providential ambassador's son. He might have diplomatic immunity, but you most certainly do not." He opens the door and follows me out. "Signor Pantaleo, you're up next." He stands and watches until I leave the classroom, not giving me any opportunity to start something with Enoch. Not that I would have, no matter how much I want to.

I'd only start something I thought I could win.

CHAPTER 6

That night Father summons me and Leo to his study.

He knows, is my first thought. But how could he when I'd pulled off the caper so flawlessly? No one had guessed anything was amiss. I walked out of my house as Leo, I walked back into the house an hour later still looking like Leo, and then Lizabetta had helped me don Mother's very expensive wig. No one had missed me.

"What do you think this is about?" I whisper to Leo as we walk down the stairs together.

"Your upcoming marriage?" He winks at me, and I slug him in the shoulder.

"Not funny."

"Ouch." He grabs his arm in mock pain. "Don't worry, sister mine, it sounds like I defended your honor amply today."

I snort. "You don't like him either. You'd have done the same thing."

"Ha! You know me, I wouldn't hurt a fly, to Father's never-ending chagrin." But there's a note of anger in his voice. "I'm glad I didn't have to listen to Enoch making insinuations about my sister though. What a *testa de cazzo*."

"You have no idea." Leo jabs me with his elbow and points at his still colorful eye. "Well, maybe *some* idea."

We stop in front of Father's door, which is taller than it needs to be. Leo touches my hair. "This thing isn't going to fall off, is it?" His nervous laughter rings in my ears as I knock.

"Enter. Sienna first, please."

Leo and I exchange a look. I grip the cold metal door handle firmly and pull. Father is standing by the glass doors that open onto the garden, talking quietly and intently with one of his aides. I stand in front of his pristine desk, hands behind my back, waiting for them to finish and staring at Father's various clocks.

The bulk of Father's clock collection is on display in this room. He's only interested in mechanical clocks with superior craftsmanship, and his taste is eclectic. A stately grandfather clock with gold and opalescent inlay stands in one corner, a carriage clock decorated with horses and dogs and rabbits sits on the mantel, and a large square clock made from different colors of glass hangs in the middle of one wall. His collection of miniature clocks cuts an exacting line across his otherwise uncluttered desk. Father likes to say you can't rely on anything like the passage of time.

The only thing given more prominence than the clocks is the family record. It sits in one corner under special lights, a tall golden rectangle. Our family name, Tascioni, is inscribed in large letters at the top, and underneath every family member's name is engraved from the time of the Founding. Mine appears at the end of the list, after Leo's, even though I'm the older twin. There is another meter of unblemished gold where our descendants' names will be recorded. I remember the first time Father showed us our names. He even let me run my grubby fingers over the letters.

Now he laughs, gives the aide a friendly nod, and watches as the young man heads into the darkness, no doubt taking the shortcut through the gardens and back to the Council Hall, a mere three bridges away. That is why Father chose this house when we moved permanently to the city.

I stare at Father's profile. He radiates power and energy, his thick head of hair still black except for a touch of silver at the temples, his jaw firmly set, his mind always working all the angles. He wants to be Doge someday—it's why he helped Zio Roberto get elected, with the understanding he'll be next—and I have no doubt he'll achieve his goal. Father always gets what he wants in the end. He turns toward me, grave and unsmiling, and I wonder what he wants from *me*. The familiar guilty feeling tenses the pit of my stomach. I never want to let him down.

"Sienna." I jump when he says my name; I can't help it. He sighs, and I have to force my arms to stay at my sides. "Your mother has spoken to me about your visit with the Royses."

I wish Leo were in the room with us. "Yes, Father?"

"She says you don't care for the Royse boy."

At least he's getting right to the point. "That's correct."

"She also says you pretended to a greater modesty than we all know you have in order to extricate yourself from the situation. And that the maneuver increased the Royse family's respect for you."

I don't feel the need to tell him the second part had been an accident. "Yes, Father."

He nods. "That was well done." I let myself relax into the warm bath of his approval. "But." My spine instantly stiffens again. "I still want you to consider him as a suitor." He holds up a hand. "I know you have objections. Your mother says you found him rude, and I know the role he played last Race Day with your brother. He is young and brash and trying to win a name for himself in a new country. You can hardly blame him for not behaving as we would behave."

I think carefully about my response. "I'm sure it must be difficult for him,"—although in my opinion Enoch is making it a lot harder than it needs to be—"but I'm not ready to get married."

I expect him to bring up Mother's age at their marriage, but he doesn't. "I don't need you to be ready to get married, not yet. We're playing a waiting game. But I need you to entertain the young man's suit. I'm opening some tricky negotiations with his father, and I need leverage. Leverage you can provide me. It's for the good of our family and our country. Do you understand, Sienna?"

I gape at him. He's never asked me to participate in something like this before, and I feel a light flush wash over my face. Father needs my help. He's asking me to contribute.

But I can't prevent the wave of distaste that fills me every time I picture Enoch Royse's smug face.

Father must see my reluctance. "My dear daughter." He shakes his head. "Your mother tells me I've been too accommodating with you over the years. That I've allowed you to spend too much time with Leo. That I've encouraged the development of unladylike ideas in your head. In short, that I've spoiled you." He approaches until he's standing right in front of me, putting his index finger under my chin and tilting my head slightly up. "You're going to have to be very clever, Sienna. Very clever, and very beautiful."

I'm shaking. We never touch. I feel the weight of the responsibility he's handing me settle over my body. When he removes his finger, I leave my chin up.

"Leo!" Father calls. He walks away from me and around his desk, settling into his throne-like leather chair, and I find myself leaning toward him like a sunflower following the light.

My brother saunters into the room, eyes darting from my face to Father's and back again. His eye is beginning to heal, turning yellow and green around the edges. "You summoned?"

Father frowns. "I have news regarding the Satori diplomatic mission. News that involves both of you."

I catch my breath. There is going to be a reception, that must be it. Maybe we'll be hosting it ourselves. I still have hopes I'll catch a glimpse of a tail poking from under a dress coat.

"The Satori ambassador here in San Marco is very interested in promoting cultural exchange between the youth of our two societies. He has brought his son and daughter with him." Father coughs. "He has suggested an informational field trip and cultural exchange in Fidelium later this year. I gather the two young people didn't have much time in our planet's famed capitol, and it should be a good educational opportunity for all involved. I have told the Ambassador you will both participate."

I can hardly believe my ears. "*Both* of us?" I've always wanted to visit Fidelium, but the chances of that happening have been remote at best, at least unless I marry the right person.

"The Ambassador wants his daughter to be involved, and it wouldn't be seemly for her to be the only female present, so Zio Roberto and I agreed you and Gianna should also be included. If you can both behave appropriately and obediently." He pauses. "We've also invited Enoch Royse. He can learn about our culture at the same time as the Satori."

Father looks straight into my eyes, and I understand what he is telling me. This is both my reward and my sentence. He knows how interested I am in the Satori, and he's giving me direct access to Satori of my own age, along with the much-wished-for trip to the Capitol. *If* I cooperate with him. *If* I continue making nice with Enoch. He's not relying on his authority over me; he never has. He's making me want what he wants.

And I *do* want it. I want to take this trip. I want to see the giant square in front of the Hall of Justice that's been featured in endless movies. I want to meet the Satori and ask them all the questions burning in my mind. I want to know what we have in common, what's so human it can't be eradicated by time or distance or isolation. I want to be at the center, not on the sidelines.

Even if it means being in close proximity to Enoch. Maybe he isn't so bad. Maybe Father is right and he's just posturing and trying to find his place in a new country. I can't pass up this chance. "Thank you, Father. I'm happy to be included."

Leo raises his eyebrows at me. He doesn't know the deal I just made. But Father does. He has the satisfied smile he always gets when he's outwitted someone.

But he hasn't tricked me. He's getting what he wants, but so am I. We've both won.

Leo looks at me with concern once we've left. "You sure you want to do this?" he asks. "I figured you'd want to avoid Enoch. Father can't be thrilled about setting you loose on the Capitol. Maybe you and Gianna could socialize with this Satori daughter here at home and, I don't know, sew together or something."

I grimace. Leo doesn't pay attention to subtext at all. And sewing? "Wow, that sure sounds like fun."

Leo rolls his eyes. "You know what I mean."

I hug myself. "A trip to Fidelium! Come on, Leo, you know how long I've wanted to see it."

Leo sighs. "It's not all that, believe me." He's been to Fidelium with Father many times. "I know you want to go, but is it really worth it?"

I shrug. "Maybe I haven't given Enoch Royse a fair chance."

Leo groans. "Father gets you alone in his study for five minutes, and you're suddenly singing a different tune about that *stronzo*. I see how it is."

I love Leo, but he doesn't understand what it's like to miss out on the fun all the time. "Everything will be fine. I know what I'm doing, Leo."

"If you say so." He reaches out with his good hand to squeeze my own, and I wonder.

Maybe he understands more than I think.

CHAPTER 7

The morning Mother announces we're paying a formal visit to the Satori ambassador's wife, I am beside myself with excitement. Leo drifts along with us, taking the excuse to miss more classes. I have trouble sitting still in the amphicar. I feel like when I cut off my hair, I set my life in motion.

We arrive at a small older house off an unfashionable side canal. Where our house is designed to be imposing, looming over guests to remind them what an important Senator Father has become, this house is modest and graceful, with wood accents and long flowing lines. Surrounded by cherry trees, the fallen blossoms make a white carpet of the front promenade. Our house looks overdone and pompous in comparison.

Mother doesn't agree with me, sniffing as we walk up the petal-strewn path. "How quaint. I wonder if Signora Lhasa requires help hiring more staff."

She knocks on the door, and there is a long pause. She knocks again. "Are we expected?" I asked in a hushed voice.

"Of course we're expected." Mother sounds put out.

Suddenly the door is flung open by a beaming woman. "Oh good, you're here," she exclaims. "I thought I heard something. I'm not used to the knocking, you know. In Satori we have the house AI announce visitors."

Mother presses her lips together, and Leo and I make efforts not to burst out laughing. This must be the lady we're here to visit, answering her own door. "I am Signora Tascioni, Senator Tascioni's wife." Mother's voice is completely smooth, betraying none of her disdain for the newcomer's lack of manners and polish. "And this is my son Leonardo and my daughter Sienna." She gives the traditional greeting nod, and Leo and I follow suit.

The woman beams at us in return. Her long dark hair flows loosely down her back, and her dress, while cut in a familiar style, is made of a lighter, less rigid fabric. "It's ever so nice of you to visit us. I'm Signora Lhasa, of course. Come in, come in. The young folks have been so eager to meet you. Ereni is already out of bed *and* dressed, she was so excited. Normally, you know"—she lowers her voice in a confiding way—"she struggles to leave her bed before noon."

She leads us into the house, pausing in the cramped foyer for us to remove our hats and place them on old-fashioned shelves. We follow her down the poorly lit hall to the back of the house, the room that would normally be the study. She's outfitted it as a sitting room with overly stuffed couches that actually look comfortable and not an instrument or sewing frame in sight. Strange dark landscapes hang on the walls, and the curtains are completely open, allowing sun to pour into the room. The glass doors reveal the riot of color of a rose garden running slightly wild. Mother stands for a moment in the doorway, mouth open.

"Please, sit down, sit down. Make yourselves at home. Ereni! Burke! Our guests are here!"

Mother has pasted a grim smile on her face that barely falters as she sits on one of the sofas and is almost sucked into a less than perfect posture. She stares at the pictures on the walls and then looks firmly away. I sit in a chair that looks slightly less squishy, knowing I'm not allowed to relax my manners even in the face of people who clearly don't know the rules. Not with Mother watching, anyway. Leo sits in a chair next to me, a broad grin on his face. "I've never been so glad to be forced into a visit," he whispers in my ear. "Just watching Mother squirm makes it all worthwhile."

She does look uncomfortable, continually shifting in order to maintain her posture. But then she's distracted by the vision entering the room. We all are. Leo springs to his feet like he's made of rubber, and I follow his lead, blinking to see if there's something wrong with my eyes.

There isn't. The young woman in front of us is the most beautiful person I've ever seen. Her long blonde hair bounces in luxuriant waves, her skin is clear and deeply tanned, her figure is full in all the right places, and she wears an expression of infinite sweetness. Unlike her mother's, her pale pink gown is the height of fashion and suitability. It's hard to believe she and her mother are even related.

I see relief wash over Mother's face. The person in front of us couldn't have been better calculated to ease her fears that her children might be corrupted by the Satori influence. "Ah yes," Signora Lhasa says with a twinkle in her eye. "My lovely daughter Ereni."

Ereni tilts her head the perfect amount in greeting. "It's such a pleasure to meet you." Her voice is as sweet as her face. "I'm afraid Burke has been detained. He'll join us as soon as he's able."

"Very well." Signora Lhasa drops herself onto the sofa next to Mother. "What do you say we allow the young people to become better acquainted? I'm sure they're curious about one another. Ereni can take them to look at the gorgeous flowers. I've heard of roses before, but this is the first time any of us have seen them, you know."

Mother inclines her head graciously. "Of course. And we can speak of how I might be of service to you. There must be so much for you to do to get settled."

Signora Lhasa gives a large sigh and allows herself to sink into the sofa, much to Mother's chagrin. "Oh, aren't you kind? What a lovely welcome we're receiving."

THE RIOT of roses looks less wild up close; open pathways carve their way around the bushes. Ereni leads us forward, Leo and I behind her exchanging telling looks. We don't have to speak out loud for me to know what he's thinking: that she's gorgeous and that she hasn't been here long enough to look like the perfect daughter of San Marco that she does. From our vantage point it's obvious she doesn't sport a tail, and Leo smirks at my disappointment.

We reach a clearing in the center of the bushes where a silver sundial sits locked in a ring of concrete, marking the regimented passing of time. Father would love it. I can't see the house from here, only hundreds of overgrown rose bushes in all directions. The morning sun beats down relentlessly with nothing to provide shade, but Ereni doesn't seem to notice. She yawns and sprawls out on a convenient bench, her proper posture evaporating in the space of seconds. "Well, we certainly gave your mother something to talk about, didn't we?"

Not so perfect after all. Leo laughs so hard he starts wheezing. Ereni watches with interest as he begins to cough, and I have to whack him on the back. "Excuse me," he finally rasps out. "I apologize."

"You certainly don't need to apologize on my account." Her face breaks out into a sudden grin. "It *is* pretty funny. I thought your mother might faint when Irisa relaxed her posture like that. Are all of you so proper here, or is your mother special in that regard?"

"Oh no, it's everyone," I say. "Welcome to Neopolitan."

Leo shoots me a sly look. "Not *everyone*."

I know he's referring to my new haircut. "Oh, shut up. You know what I mean."

"Judging by your reaction"—she gives Leo a friendly smile—"I'd have to agree with you. Not everyone at all." She raises her arms to include us both in her gesture. "It is truly a pleasure to make your acquaintance. You know, this might be the first casual conversation I've had since we landed? Outside of colleagues, of course. It's been all formality and ceremony."

"Well, we did think you might have tails," I can't resist saying.

She bursts out laughing. "Is that what you heard? Lord, tails haven't been in fashion for generations now. Oh, I like you two."

A young man emerges from the bushes to our left. He's heavily muscled and taller than Leo, but then, almost every man is taller than Leo. His dark hair frames his face, a little longer than the current style, and he's as tan as his sister. He's wearing a casual white linen shirt tucked into his formal pants. A bit of his chest is exposed where his shirt opens, and he's not wearing any gloves even though we've never met. I blush and look away. "It's about time," Ereni says. "Burke, meet my two new friends, Sienna and Leonardo. Senator Tascioni's children. You'll be relieved to hear they're a true delight."

He folds his arms across his chest and nods. "Thanks for visiting us." His eyes meet mine boldly, unlike any properly bred young man. He stares at me, almost as if daring me to object, and my chest squeezes. I know it's nothing. He didn't grow up here. He doesn't know what he's doing. I both desperately want to talk to him and have no idea what to say.

He finally looks away, and I can breathe again. Ereni is watching me, a little smile on her face.

Leo tugs at his gloves uncomfortably, flexing the fingers of his injured hand. He's had to cut off one finger of this pair of gloves to accommodate his splint. I wonder if he wishes he could behave with the same forwardness as Burke. "How are you finding San Marco?" he murmurs politely, staring at the yellow rose bush in front of him.

Burke shoves his bare hands into his pockets, but not before I notice the dark hair covering their backs. I avert my eyes. "It's an interesting contrast to Fidelium."

Ereni leans forward, all enthusiasm. "San Marco is charming. Not as modern as Fidelium, to be sure, but I think that's a point in its favor. It feels like a city lost in time."

"Father says it's a city that treasures what's best from the past," I volunteer. "He says as a species we are too quick to charge forward and not appreciative enough of the strengths we've already discovered." Ereni makes a noncommittal noise in her throat. "I've never been to Fidelium," I continue, not wanting the conversation to peter out. "But thanks to you, I'll finally get to visit." I'm still having trouble believing I'll finally see the Capitol about which I've heard so much.

Ereni gives me a blank look. "Thanks to me?" she repeats.

"The cultural exchange trip that's being planned on your behalf,"

Leo says helpfully. He sounds relieved to have something he can explain.

Burke snorts, and Ereni gives him a quelling look. "Of course," she says smoothly. "How silly of me to forget. I'm very much looking forward to spending more time in Fidelium, and especially in such pleasant company." She includes both Leo and myself in her smile. "It's very different in Satori. We as a people are not overly enamored by the past. But it's easy to see the appeal."

"Ereni can find the good in anything." Burke manages to make this sound like a drawback. "It's one of her many talents."

Ereni doesn't react at all, almost as if she hasn't heard her brother. Instead she pats the bench beside her. "Come, Sienna, sit and tell me about yourself. What profession do you hope to pursue?"

I blink at her in confusion, buying myself time by sinking onto the bench as she's asked. "I'm afraid I don't know what you mean."

Burke settles onto the bench opposite us, all outstretched limbs and relaxed poise, his hair glinting in the sunlight. "She means, what do you want to do with your life? What career would you choose if you could do anything?" He gives me an unsettling smile, as if he expects me to say something shocking.

I look at Leo, but he's no help. He's looking at me curiously, as if he's interested in my response. "We don't have careers here," I stammer out. "I mean, women don't. I mean, women of a certain class. Like me. Someday I'll marry, probably someone like my father. A politician." Or an ambassador, I don't say, thinking of Enoch.

Ereni turns to Leo. "And you?"

He doesn't hesitate. "I'd apprentice with an artisan." I catch my breath at his boldness. This is Leo's biggest secret, and I can count the number of people who know it on the fingers of one hand.

"Ooh, an artist! How thrilling," Ereni says. "I can't wait to see some of your work."

He shakes his head. "You misunderstand. I'm speaking only in hypotheticals. I will of course follow in my father's footsteps: get a law degree, help him manage our family's business affairs, and then enter politics at the appropriate time. For me, art will always be just a hobby." The words he could never say to another Neopolitan ring with a depth of bitterness that surprises me.

"And what about you, Sienna? What will take up your time when you are a…wife?" Burke pronounces the word as if it's foreign.

"I'll run my husband's household and play a role in polite society. Eventually I'll raise our children." I pause, wondering what they'll make of my words. "And I'll help my husband with his career, of course."

Ereni blinks. "Oh, so you're interested in politics? That makes sense, coming from your family. Would you run for office, if you could?"

Would I? This is not a question anyone I've known would ever ask. "I…I don't know." I ought to have a better answer. Both the people in front of me have left their home, their entire planet, to be here. They probably have such interesting answers to questions like these, questions I've barely considered. Burke raises an eyebrow at Ereni, and I wonder if it's his way of saying "I told you so." Am I exactly what they expected? I find myself wishing I were more.

"I'd like to do what you do," I blurt out. They both look back at me. "I'd like to travel to different places, learn about other cultures, negotiate with and learn from people, build relationships." I look from Ereni to Burke. "Isn't that what you're here to do?"

"You're certainly not here to establish any kind of meaningful trade relationship." Leo flashes a sardonic smile, and I'm surprised all over again at how open he's being with these people. "Unless your star-faring ships are much better than you say."

Ereni shrugs prettily. Everything she does has an ornamental quality to it. "If only." She spreads out her hands. "But no, as you say, we're not here primarily for trade. We've already said so. We have nothing to hide."

"Why are you here then?" I ask. The question is rude in its directness, but I'm too fascinated to stop myself.

"Would you believe that we're curious?" Burke gives me a sly smile that brings unexpected heat to my cheeks. He's paying so much attention to me. Too much attention. Leo feels like an insufficient chaperone against Burke's encyclopedia of meaningful looks.

"Humanity has scattered over so many systems at this point, and yet there is no functioning widespread communication network. The Satori strive to collect information about the many branches humanity has taken since the diaspora. We believe we can learn from one another, that each civilization has something valuable to offer to the others." Ereni laughs. "So yes, Burke is correct. We're incorrigibly curious."

"I take it you think you have something to offer in return." His words are a challenge, but Leo still doesn't make direct eye contact with her. This is not a proper conversation for a young man and woman to be having.

"Well, for starters, we update and maintain the most comprehensive repository of human knowledge in existence today." Burke's face softens. "It's not actually an infinite library, of course, but sometimes it seems that way."

"It's different on every planet we visit," Ereni interjects in a way that makes me think Burke would have otherwise waxed long about their library. "For example, the Etripedes on the planet Sahara were very excited about the more efficient desalination techniques we were able to teach them. But here, you have no pressing need for such technology. And there are always potential technologies that could unfavorably disrupt the balance a civilization has achieved. We don't wish to cause harm where we travel. It's a fine line we must tread."

"Do you know how you can help us?" I ask.

"We're still assessing—"

"Medicine," Burke interrupts her. "Our medical technologies are vastly more developed than your own, and we can have a deep impact on the overall quality of life of your people. We want to set up clinics, provide new technology, and offer advanced training to your medical personnel."

"If that help is desired," Ereni says sharply. "Everything has to be done through the proper channels."

Burke rolls his eyes. "Who wouldn't want to live longer and healthier lives? Please."

I think of Mother's long illness, its ebbs and flows, and I have to agree with him. "That's wonderful," I say. "So you travel from planet to planet making peoples' lives better." It sounds like a dream come true.

"And learning from them," Ereni says. "We prefer to participate in an exchange of ideas. Everyone has something to offer."

And they're both going to spend their lives doing this. A sudden pang of jealousy jolts through me. "How lucky," I murmur.

Leo gives me a sharp look, but Ereni smiles. "You think so, do you? It sounds like you're a budding diplomat yourself."

I shake my head at the absurd idea, even though I wish it could be true. Ereni bounces up and strolls over to a rose bush sporting bright orange flowers, stroking the petals with her long fingers as if they're precious.

Burke leans forward, a sudden intensity in his gaze. "The diplomat's life sounds exciting and exotic, but nothing is perfect. It can be lonely, spending your life away from your home world."

"You have your parents and your sister," I point out.

He makes a noncommittal noise. "But I'll never return to Satori. And no other planet will be quite the same." He shrugs. "The air here feels different. It *tastes* different. It's hard to explain unless you've experienced it."

"You don't think you'll ever go back?"

"Why would I? Even if one of our ships departed tomorrow, by the time we returned over sixty years will have passed since I left. I'd still be young, and everyone I knew would be much older or off-planet. Nothing would be the same." He shudders. "Some people go back to retire and add information to our library, but I'd rather have the undiluted memory of home."

I hadn't considered the realities of Burke and Ereni's lives. I know about time relativity and space travel, of course, and the limitations these place on interplanetary trade and diplomacy. But speaking to people who have left their home forever is a different matter altogether. "I'm sorry." I remember his mother answering her own door, setting up the house to suit herself instead of following tradition. Eventually she'll learn to fit in, but will she always miss her way of doing things? Will she always feel like she doesn't belong? "Did you… choose to leave? Or were you required to accompany your parents?"

He gives me a strange look, then laughs. "Oh no, I chose to come. On Satori, it's a great honor to be part of a diplomatic mission like this one. I'm lucky to be here so young. My brothers and sisters were spitting with jealousy."

"Oh? You left brothers and sisters behind?" I wonder how large their families usually are.

But Ereni, having wandered over to a bush a row over, interrupts us. "Isn't this just lovely? Come see, Sienna."

Burke shakes his head. "You shouldn't let her tell you what to do, you know," he tells me.

But I want to be friends with Ereni. I'm flattered she wants to talk to me. I don't have any female friends except for my insipid détente with Gianna, with whom I can't have an honest conversation to save my life. And Burke's attention, while it makes my heart race, is unsettling. "I don't mind."

Burke raises his eyebrows but doesn't object further, and I hear him ask Leo an innocuous question about racing as I hurry over to the bush Ereni is examining. The roses really are beautiful, so large and richly colored. We have one rose bush at home, carefully culti-vated, with small white flowers. Most of them are removed from the bush before the blossoms have a chance to open.

"If you're interested," Ereni says, giving me a sidelong look, "we could share some diplomacy…tips and tricks of the trade. I have a lot to learn about the way you do things in your culture. And I'm sure you know a great deal, having grown up in a political household."

I like how she's putting us on an equal footing, even though she's a trained diplomat and I only know whatever I've learned from reading and observing. And I'll take any excuse to speak further with her. "What's a basic diplomatic principal you use all the time?"

"Hmm." She absentmindedly fingers her lace cuff. "Names. Both good politicians and good diplomats always remember names the first time they're introduced. They figure out a pneumonic device if their memories aren't naturally sharp…or they don't have technological assistance." She winks at me. "How are you with names, Sienna?"

I lick my lips. "Excellent." Mother would chide me for bragging, but it's true. I've watched her and Father greet people they barely know correctly by name for as long as I can remember. A few years ago I started keeping a little notebook where I write the names of everyone I see that day by hand. I look through it briefly every night. Writing out the names helps set them in my memory.

"Of course you are. You see? I could tell you're a natural diplomat."

She's taken off her gloves to fondle the rose petals, and she reaches out as if to pluck the flower. "Be careful! The thorns are sharp." But I'm too late. She draws her hand back with a gasp, a drop of blood welling from her finger. She stares at it for a moment before drawing a handkerchief from her pocket and wrapping it around her finger. We watch as the redness spreads over the white cloth.

"I suppose I needed this reminder." She's still staring at her injured finger. "We should always beware first impressions. Just because something looks beautiful doesn't mean it can't also be dangerous."

She blinks down at me with her wide, limpid green eyes, and I wonder if she's talking about the rose or herself.

CHAPTER 8

*M*other gushes about Ereni enough on the way home I take a chance and suggest I invite her to the upcoming Mask Maker's Festival on Paraval Island. Mother is so taken with the idea she forgets to suggest I invite Gianna as well. Ereni might not believe in first impressions, but she's certainly succeeded in making a positive one on Mother.

As soon as the door to the playroom shuts behind us, Leo grabs my shoulder. "You have to help me."

I'm instantly on alert. "What's wrong?"

His face contorts. "I can't race tomorrow."

"Why not? Is that what the doctor said?"

He doesn't meet my eyes. "No, he said it's fine."

"Well, your finger *is* still in a splint, so just skip it." My scalp itches, and I can't do anything about it while I'm wearing this wig. If I hurry, I can take it off and get some relief before my dance lesson. "You've missed Race Day plenty of times."

"Enoch Royse's been talking about me to the other guys. Making threats, that kind of thing. If I don't show up tomorrow, they'll think I'm a coward." Leo looks at me with pleading eyes. "Come on, Si, you've got to help me. If you hadn't almost gotten into a fight with him, he wouldn't even remember I exist."

He has a point. "Fine, what do you want me to do?"

"Race in my place."

I stare at him. "Excuse me?"

"You train just as much as I do in VR, and we used to ride speeder bikes all the time in the country." I can't believe what I'm hearing. "It's not like I ever place anyway. You don't have to do well, you just have to show up and lap around the track a few times. You can keep a helmet on the whole time. No one will notice or care, I can promise you that."

I'm burning to say yes, to get on a real bike again. The VR simulation is top-of-the-line, but it's still not the same as the real thing. But guilt gnaws at my insides. I know exactly how disappointed my parents would be if they found out. I don't know what they'd do to me, but it's not the punishment that gives me pause. It's the way they'd look at me. "Racing in public? I…can't do that."

But Leo is stubborn when he wants to be. Especially when he wants to get out of something. "Why not? We both know you'd love to race. And you took my exam for me, didn't you, and no one could tell the difference."

"Yeah, but I wasn't there very long," I argue. "Just because I succeeded for ten or fifteen minutes doesn't mean I'll never get caught. Besides, you guys have your pre-race rituals." I don't know exactly what these entail, but I've heard rumors they do a naked cold plunge.

Leo makes a face. "Skip that. Be late. I'm late all the time."

I try to push down the temptation. "I don't understand why you don't want to race. Is it Enoch? Are you afraid he'll beat you up? Because you have friends too, you know."

"It's not Enoch," he scoffs. "I can take care of him no problem."

"Well?"

He turns away from me, walks to the window overlooking the canal. He stares out for a long time. "It's the racing, okay? I don't want to get back on the track."

I suddenly remember Leo's first proper race. I'd been helping him get ready at home, and he'd had to run from the room to vomit. It happened every Race Day after that, sometimes beforehand, sometimes afterwards. He's always had racing nerves, and he's never had such a spectacular accident on the track before. I put my arm around him. "The force fields are there for a reason," I say softly. "There hasn't been a race-related fatality in years and years."

"I know." He sounds miserable. "But this finger…I'm going out of my mind not being able to work on my masks. What if I hurt another finger this time? The force fields aren't foolproof."

"Well, yeah, but it's not going to get any easier to get back out there."

"I know. Contrary to popular opinion, I'm not a complete *coglione*. Even though you and Father would disagree."

"That's not true." Although I have mercilessly rubbed in the simplicity of that oral exam. "You're my brother. I'm supposed to give you a hard time."

"Then do me this favor." He holds his body stiffly underneath my arm. "Come on, Si. You're a better rider than I am, anyway. Just do it this once, that's all I ask."

For now, I don't say. For as long as we've been alive, my brother has asked me to do favors for him. Cleaning up his room, helping him practice, doing research, writing a paper, taking an exam. But he shows up for me too. It's part of our twin pact. He only started racing in the first place because I was so interested in it, and he listens to me go on and on about whichever subject has captured my interest, whether it's an obscure city law or speculation about Satori tails. And he's the only one who understands the particular frustrations of Mother and Father.

I can't tell him no. Especially not when he's asking me to do something I've dreamed about anyway. "All right, all right, I'll do it."

He throws his arms around me. "You're the best sister. And I'll get back out on the track soon, you'll see."

"I'm sure you will." My words come out muffled, which is appropriate considering I don't believe they're true.

~

I TELL the amphicar to drop me off at the track exactly fifteen minutes before Leo's race, and I have him send a frantic message to a few of his friends about how late he is. I change into his racing suit in the car. No locker rooms for me: even wearing the tough base layer, my wrapped breasts are too obvious.

Leo's eye has healed to the smudged brown and yellow stage, a lot less attention-grabbing, much less likely to distract people from noticing I've taken his place, and I'm grateful for the helmet. No one is looking for an imposter, I remind myself as I wait in the car, the timer ticking down. I've never worn a proper racing suit before, and I'm surprised how stiff it is.

I have to steel myself to step out of the car. I wish Leo hadn't decided to go quite so flashy with his suit. The door lifts up, I scoot out, helmet under my arm, and suddenly all eyes are on me. Even if he's not a top racer, the *Ragazzo d'Oro* gets noticed.

Someone starts chanting my name, and I can see a few cameraflies diving down for a closer shot. Great, all I need is photographic proof of me in Leo's place. I slide on the helmet and wave just the way Leo does. I'm not Sienna Tascioni, not anymore. I stride through the crowd to the racers' door, and people move aside for me. A few reach out and touch my sleeves, as if for luck. I feel tall, invincible, like people are really seeing me. Which is a joke, considering they're all seeing my brother.

I make my way straight for Leo's garage, where I've snuck more than once at the end of Race Day to drool over his latest bike. Leo changed the garage lock settings to include my retina ages ago. Someone grabs my arm and tries to stop me before I get there, but all I have to do is point at the huge projection in the air above the track, showing eleven minutes left before the race, and they let me go on my way.

The garage smells like dust and grease and metal. Leo stores several bikes here, but I make my way to my favorite, the Lucetti Comet Z. I unplug it while admiring its sleek frame. The fairing is painted a shimmery gold, of course, and completely hides the best part of the bike: its sweet engine that packs a massive punch power-wise. I maneuver another, older bike out of its way and climb aboard. The bike molds to my body, making it feel like I've been caught in a full embrace, and just like that, any nerves I may have been feeling vanish. The race doesn't matter. All that matters is getting a chance to ride this beauty as fast as possible.

The bike recognizes my fingerprint set, and the windscreen lights up with all the information I could need. I kick on the ignition, lean forward, and raise the bike about a meter from the ground. I twist the throttle and ease slowly from the garage, mindful of pedestrians even in this less crowded staging area. Four minutes to go.

I twist the throttle harder and drive down the stretch of garages and around the corner to the entrance to the track. I pull into my position—the worst one since Leo was the only one who didn't finish the last race—just as the countdown clock reaches two minutes. The crowd roars, whether for me or in general excitement, I can't tell. The racer next to me nods in greeting, but I can't remember who he is. I peer through the ranks to see Enoch in pole position, sporting the now familiar yellow insignia against a black background.

I force myself to drive Enoch from my mind, and Leo, and the fact that I'm a girl in a crowd of boys, about to illegally race. I focus on the way the bike purrs under my body, the way it responds to my movements, the drivers in front of and beside me. There's no one behind me, that's how bad my starting position is. But that's a good thing, it means no one expects anything from me. It means I'll be a surprise.

Please let me be a surprise.

The countdown flashes both above me and on the windscreen. 3...2...1...go! I open the throttle fully and give myself an extra boost with my left foot pedal. I swerve aggressively between the two racers in front of me, getting both ahead of them and closer to the inside of the track. I elevate an additional defensive four meters to cause maximum difficulty if either wants to cut above or below me.

That's really Leo's problem. He's a competent racer, but he's nice down to his marrow. Not me. Not when I'm on a bike.

My engine hums softly. I could rev it if I wanted to, but that would just give my fellow racers a warning I'm coming for them. That's Leo's other problem. He shows off too much and gives away his advantage. I hunch over the handlebars, refamiliarizing myself with the physical realities of flying. This is a medium length race, so I have a little time.

But not that much. Not with such a poor starting position. The racer in front of me is flying slightly higher than optimal, and he's distracted by another racer crowding him to his right. At the apex of the next curve I dart under him and give myself another boost of speed. I clear him with less than half a meter to spare. Think you don't have to worry about me, buddy? Think again.

I need to get that innermost position if I'm going to catch up with the frontrunners. And I'm only going to get it by playing rough. The rider in front of me goes a hair wide on the next turn, and I exploit his mistake, jamming my bike in between him and the inside rider. All three of us race knee to knee the whole straightaway, no one able to take the lead.

Time to be ruthless. At the next curve, I crowd the inside rider, my knee literally touching his. He loses his nerve and corrects too tightly, careening into the inner barrier. I pull up to avoid his bike, and now I've got the coveted inner position.

I see Enoch's back curved low over his bike now, but there's still a racer between us. Not for long. I close in on him, waiting for a mistake I can exploit. But the racers in these prime positions are better, and they don't make many mistakes. We complete one lap, then another, and I'm still waiting. I don't know how I'm going to get around him.

Meanwhile he's crowding Enoch from behind, his engine making aggressive noises. I could tell him it's not going to work; Enoch has nerves of steel, and some loud noises aren't going to throw him off his game. They do make him angry though. As he accelerates away, his bike releases a big puff of gray smoke. The rider in front of me appears startled, and he misses the apex on the curve we're riding, blocking the rider to his right while he's at it. I dart into the space he's left, accelerating right on the apex, and leave him behind.

Now I'm riding on Enoch's tail, and there are only three riders between me and victory.

As I look for openings to get around him, I can't help admiring Enoch's form. My arms and wrists ache from leaning forward, but he doesn't seem to be tiring. He unerringly chooses the best line for every turn, and I have to admit I'm learning something by following him. The two racers on his right do their best, but they are unable to cut him off, and he always stays just a touch ahead.

We're heading into the last lap, my body quivering with fatigue and adrenaline. It's all I can do to keep my place. A bike is right behind mine, and another hedges me in on my right. I bob up and down to prevent them from passing me, but I feel boxed in. There's not enough room to maneuver.

I grit my teeth and lean harder on my long-suffering arms, ignoring the pain. All that exists for me is the race, my bike, Enoch's yellow insignia mocking me, calculating a turn, another turn, the last straight away…and we've finished. I pull up and out, bleeding off speed, as I raise my eyes to the rotating screen. Enoch won, that's no big surprise, but as I quickly scan the results, I see my name in huge golden letters. Fourth place. Fourth place! That's the best I've ever done!

I shake my head to bring myself down to earth, bringing my bike to a stop. The best *Leo* has ever done. It's Leo's name up there, not mine. Get it together, Sienna.

But whoever's name is up there, I'm the one who put it there. I gradually become aware of the screaming, churning crowd. They've been here this whole time, but I completely forgot about them until this moment. I hear Enoch's name being screamed, and then I hear something else: "*Ragazzo d'Oro! D'Oro! D'Oro! Ragazzo d'Oro! D'Oro! D'Oro!*"

I can be the *Ragazzo d'Oro* just as well as my brother can. I pull off my helmet, my hair and face damp with sweat, and I join the crowd's chant. "*Ragazzo d'Oro! D'Oro! D'Oro!*" I pump my fist in time with the words. The crowd loves me, and I love them. I feel like I might burst into a thousand pieces from the joy of it.

A heavy hand claps onto my shoulder. "Getting ahead of yourself, aren't you, little pup?" It's Enoch, tall and blond and beefy. He puts an arm around me, and the crowd gets even louder, loving the visual of the big pale foreigner palling around with the slight dark boy from home. But for me it's like being doused with ice water.

Enoch gives me a pat that will probably leave a bruise. "Keep practicing, and you might make it to third." Then he struts around the track by himself, leaving me steaming at his words. Oh, I'll do better than third. I'll beat his arrogant ass before he knows what's happening. I'll….

A camerafly swoops into my face for a close-up shot, and I remember myself. Who knows how many photos have been taken of me celebrating? Better hope I can keep hiding in plain sight. To be safe, I cram the helmet back on my head and return to my bike. Time to slink back to the garage and then home before anyone notices the differences between Leo and I.

It takes me a while to extricate myself from Leo's excited race mates, all of whom want to congratulate me and ask me what my secret is. Do I have a new training regimen? Did I fix up my bike? Pretending to be Leo is exhausting. I have to take a brief pause before I speak every time to make sure I'm choosing the right words. Leo's words. I'm relieved when I can finally get away, lying that I'll probably drop by the post-race party soon.

The crowd's cheers diminish behind me as I fly slowly back to my garage, and my shoulders relax. I'm not used to being the center of attention. I wonder how Leo does it day after day. His "man of few words" pose makes more sense than it used to. I'm almost on top of the garage, the door already scrolling open, when I see the person leaning against the wall, muscular arms crossed.

It's Burke Lhasa, dark hair falling into his eyes. He follows me into the garage, watches without a word while I maneuver the bike into its spot, dismount, get a diagnostic started running, and plug it in. Finally I turn to him, wondering why he's here. He's attractive, that much hasn't changed, and I don't want him seeing me like this, sweaty and wrung out.

"It's hot," he says. "You wanna take that helmet off?"

I don't see how I can avoid it, not when he's called it out so explicitly. I do it slowly, relishing the cool air on my overheated face, tossing my head just a tiny bit as though I still had hair to shake free. And because I'm trying to play a part, I strip off my gloves as well, flexing my hands in relief.

Burke grins. "Nice race, Sienna."

CHAPTER 9

The world shakes, and I grab onto the bike next to me. I must be dehydrated. I clear my throat, struggling to bring my voice sufficiently down in pitch. "Excuse me?"

"Don't try to brazen it out," Burke says. "Please. Save us both some time. I know you're Sienna, not Leonardo."

I stare at him openmouthed, trying to collect my thoughts. If he knows, there's nothing I can do. "How?" I ask instead. How many people have guessed my secret? Can I get ahead of the news? What kind of damage control might be possible? I need to talk to Leo right away.

"Calm down. We should have a little chat." He gives a pointed glance at the still-open garage door. "In private, don't you think?"

I trigger its closing mechanism and wait until it shudders into stillness. "How did you know?" I don't bother to disguise my voice, and it sounds strange.

Burke leans back against the work counter, folding his arms again. "I'm trained to notice things. Part of the job description. You and your brother do look very similar, it's true, but there are differences. You're relying on people making assumptions."

I'm getting angry. "Well, it's worked so far."

"Relax, I didn't mean it as a criticism." I can't tell if he's laughing at me. "In general, people see what they expect to see. And they certainly don't expect to see you on the racetrack instead of your brother." He shakes his head as if impressed by my audacity. "But I'm not from around here, and I'm trained to see things with fresh eyes."

I need something more concrete. "And?"

"And what?"

"What gave me away?"

He looks up and down my body then, and it takes all my anger to avoid shrinking in on myself. "You don't move right," he finally says. "The men here, they plow forward. Their movements are big, almost exaggerated. When they sit, their legs spread out so far it distorts their posture. They take up space." He takes a few steps forward, and I shrink back. I can feel myself doing it, but I can't seem to control it. "You, Sienna, take up as little space as possible."

I won't step back. I will fill this space I'm standing in if it kills me. But it feels so uncomfortable, so wrong, I can only hold out by taking a step forward. We're standing too close to each other now; I can see the individual hairs on his face. He needs to either shave or grow out a beard, not this in-the-middle nonsense. His eyes lock onto mine, a murky gray. "Also," he breathes, his voice quieter now, "you don't have an Adam's apple. Next time, wear something that covers your throat.

He takes my hand in his, and I freeze. He's touching me. I'm not wearing gloves, and a man is touching my bare skin. He pauses but doesn't move his hand. "Are you okay?"

His hand is warm, much more so than mine, and slightly rough. He smells crisp and clean, like the pine trees that grow around our country home. Under his jacket, his shirt isn't buttoned all the way to the collar, and a triangle of skin peeks out just under his throat. I stare at it for a moment before pulling my hand away.

"Next time?" I ask. "Does that mean you're not going to tell anyone?"

My whole body tightens as I wait for his answer. I'll be in terrible trouble if my parents find out, but that would be nothing compared to what would happen if my exploits become public. What had Leo and I been thinking?

"I don't think there's anything wrong with women racing. I say good for you for figuring out a way to do it." His sudden smile makes my breath hitch. "I admire you, Sienna. You have a lot of courage."

He's still close, too close, and every nerve in my body twitches with alertness. "I'm just like everyone else."

He laughs. "Liar." I look down at Leo's suit on my body and I have to agree with him. "Don't worry," he says. "I won't tell any of your people."

He turns away then, and I'm almost disappointed. I want to reach out and touch him. But I have to be smart. I can't let the headiness of racing lead me to recklessness. "What do you mean, any of *my* people?"

"None of the Satori have any interest in exposing you, Sienna. Your secret is safe with us."

And then I understand. He's going to report what he's observed to his parents back at the embassy. Maybe even to Ereni. "Are you sure that's a good idea? Telling other people?" He must know I want him to keep his mouth shut.

"Unfortunately, it's my job." He walks to the back door. "Be careful, Sienna. I'm probably not the only person watching you."

He leaves me staring after him, wondering exactly how much trouble I'm in.

THE NEXT MORNING I'm on edge, worried about how much I can trust Burke. He didn't seem shocked by my behavior. If anything, as hard as it is for me to believe, he seemed to admire me for it.

It's a heady feeling to know a stranger has seen such a secret side of myself and is taking it in stride. Burke relates to me in a way no one from Neopolitan could understand. I want to see him again.

So I'm disappointed when he's not present when I come to get Ereni for our outing to the Mask Maker's Festival. But Ereni is all charm and delight at seeing me again. I'd thought maybe I'd exaggerated her beauty in my memory, but she is just as absurdly, inhumanly gorgeous as the first time I met her. I marvel at how unconscious of it she seems.

Once we dock at Paraval Island, I take charge. "First things first," I tell Ereni. "We need to choose what masks we'll wear today." We disembark into the crowd of people, most of whom are already masked in honor of the day. Ereni zeroes in on the beggars sitting respectfully with their backs to the shops' walls, refusing to make eye contact. I don't notice them anymore, they're so common around San Marco, but Ereni stops and gives something to each one we pass. "So much needless suffering," she murmurs, shaking her head. "I can't wait until we get permission to open our clinic. Just think, we can give these people the best medical care on the planet."

"But they can't pay," I say, surprised.

"It will be a free clinic. We're not here to make money." Ereni makes money sound like a dirty word. "There are several diseases and disorders here on your planet we've managed to eradicate altogether on Satori, or that are only mild inconveniences. I hope we'll see the same thing someday on Sanctum."

I think of Mother, of her fainting, her headaches, the terrible crawling pain she endures on a regular basis. "There are some illnesses that just can't be fixed."

Ereni gives me a knowing look. "You're speaking of your mother."

I answer her with a shrug. It's common knowledge Mother isn't well. Ereni has done her homework.

As we make our way to my favorite mask shop, we pass every kind of mask imaginable: half masks and whole, smiling and frowning, masks created from joining two completely different masks right at the middle, black and white masks and brightly colored ones, along with metal masks and masks adorned with jewels and glitter and feathers. There are masks meant to convey different animals and different storybook characters, masks more than a meter long, masks that include elaborate headdresses and bonnets and costumes.

"They're all made by hand," I say. "And none of them are allowed to incorporate advanced technology. That's why there aren't any holograms or flashing lights or anything like that. They would be counter to tradition."

When we enter the shop, crowded with festival goers who have left their mask selection until the last minute like us, Ereni spins around, taking in the dizzying array of masks displayed on the walls and every available surface. Even I pause for a moment, appreciating their beauty. I've been collecting masks my whole life, and they've never lost their magic for me. They take up an entire wall of my bedroom, and I can remember exactly when I wore each one.

"I don't know where to start." Ereni picks up a purple mask with feathers erupting in an elaborate headdress and holds it to her face, then discards it for a full-faced porcelain rainbow mask that is twice the size of her own head. "How do you choose?"

"It depends what you're looking for." I finger a cleverly constructed leather fox face. "Do you want something elaborate? Something unique? Something trendy?"

Ereni tries to hold two masks to her face at once. "What do *you* look for?"

I hesitate. I have trendy masks, but they were all purchased for me by Mother. "When I'm shopping, I always try to find a mask that reflects a truth about who I am."

Ereni gestures to all the masks surrounding us. "But you don't know me well enough to guide me. I want to try on every single one." She grabs my arm, giggling, and I do my best not to flinch at the sudden touch. "Help me, Sienna, I'm depending on you."

I laugh at her confused rapture even while I try to discretely retrieve my arm from her grasp. "If you're not sure, then why don't you start with something simple?" I hold up a black half-mask that winks with small aquamarines that match her dress. It is plain other than some basic golden scrollwork and the jewels, but I think it will set off Ereni's intense beauty better than something loud and fussy. "You can always choose more later. You'll need several for Carnival, after all."

She takes the mask from me and ties the ribbon carefully around her hair. She gives herself a quizzical look in the mirror, tilting her head at different angles. "And when is Carnival?" she asks.

"It's based on the Old Earth calendar, so it changes every year. Sometimes we even have it twice a year, Masked Years, we call them. They're supposed to be lucky."

Her eyes dance. "Is this year a Masked Year?"

I shake my head. "I'm afraid not, but Carnival isn't long from now. It's a good chance to cut loose before Lent starts." I sigh at the very thought. If I think my life is claustrophobic now, it's nothing compared to how things are during Lent. No Race Days or parties, and I'm only allowed to wear dark colors and eat bland food. It's always a bleak time.

Ereni is still posing in front of the mirror, fluttering her eyelashes at herself. I take the opportunity to search for my own mask. I make my way to the back corner, brushing various masks with my gloved fingers as I walk past. None of them are quite right.

I begin sorting through a pile of masks, rejecting one and then another. And then I see it, the second to last in the pile. It's a half mask, all glittering gold, crafted from buttery leather. Golden feathers decorate the outer edge of the mask like the sun's rays or a lion's mane. It's not until I see Leo's secret mark on the inside that I understand what he has made. It's the *Ragazzo d'Oro* in mask form.

I clutch it in my hand, trying to convince myself to let it go. I've never allowed myself to buy one of Leo's masks before: the secret is too precious to risk. But surely I can buy one just this once? I tie it over my face, where it sits comfortably, showing only my mouth and chin. Its flaring design at the temples makes me look mysterious, older, but still feminine. The dark curls of my wig contrast well with its brightness. This mask lets me be everything I want to be.

When I return to Ereni, she's snapping photos of herself with her qualpad. "What do you think?" I ask her.

"This mask is charming, and I love it. Thank you, Sienna, for being such a good guide." She lowers her qualpad and turns to me. "Oh, and what have you found for yourself? How lovely." I think she's going to reach out and touch the cheek of my mask, but her hand simply hovers between us. She's not flawless, I realize as she draws it back. Even Ereni is having trouble adjusting to a new place, a new culture, a new set of rules.

And there certainly are enough of them.

~

WE WALK along the main promenade on the island, too hot in our masks and dresses. Ereni keeps reaching for her hair as though to pull it from her neck before remembering where she is. She also continually fusses with her gloves. I buy us lemon ices to help us keep cool.

We make it to the pier, and a breeze plays with my hair while Ereni stops at each booth and asks me questions. She speaks with a very slight accent, a subtle burring of her r's, an inability to make a pure "e" sound, an "s" that goes on longer than it should. "What language do you speak back home?" I ask her.

With her face hidden behind her mask, I can't tell what she thinks of my question. "You wouldn't have heard of it," she says, looking out over the water. "It's a lovely language. I still dream in it."

"Don't you still speak it with your parents and brother?"

She shakes her head. "Oh no, we're here to do a job. It wouldn't do for us to forget where we are. It's part of our Principles."

"What principles?"

She takes a delicate lick from her ice. "The Satori Foundational Principles. We take them rather seriously, I'm afraid." She winks at me. The dark mask sets off the emerald green of her eyes. "I've had them memorized, along with our Code of Conduct, since I was eight years old."

It didn't surprise me she'd been a precocious child. "So you always wanted to be a diplomat then?"

A group of young men on a boat motor below us, all wearing the same white masks, singing a sailing song in loud discordant voices. Their eyes watch us, and one of them toasts us with his flask. She gives him the exact right degree of smile: enough to acknowledge him without encouraging him further. It's a balance I have trouble striking, but then, I grew up in the country where everyone is more relaxed.

"Yes, ever since I can remember. I used to run through multiple AI scenarios per day, trying to learn how to be likeable."

I laugh. "That's not something you learn. That's something you *are*."

She cocks her head. "Is it, though? Of course some people are gifted with natural charisma or a knack of knowing the right thing to say, but that doesn't mean you can't also learn how."

I decide to play along. "All right, how do you go about learning to make people like you?"

She begins to tick off ideas on her fingers. "Well, in a culture like yours, it's important to learn to be as attractive as possible. Why do you think I chose this body for this mission?"

I gape at her. "What do you mean, you chose that body?"

She gives me a look. "You were expecting tails, isn't that right?"

"Yes...."

"We consider tails to be somewhat outlandish these days, but that doesn't mean we don't alter anything." She reaches up and touches her hair. "Aren't I very beautiful?"

I've never heard a woman say such a thing. We are supposed to be modest. We all care very much about our appearances, it's true; we all know how important it is to look our best. But to speak of our own beauty out loud? I look around to see if anyone is listening to us, but people flow by in a steady stream, talking and laughing and snapping photos of their favorite masks. "Yes, but...."

"But what? You think that's an accident? I had it done so I'd be likeable when I came down to the surface. That's the dedication of a diplomat. At home, none of this—the blond hair, the curves, the skin color—it wouldn't matter in the slightest. This isn't what we strive to be. But here it's important. It made your mother like me, didn't it? It's why we're here today, just the two of us."

She has a point. I try to swallow my shock that she has deliberately changed herself all the way down to her cellular structure. That she wields her beauty not as a burden she must perform, but as a tool. I don't understand, but even in my confusion, I want what she has.

"I can't change like that," I say. "We don't do that here."

"But you understand the principle well enough." She nods at me. "You're wearing that wig, after all."

So Burke told her. I reach for my fake curls, suddenly self-conscious. The truth is, I love this wig. I love that Lizabetta can style it while I do something else. I love that my scalp is no longer constantly sore from her ministrations. And most of all, I love the freedom of shedding the wig altogether. Not just when I'm pretending to be Leo, but at night when I go to bed. It's a tangible thing that reminds me I have a secret. That I'm not exactly who everyone expects.

"I'm not sorry." I say the words boldly, even though I'm terrified she'll expose me.

"I wouldn't be either." She leans on the rail with her elbows. "Don't worry, Sienna, we're all pretending to be people we're not. It's not just you." Another boat of rowdy boys passes. One of them whistles up at us. Ereni shudders. "I don't know how you manage as well as you do," she says.

I lean on the rail next to her. "So likeability is all about appearance then?"

"Not at all. That's one aspect, and in certain cultures, it carries particular importance. In Neopolitan, with your strict gender binary, it's the women who bear the brunt of these expectations. In other places, it's quite different." I try to imagine a culture in which it is the men who are expected to be beautiful at all times, but I can barely comprehend the idea, let alone picture it. "But there are other tricks to learn. Finding something in common with whoever you're interacting with, for example."

"You mean like you telling me we're all pretending?"

"Exactly!" She sounds cheerful, not at all put out by me calling her on her own words. "You see, you know what I'm talking about. Giving compliments can also be helpful. You have to be sincere, but if you put your mind to it, you can always find something positive to say."

Gianna and I are constantly giving each other compliments, but they never seem to make us like each other better. But then, neither of us mean a word we're saying. "Anything else?"

"Showing your appreciation. People like to feel important, like you've recognized their worth. Oh, and thanking them ahead of time. With money or favors if need be. It makes them feel obligated to help you."

"How do you know people on Sanctum will find the same things likeable?" They will, I can hear the truth ringing through her words, but I'm curious what she'll say.

She laughs again. "Oh, people are people wherever you go. The Satori have traveled to so many settled planets, and it's always the same. The trappings might be different, the traditions, even the basic values. But when it comes down to it, we're all still from the same species, and by and large human psychology remains predictable. Which is a lucky thing for us."

Another boat goes by, this one with two poorly dressed men at the oars. Four young men lounge on the seats, sipping wine from glass goblets. They look up at us, but they are too well bred to shout or make rude gestures. A sudden shock of recognition sweeps over me: the one with the black and white checked jester's mask is Enoch Royse.

Ereni straightens. "Now there's a snake in the grass," she says softly.

"My parents want me to marry him." Whatever Father says about a waiting game, I know he'll push for marriage if it benefits him and our family. And isn't this who I've been raised to become? The perfect diplomat's wife?

"And will you?" Ereni cocks her head in curiosity.

I shouldn't have mentioned this, and now I have to play it off. "Well, I have to marry someone." She doesn't say anything. "I hope not." The words come out scarcely louder than a whisper.

Ereni pushes herself from the rail. "Shall we take a stroll to the end of the pier?"

We walk in the small bubble of space our status as well-bred young ladies affords us. The competing smells of sweet popcorn, iced cakes, and roasting skewers of meat assail our nostrils, and I find myself getting hungry even though I just finished my ice. I buy Ereni a traditional glass and brass necklace; the glass beads are the same color as her hair. I'm about to suggest we stop for a snack when another group of young ladies passes us. Even masked, I recognize

Gianna in a heartbeat: her trademark ringlets, the mincing way she walks, the flurry of pale pink ribbons cascading down one side of her mask. I slouch down, hoping she won't see me.

No such luck. Her head whips around, and I feel her glare as a physical force. She marches over to me, and the crowd automatically makes room for her. She stops directly in front of me, a wide, tight smile showing underneath her mask, flanked by her two friends, one of them doubtless her little sister Isabel. "Sienna! What a pleasant surprise. When I didn't receive your invitation to come with you to the festival today, I feared you wouldn't be able to attend. And I know how much you love gallivanting about in a mask."

I return her smile. "You're the one who taught me the importance of being seen, Gianna."

"Since we *always* come to the Festival together, I didn't know what to think." She can't actually be disappointed I didn't invite her, can she? This is the first year we've attended separately, but she could have invited me for a change. No, she's taking another opportunity to find fault with me, that's all this is. She's been disapproving ever since we moved to the city and she ditched me for her stylish new city friends, spreading stories about me so I'd never have a prayer of fitting in.

We face off, both exuding cordial hostility. I'm forming another cutting comment in my mind when Ereni intervenes. "Oh, Gianna, is that you? I didn't recognize you in that gorgeous mask." Gianna's pause gives away her own lack of recognition. "It's Ereni Lhasa. We met two days ago when your family paid us a visit at the new Satori residence."

I would give a lot to see Gianna's shocked expression right now, but the mask hides any reaction. "Oh. What a pleasure to see you again." She fails to sound happy. In the social order we move within, I've achieved a coup by bringing Ereni to the Festival as my sole guest, and we both know it. "I didn't realize you were acquainted with Sienna."

Either Ereni is also aware of the social eddies of the situation or she just smiles a lot. "Oh, Sienna and I are becoming fast friends," she says. "As soon as we met, I knew she'd be the perfect person to help me navigate this city. Isn't the festival charming? She helped me buy my first mask, do you like it?"

Maneuvered into publicly admiring the mask she knows I chose for Ereni, I have to admit Gianna behaves with grace, even if the glances she throws my way are cutting. We force the crowds to spill around us as we admire each mask in turn, a delicate dance of courtesy and insult.

Until Gianna reveals her trump card. "I was so pleased to hear about our trip to Fidelium later this year," she simpers. "I've been many times, of course. It's such a diverting place to visit." Zio Roberto is less strict with his daughters than Father is with me. Father believes I must be protected like a hothouse flower. I know he would have never agreed to have me accompany the others on this trip to the Capitol if Zio Roberto hadn't convinced him it was a political necessity.

"Poor Sienna still hasn't been though, have you, Sienna?" Gianna knows how much I've been dying to go. We used to build miniature versions of Fidelium in her playroom, back when we were friends. She'd asked her parents for clear blocks so we could make the skyscrapers look more realistic. We'd keep stacking the plastic squares on top of one another until the entire structure would come tumbling down.

"You simply must let me show you around while we're there, Ereni." Gianna makes eye contact with me while she says it, underscoring the hierarchical order in which I'll always come in second place. "I'm happy to act as your private tour guide.

Ereni's friendly demeanor doesn't falter. "What a kind offer. I'll certainly keep it in mind." Polite but noncommittal. "We mustn't keep you any longer," she continues brightly. "But what an unexpected surprise to see you here."

"Anyone who is anyone comes to the Mask Maker's Festival," Gianna replies airily. "We should get together soon. I'd love to take you to lunch tomorrow, if you're free."

Another snub, but this one leaves me unscathed. A lunch doesn't compare in any way to an entire day at a festival. But Gianna has already bested me with her knowledge of Fidelium, so she can afford to make a soft play.

Ereni clasps her hands as if she'd like nothing more than a lunch with Gianna. "Oh, I wish I could. But alas, I've already asked Sienna to accompany me on my charity work tomorrow. Isn't that right, Sienna?"

Oh, she's good. She's been following the subtleties of the interplay all along, and I don't even care that Mother's approval of this new outing is hardly a given. "Yes, I'm looking forward to it," I say. I don't bother to send a look of triumph Gianna's way. The message is clear: Ereni has chosen me.

"But let's get together soon, shall we?" Ereni gives Gianna a sunny wave and begins to walk.

"I'm counting on it," Gianna calls after us. I can tell she's gritting her teeth at being outplayed.

I wait until we've put some distance between our two parties before leaning close to Ereni. "That was impressive. Although I don't think you've gained a new friend." But Gianna respects the power Ereni wields, a different but possibly equally useful tool.

Ereni gives me a conspiratorial smile. "Oh darling," she says, "you haven't seen anything yet."

CHAPTER 10

The next day Ereni takes me into one of San Marco's poorest neighborhoods. When she hears about our plans, Lizabetta insists on accompanying me, so our party consists of her, myself, Ereni, and a Satori medical doctor, Dr. Reddi. A woman doctor! She is small and plain and quiet, the complete opposite of Ereni.

The Satori amphicar can only take us so far by canal, and we have to proceed through a warren of narrow alleys on foot. Lizabetta hovers close to my side as if she's a bodyguard. Laundry bakes on lines above our heads, blocking what little light sneaks in from the narrow gaps between buildings. Further from the water, you'd think the smell would improve, but instead it worsens, a foul rotting stench that makes it difficult to breathe. "There's no regular garbage collection here," Ereni tells me in an undertone. "And they've been having problems with the sewer system."

The odor will only get worse as the temperatures increase over the spring and summer. "Is it scheduled to be fixed soon?" I ask.

Lizabetta snorts, and Ereni shakes her head. "The residents have been told it's not an urgent priority."

I'm embarrassed she knows these sorts of things about my city when I don't. I'm allowed to do charity work on Race Day, but I never get to see where that money is going. If Mother knew where I was right now, she'd be bedridden for days. Luckily she thinks I'm safe and sound taking tea at the Satori embassy as a thank you for the Mask Maker's Festival excursion yesterday.

We've been walking for less than five minutes before I doubt my ability to find my way back to the amphicar. Ereni takes the turns confidently, not even pulling out her qualpad. "How do you know where we are?" I whisper.

She taps the side of her head. "We have an intracranial interface that feeds us the information we need. Not unlike your qualpads, just faster." She flashes me a smile as if having a computer communicating directly to her brain isn't profoundly alien. I wonder what it's like to have the entire net just a thought away.

The alleys are mostly empty except for the occasional woman doing errands. Popular music blares from a few of the upper windows, along with the occasional baby crying. Piles of stuffed garbage bags, the entrails of these people's lives, sit beside each and every stoop.

We stop before a random brick building, white and pale blue sheets flapping from its windows as if to argue with the notion these people are fundamentally dirty. Father loves to say: "God helps those who help themselves." He's probably never seen this part of the city.

"Have you been here before?" I ask Lizabetta in an undertone.

She shakes her head. "This isn't my neighborhood." Then she shrugs. "Although it might as well be."

A fresh bloom of embarrassment unfurls inside me that I didn't know how badly off her family has been.

We climb three flights of stairs and knock on a door with peeling paint. A short woman in a bright yellow apron, streaks of gray in her flyaway hair, answers and smiles at us shyly. "Won't you come in, signorinas?" She rubs her bare hands frantically on her apron. "Please. Forgive me. Signorina Ereni, I spoke with all the neighbors, just as you said. Some of them...." She shakes her head. "They aren't so sure about you. But many came, yes, here they are, waiting for you." She opens the door wider, allowing us to see the cramped sitting room behind her, where there must be twenty of her neighbors, all women, all dressed in similarly modest but old garments and bright aprons. None will meet our eyes as we enter the room. None are wearing gloves.

Quietly, deliberately, Ereni pulls her own gloves off and stuffs them into her reticule. Dr. Reddi follows suit. Lizabetta looks at me, then the women, then back at me, and then with a little sniff she removes hers as well. I put my own gloved hands behind my back. The women watch us, and nobody says a word. The woman with the yellow apron closes the door behind us.

"Thank you for coming," Ereni says. A baby starts wailing, and she waits while the mother makes shushing noises and bounces it up and down. "Dr. Reddi and I have come to talk to you about women's health."

She and Dr. Reddi proceed to give a presentation on contraception, pregnancy and childbirth, menstruation, menopause, mental health, and various treatments and screenings they plan to offer free of charge at a clinic in the neighborhood, including medical care for children. The women listen in silence, occasionally exchanging glances when the Satori say something especially outrageous. Finally, Ereni offers any woman present a free contraceptive treatment on the spot that will last three months.

The woman in the yellow apron clears her throat. "We appreciate what you're trying to do," she says, "but many of us have questions. Contraception is hard to come by, yes, but it's also against the Church's teachings. Our men would not approve." Some of the women are nodding their heads. "But I lost my daughter Lara in childbirth last year. She was only twenty-two years old. She never recovered from her previous birth. It was too soon." She fingers the small gold cross around her neck. "We want to be sure we're doing the right thing."

Ereni looks at me as if expecting me to answer. I touch my own gold cross necklace with my gloved fingers. I think of this woman's daughter, less than five years older than me, already many times a mother, and dead. I think of what Mother and Father would say, how adamantly opposed they would be to the idea of providing contraception to these women. I think of the baby who will never know its own mother.

I have no idea of the scope of difficulties these women face. I turn to Lizabetta. "What do you think?" I ask her.

She shrugs. "It's a personal decision. Deception of this sort isn't to be undertaken lightly. We all know what the consequences could be." The women are nodding again, murmuring amongst themselves. "But"—Lizabetta's voice cuts through the room—"if we want to be good wives and mothers, and good people in general, we need to be responsible. And that means taking care of our own health too." She rubs her hands together, taking in the group of women in front of her. Women, I realize, that are just like the ones she grew up with. "You can't take care of your families if you're too ill to get out of bed. You can't feed your families if there are too many mouths and not enough food." She nods at the yellow-aproned woman. "Your grand-children will never know their mother. There's nothing moral or right about that. Senator Tascioni likes to say God helps those who help themselves. By taking care of our health, that's exactly what we're doing."

The yellow-aproned woman has tears streaming down her face, and the women break into discussion. Several have questions for Lizabetta. Ereni gestures for me and Dr. Reddi to follow her into the kitchen to give them some privacy.

"Well, Sienna, it looks like you knew the right person for this job." Ereni leans back against the sink in the tiny space. "I'm glad I asked you to get involved. I couldn't have done it without you."

I rather doubt that, but I can't prevent the warm glow that suffuses my body at her words of praise.

DR. REDDI GIVES the contraceptive shot to several women before we leave, and the general consensus about the new health clinic seems positive. Lizabetta asks to stay longer to speak privately with some of the women who are undecided, and Ereni invites me to take tea with her back at the embassy residence to celebrate our victory. "And to keep up your cover," she teases. "After all, you did tell your mother we'd be having tea together."

Once we return, she goes to the kitchen, leaving me to fend for myself in the strange sitting room, staring out at the festive roses and wishing in vain Burke would make an appearance. She brings back a pot of tea and some stray cookies and crackers on a chipped plate. It is the most unorthodox tea I've ever seen, but I enter into the spirit of being diplomatic and take a bite of slightly stale cookie without complaint.

"Thank you again for your help." She pours tea into my cup. "Some of those women will still be alive in a year because of what we did today."

She's exaggerating—isn't she?—but I flush with pleasure all the same. I've been able to achieve something, however small. "It was nothing."

"On the contrary. It was remarkable, especially given the current political climate." She reaches for the knife to cut some cheese slices. "Your government is getting quite cozy with the Providentials, you know. And as I understand it, the Providentials would have shot those women dead just for meeting with me today."

I don't know if that's true, but the Providentials *are* quite traditional and always have been. It's as if, arriving late as they did, they've felt the need to compensate for it. "Have you met the new Providential ambassador?"

"My parents have. And I hear your father spends a great deal of time with him."

I shrug. "Perhaps. But Father is a busy man. He never has much time for anyone." Except Zio Roberto, of course. Father always makes time for him.

Ereni makes a noncommittal noise. "Did you know late last week, the Providential government passed a law making it illegal to read or watch Satori media of any kind?" She puts a slice of cheese on a cracker and bites down.

"I didn't." I don't follow Providential politics, but given I've agreed to be courted by Enoch, perhaps I should start.

"And did you know that this morning, your own government

passed a very similar law? With certain passages that are almost exact duplicates?"

I hadn't known. There's been no time for me to get up-to-date with my qualpad. "I'm sure they have good reasons for the legislation."

"Your father was its biggest proponent on the floor." She glances sidewise at me before taking another bite.

"He champions all kinds of bills. That's his job."

"Are you saying you wouldn't like to see Satori movies? Read Satori literature? Learn about our history and way of life?"

"You know I would. But it doesn't matter what *I* want." I reach for another stale cookie.

"I could lend you a few books if you'd like." Her offer has unexpected teeth, given she's made sure I know it's now illegal for me to read those books.

But who would find out? "I'd like that."

Ereni beams at me. "A trait you share with successful Satori diplomats is that sense of burning curiosity about the world around you."

I don't know that the diplomats here on Sanctum would agree with the virtue of such a trait. And being a Senator's daughter, I know when I'm being flattered. Ereni is telling me exactly what I want to hear. And her huge green eyes don't hurt either. Altered eyes, I remind myself. She chose to have such beauty to have the effect she's having right now.

But I can't help liking her, even knowing that.

"Would you be willing to do more to help our cause?" Her words ripple through me as I consider the possibility of someone thinking I'm useful. "I'd understand if you're too busy."

"What do you have in mind? More visits like today's?"

"Not exactly." She walks over to the mantle, runs her fingers along it, stops when she reaches the mask she wore yesterday, now on display. "You must have access to all kinds of information, living with your father."

It takes me a moment to understand what she's implying, but

once I do, I spring up and back away as if she's suddenly sprung fangs. "You're asking me to spy on my own father?"

She laughs as if I've made a rather weak joke. "No, no, I wouldn't put it that way at all." She runs her finger over the contours of the mask. "You would just be passing on relevant information from time to time. Whatever you're comfortable with, of course."

That sounds like spying to me. "I don't know how things are in Satori," I say through clenched teeth, "but here in Neopolitan we are loyal to our families. I owe everything I have to my father."

"I know, and I wouldn't want you to do anything untoward." She gives a thoughtful tug to one of her curls as she walks back to the table. She picks up another cracker. "I hope your tea isn't getting cold."

I settle myself back into the chair across from her, watching her with a new alertness. The silence between us stretches thin. "I don't know anything that isn't common knowledge," I finally say. "My father keeps his private family life separate from politics."

"Of course. A practical arrangement for all concerned. Very Neopolitan." I can't tell if she means it as a reproof or a compliment. I take a sip of my lukewarm tea. "I was only thinking: if Neopolitan were to become slightly less friendly with Providence, arranging a marriage with a certain diplomat's son might seem less advantageous. You never know, Providence might even be inspired to call back the Royse family and reinstate the old ambassador." The end of Enoch? The entire city of San Marco would thank me. "And it would be good for everyone if your government were more inclined to cooperate with the Satori. I've spoken to Dr. Reddi about your mother. She has some ideas about her health issues and might be able to help her. If, of course, the Satori are allowed to begin practicing medicine here in San Marco. If we're allowed to open our clinics."

What would that mean, if Mother were finally well? I can't remember a time when she wasn't sick. For her to finally be free from her suffering…Ereni is offering something I don't want to refuse. And to be rid of Enoch Royse in the bargain? It sounds too good to be true.

She sips her own tea calmly, as if we're having a conversation about the weather. She's offering me more than I could have imagined even ten minutes before. But I don't trust her. How can I? "What will you do if I say no?" Expose my charade at the races? With that secret in hand, she can force me to do whatever she wants, and she must know that.

But she shakes her head. "I want to help you, Sienna, not hurt you." I want to believe her, but how can I when she holds my deepest secret? "Why don't you think about it? If you don't want to help, that's fine. I wouldn't want you to do anything that makes you uncomfortable. But since our interests align, I would certainly appreciate your help if you'd be willing to give it."

I drain my cup in an unladylike way and set in down with a clank in its saucer. "Let's say I did tell you things from time to time. I'm not saying I will," I rush to add. "I'm speaking hypothetically."

"Of course." She gives me an encouraging smile.

"Would everyone know?" I gesture at the residence around us. "Burke seems to have had no qualms about sharing my secret."

Ereni snorts. "Well, that's Burke for you. I certainly won't be telling *him* anything. Some of us have learned the importance of protecting our friends." She leans forward, hands clasped as if in prayer or promise. "It would be private, Sienna. Just between you and me. I swear it."

I look away. I know she's trying to manipulate me, but I'm so tempted to say yes. "I'll think about it," I finally say.

"Take all the time you need." She rises from her seat, all graciousness. "Now, let me see about those books for you to borrow."

She kneels beside a low set of shelves and pulls out a few paper volumes. Imagine traveling from another galaxy and bringing along paper books. These must be a rare luxury for the Satori. But even knowing that, I take them eagerly, hiding them in my own reticule.

I can't resist the burning curiosity Ereni knows I possess.

CHAPTER 11

$\mathcal{A}$ few evenings later, I'm sitting at a table with crisp white linens and gleaming settings. Across from me is Enoch Royse, his pale hair glowing in the candlelight, his eyes continually straying to my well-covered bosom as if he thinks I'm too innocent to notice. Everything about him is larger-than-life: his booming voice, his great slabs of hands balancing the restaurant's delicate cutlery, the way his presence in the room seems to devour all the space.

We are on a parent-sanctioned date. Lizabetta has accompanied us as our chaperone, but she's been relegated to the kitchen, where I hope she's being fed as well as we are. She's been making jokes and sly comments about my prospects all day, and when she got her first look at Enoch, she winked at me.

The restaurant Enoch has chosen is tiny and exclusive, with space for only five tables in the candlelit dining room. My feet sink into the plush rug, handmade by artisans from Aswan, and the walls are covered with gorgeous mosaics in earth tones. He has reserved the entire place, thus getting around the normal rules for a date such as this one. Technically we aren't alone since we are out in public. But the waiter keeps disappearing for inordinate amounts of time, and I know he's been bribed to give us space.

I try to be cordial, I really do. I have my deal with Father to consider, and I'm trying to focus on the positive aspects of being an ambassador's wife. I'd certainly get to travel more than I do now; instead of one special and well-chaperoned visit to Fidelium I might go there all the time, becoming part of the international elite. I could make a difference behind the scenes, collecting information and dispensing it as I see fit. It's more interesting than most of my future scenarios.

If only it didn't involve Enoch. He talks nonstop, but I'm used to listening, and this way I have an easier time maintaining the façade of my prodigious modesty. I keep reminding myself of the promised trip to Fidelium if only I can keep Enoch interested in me.

But what he says takes away my appetite. "You treat your maid awfully well," he observes at one point.

I dutifully look at my plate. "She's like family."

He laughs, and I look up sharply. "You women are so notoriously soft-hearted. 'Like family.'" He uses a ridiculous high-pitched voice to mock me. "She's only with you because you pay a good wage. It's not as if she's one of us."

"One of us?" I take a careful sip of water.

"Breeding shows," he says. "You and I both come from impeccable family lines, directly traceable to the Founding Families, so perhaps you haven't noticed. Your parents do take the precept to shield your innocence very seriously, I can tell. I approve of the old-fashioned ways. Too many cares placed on a woman's shoulders and her beauty fades away more quickly."

I wonder what he'd say if he knew I'd raced against him and almost beaten him. Would he think less of my beauty then? I quash the temptation to tell him just so I can see the look on his face.

He talks a lot about his friends back in Providence, and I get the sense he is namedropping, only I don't know the names. He talks about the house his father will be giving him soon. He talks about his brief time in Neopolitan, not bothering to hide the occasional sneer. He thinks he's better than we are, that his country is better than ours. I wonder why he's willing to consider me as a prospective marriage partner. In his own way he must be as dutiful to his father as I am to mine. I try to like him because of it, but watching his jaw swing open as he gabs continuously, his attention fixed entirely on himself, I can't feel anything more benign than impatience.

At least the food is good.

He doesn't start going after Leo until the dessert course is served: a big slice of chocolate cake for him, a small dish of strawberry-glazed panna cotta for me. He chose both, and I take a tiny spoonful of panna cotta even though I don't like it. "Your brother's quite a piece of work," he says around a mouthful of cake. I watch him chew, little crumbs of cake escaping to land on his chin. "I don't think he likes me."

"He doesn't know you." I'm proud of my tactful response.

"He tried to fight me one time." Little does he know he's talking about me, not Leo. "And he drove recklessly trying to beat me on the track." Also me. And he's wrong. If I'd been reckless, I would have ended up in an accident, not taking fourth place. "I think he's jealous."

"Jealous of what?" I allow a small amount of incredulity to creep into my voice. "Leo's just Leo. I wouldn't worry about it."

"In Providence sometimes it's left to the older brothers to train their sisters for their wifely duties."

I stare at him with my mouth wide open as the full meaning of his words hits me. What he has just said is so offensive and disgusting I can't think of a single response. No promised trip is worth this much suffering.

Enoch smiles. "Oh, come on, Sienna. I know you're not as virtuous as all that. I'm not an idiot. I've talked to my new friends here. You don't have a special reputation for modesty. You have one for talking too much and having entirely too many opinions for a proper young lady. Your father hopes to pawn you off on me because no one here will have you. But hey, I'm a good sport. Maybe we can have some fun, and if everything goes well, I'll consider his proposal more seriously." He reaches underneath the table and squeezes my knee. My knee. It has his *hand* on it.

The worst part is he's completely serious. He thinks he can insult me in multiple ways, and I'll just play along. That I'll make excuses for him, that I'll chalk it up to his foreign ways, that I really am that desperate since I am apparently already unmarriageable at age seventeen.

I put my hand on his, and he grins, specks of brown lodged between his teeth. He thinks I'm falling for it. I'm so angry every second is an eternity. I shove his hand off my leg and stand up. For once I'm taller than he is, and I revel in it. I reach across the table, grab his icing-covered cake that is so much better than my own dessert, and shove it right in his face. It makes a satisfying squish.

He's so surprised his eyes bug right out of his head. I'd be laughing if I weren't so mad. He splutters, trying to wipe cake from his face. I grab my bland panna cotta and dump it over his head.

I wipe the icing from my hands with my pristine napkin, one finger at a time while he struggles to wipe pink goop from his eyes. "I understand you come from a different place, and allowances need to be made." I speak every word with the crispest diction. "But the next time you insult me, you'll get a lot worse than some dessert."

I look up to see most of the staff crowded at the kitchen door, watching us with a comical array of shocked expressions. Except for Lizabetta, who is silently laughing. She helps me with my coat while Enoch keeps up a steady stream of swearing, the rest of the staff hovering around him in ineffectual dismay. We leave the restaurant even though we don't have an amphicar waiting for us.

"Lord, I'll never forget this, not for the rest of my days," Lizabetta gasps as we round a corner. "You never take the easy way, do you, Signorina?" Her lips quirk, I snort, and we both burst into gales of laughter. For a moment we are more bonded by our womanhood than separated by our stations. Just as we're calming down, she says, ""That pink goop all over his face!" and we break into hysterics again.

We call for an amphicar a few blocks away, once we've put a safe distance between me and the raging boy I've left behind.

WHEN WE ARRIVE HOME, Mother is waiting for me in the foyer. Collapsed onto one of the benches beside the door, she leans her head against the wall, her skin looking pasty in the low light. She must be having another of her spells. When she sees me, she stands up straight, looking like she's tasted something rotten. "Your father wishes to speak to you."

They must know. Enoch certainly works fast. "Father's home? I thought he was out."

"He was," Mother hisses. "The Ambassador cut their evening short."

Translation: Father is even angrier than I am right now.

"Lizabetta, go upstairs. I'll need you later." Any trace of mirth has disappeared from Lizabetta's face as she hurries to obey. Mother escorts me to Father's study as if she's afraid I'll run away, our shoes sounding loud against the tile. She pushes open the door without bothering to knock. Father stands up behind his desk at our entrance, and we all stare at each other.

Then Mother sinks into a chair, and Father heaves a huge sigh before standing to get her a glass of water from the bar cart. "The Ambassador of Providence has informed me you assaulted his son this evening."

Assault? I bridle at the overblown accusation. "That's hardly what happened. He propositioned me. He implied I have a poor character and suggested I grant him certain…favors in exchange for his willingness to consider me as a potential marriage partner." I force myself to continue in spite of my embarrassment. "He also suggested I already give those favors to Leo." I pause, ready to hear their shock and indignation.

"Foolish girl." It's Mother who speaks, while Father circles back behind his desk. "Have I taught you nothing?"

I struggle to hide the hurt caused by her harsh words. "You taught me how important it is for me defend my virtue. That nobody will marry me if there are rumors of me being alone with a man or behaving inappropriately."

"I taught you to do what's necessary to seal the deal." Mother takes one small sip of water before setting the glass on a coaster. "Instead you disgraced our family."

"That's not fair. I acted to avoid disgrace. And it's not as if I hurt him."

"You hurt his pride, Sienna." Mother says the words as if I'm the biggest idiot she can imagine. "What have I told you about a man's pride?"

That at all costs I must allow a man to maintain it. "But what about my pride?" I burst out. "What about the other things you've taught me? How am I supposed to behave properly when I'm not given any options?"

"Not given any options?" Father leans on his desk, his powerful forearms bulging. "Surely you've had a better education than that. You should have spurned his advances more diplomatically. With tact and precision, while flattering him and implying there could be future favors. Not by"—his face was turning red—"dumping both your desserts on his head."

So he already knows there was no violent assault. "I told you it was a bad idea for him to court me. I don't like him. There's something wrong about him."

"It doesn't matter how you feel." His voice thunders through the office, and I shrink back. Father rarely expresses his anger, but when he does, he makes it count. "You have embarrassed me in front of one of our most important Ambassadors. You've made it look like I can't control my own daughter, let alone follow through on the political commitments I've made. Because of your actions, going forward I will have a weaker position in our negotiations. Do you understand the harm you've caused?"

I can feel tears threatening, but I swallow them down. "I didn't mean to."

"As if intentions count for anything in this world." Father thumps his desk. "You will apologize to Enoch Royse first thing tomorrow morning. You will take full responsibility for what happened tonight, you'll apologize at length, you'll grovel on the floor if that's what it takes to appease him. And then you'll allow him to court you properly and keep him happy until I tell you to do otherwise. Do you understand?"

I stare at him, aghast. I don't want to apologize for something that wasn't my fault, and especially not to someone as odious as Enoch. He won't accept my apology anyway, not unless I humiliate myself and proffer those favors he's so obsessed with. Father might think I should have been able to manipulate him into cooperating, but even were I capable of such a thing, that opportunity is now gone.

"I won't do it."

Father's eyes narrow. "Your mother's judgment has been sound. I've allowed you too much leeway. It was a mistake to let you share in Leo's education before we moved here. Your reputation is not what it should be."

"My reputation is spotless!"

"You talk too much and too loudly, you have too many opinions, and you have a temper." Mother lists my faults dispassionately, as if she's not thrusting a knife into my heart with each one. "Not to mention you lack a certain pleasing pliability of temperament."

"So you want me to go and give your precious suitor exactly what he wants? Is that it?" I can't believe what I'm hearing.

Father sits down heavily. "What I want, Sienna, is for you to be an asset to this family. You will apologize."

He doesn't answer my question, which tells me everything I need to know. I picture Enoch's fleshy face, the look of naked acquisitive hunger in his eyes when he looks at me, and I can't help shuddering. Is this really the only option before me? I try again. "Please, Father." I clasp my hands in supplication. "I don't know how to be who you need me to be. Please."

He stares at me impassively. Nothing I say will change his mind. I'm about to capitulate when I think of Ereni, who is the complete mistress of her fate. I want to be like her, not like myself. I swallow hard and try not to shrink back from the united front of my parents' rigid postures. "I can't apologize," I whisper.

Father squeezes his hands into fists, and then I do cower. But he doesn't move from behind the desk. "Then you leave me no choice. Your bedroom will be moved to our wing of the house where your mother can more closely supervise you. You will spend less time with your brother since you seem unable to understand your different positions in life. You will no longer be involved in any charity work, including the Race Day booth. And you certainly won't be traveling to Fidelium this spring, not when you can't be trusted to behave properly."

My tears come closer to the surface, and I fight to hold them back. "But I haven't done anything wrong. I'm being punished for what Enoch Royse did. It's not fair."

"Don't speak to your father like that," Mother interrupts. "I've tried my best with you, but with my illness…." She trails off, and I feel like the worst daughter in the world. "Enoch Royse can't be expected to control his baser impulses; it is up to you to regulate them for the both of you."

"But he said—"

"I know what he said." Her voice is sharp. "You had many choices of how to respond, and instead of choosing a ladylike one, you gave into your temper. That is hardly Signor Royse's fault. And if you refuse to respect your father and apologize, you must be punished accordingly." She sniffs. "It's for your own good. We have a lot of catching up to do for you to be able to fulfill your responsibilities to this family."

Father swivels his chair so his back faces me. "We are done here," he says. "You are dismissed."

They're taking away everything I care about, all because Enoch Royse is a first-class nightmare. There's no point in arguing further. I've never been able to change Father's mind.

The injustice of it burns. I writhe with it as Mother escorts me to my new room, one of the guest rooms down the hall from her and Father's suite. "We'll move your things tomorrow." She opens a drawer, showing me a nightgown kept there for guests, and leaves without saying good night.

I sit fully clothed on the bed that's not my bed. It's too big and too soft. The direction of the windows means I'll get full sun streaming in every morning, the curtains insufficiently thick to block it. A huge full-length mirror dominates the wall in front of me, making me feel like I can't get away from myself. I struggle to take off my wig, and I look at myself. My bare self. The person my parents want to snuff out and replace with the ideal daughter, someone I will never be able to become.

Except with some help. If Ereni is able to sour relations between Providence and Neopolitan, then this will no longer be my fault. My behavior to Enoch will be forgotten. It will be the least of Father's problems. Enoch will return home where he belongs, and I'll have another chance.

And Mother is becoming worse again. It's obvious, all the little signs, now that I'm looking. The fatigue, the sharpness, the long afternoon rests. I catch her with eyes closed, pain etched in the lines on her face, when she doesn't think I'm looking. She needs Satori medical intervention, whether she knows it or not.

And like Ereni said, it's not like it's spying. Not really. It's just sharing some information from time to time. My parents want me to become better at manipulation and diplomacy, don't they?

Well, here is my chance to become better than they ever imagined.

CHAPTER 12

My gown for the reception honoring the new Providential and Satori ambassadors, an appropriate pale lavender, squeezes me like a straitjacket, and Lizabetta spends more than two hours arranging my hair. I've never been so grateful to be wearing Mother's old wig, even while I'm glad of the excuse to hide in my room. Mother has gone to great lengths to instruct me on my behavior at the event. Now that I've offended Enoch, she doesn't trust me to remember the most basic manners and protocol.

On the other hand, at least she's letting me leave the house. Except for a carefully monitored visit with Gianna, I haven't left the grounds since the disastrous dinner with Enoch. I've barely even seen Leo; after a few days he succumbed to the boredom of my absence and returned to school. I don't know how Enoch has been treating him because I don't dare to ask in Mother's hearing.

This reception will be the perfect opportunity to tell Ereni about my change of heart.

I'm ready to take matters into my own hands.

PROVIDENCE IS HOSTING the event at their embassy, adjacent to the Royse's residence. Hundreds of glow balls circulate above our heads, making the huge room as light as day, and a small orchestra plays softly at one end of the room. Our hosts have chosen a slightly chilly temperature, causing goosebumps to develop on my exposed arms. The odors of a hundred sweet perfumes mix with the scent of the roasted meat hors d'oeuvres, making me momentarily queasy. Cameraflies zoom around the room, recording the luxury for all those not fortunate enough to be present.

My parents sweep into the reception line with the grace of long practice, at ease amongst their friends and colleagues flaunting their most formal outfits and glittering jewels. Leo and I go more slowly; all of Mother's advice has been wrapping itself around my brain like a boa constrictor, making me cautious. "Everything okay?" I murmur to Leo as our parents speak to Ereni and Burke's parents.

"Just fabulous." He waggles his fully gloved right hand. "Got the splint off earlier today. Finally! The doctor says I have to be careful for another week or two, but I bet I can get away with a little painting at the very least. I can't wait to get back home."

He looks happier than he has since the accident. "Speak for yourself," I tease. "If I didn't get out of that house tonight, I was going to start beating my head against the front door."

Leo laughs. "I'm surprised you and Mother haven't strangled each other yet. Is she letting you do anything by yourself?"

I roll my eyes. "The other day I thought she was going to follow me into the bathroom."

We're introduced to the Satori Ambassador to Neopolitan—and Ereni and Burke's father—Arum Lhasa. He's tall, with a thick silver mane of hair and a wide nose, his skin olive like my own. I know he's chosen to look this way, and I approve. His wife thanks me for my kindness to her daughter, and then we're face to face with Ereni and Burke themselves.

Ereni winks at me, and I notice she's wearing the golden glass necklace I gave her. "I hear you don't have a fondness for cake," she says softly. Her eyes sparkle with mirth.

How does she know what happened? "Actually, my objection is to panna cotta," I say. Leo snorts beside me.

"Well, I'm glad they let you come tonight. You're my favorite Neopolitan, after all." Ereni glances across the room, where Gianna huddles with her sister and a few of their sillier friends. "Even Burke has missed you. Haven't you, Burke?"

"I don't know how I've managed to keep myself occupied in your absence." He flashes his crooked smile. "Although I've appreciated living without risk of being attacked by desserts. I'm still learning your strange customs, you understand."

I smile back. "Just wait until you're forced to participate in one of our formal dances."

He groans. "Unfortunately, I've already been briefed on that particular facet of your culture. But I doubt I have the skills to join."

Once again Burke shows his discernment: in order to be proficient, I've been studying our formal dances since I could walk. "Perhaps remaining an audience member is best," I say.

His lips twitch. "I hope to see you again later this evening."

It's Ereni I need to speak with, Ereni with whom I need to make plans. But it's Burke's smile that gets stuck in my head. "Me too." We nod at each other before Leo and I continue down the line after our parents.

"He pays too much attention to you," Leo whispers.

I know he's right, but Burke makes me happy, and there's so little that does these days. "He's harmless."

"You're wrong." I'm surprised by the heat in his voice.

But then we're standing before Enoch's parents, who greet me with frowning faces. His mother openly glares at me. I give them the tiniest smile and nod and let Leo do the talking. By the time he's through with them, complimenting everything from Enoch's mother's gown to Enoch's racing prowess, they've thawed slightly.

Enoch glowers beside them, tall and blond and bearish, and I wish we could skip greeting him, but that's out of the question. "Good evening." I say it with the customary nod.

"Evening," he drawls. He's doing a terrible job pretending not to be angry. His left eye twitches with the effort of holding in his feelings. "Tascioni. Will I see you at the track tomorrow?"

"Naturally." Leo grips my arm tighter and leads me away. "Are you going to be able to sneak out tomorrow and take my place?" he whispers.

"With Mother keeping me under lock and key? Doubtful."

Leo sighs. "I'll have to find an excuse to withdraw."

Any excuse he makes will play as weakness. "Are you sure you can't just…race? You can stay far away from Enoch Royse. Play it safe so there's no chance of another crash."

He releases my arm. "Don't worry about it, Si." This is Leo's way of outright rejecting my suggestion.

But I can't let it go. "Do you want me to practice with you? It'll be hard to evade Mother, but I can sneak up to the playroom tonight after this is over, and we can—"

"I'll handle it." Great. Now I've annoyed him.

"She won't be my jailer forever," I say in a rush. "You know how she is, she'll get distracted sooner or later." Or sick, I don't need to say.

"I said don't worry about it. *Merda*, I wish I didn't have to be here." He walks away abruptly, leaving me at Mother's mercy.

Luckily Gianna bears down on me soon afterwards, her tall willowy figure clad in a daring gown even more unyielding than my own, all sparkling gun metal gray. Her collar bones stick out above the neckline and her elbow length gloves are made of matching but translucent gray lace, two new risqué trends Mother would never allow me to follow. Mother returns to Father's side after giving me a particularly trenchant look of warning.

"Gianna!" I force my lips into a bigger smile. "What a remarkable color."

She wrinkles her nose, not sure if I gave her an insult or a compliment. Gianna is so easy to bait, it's hard for me to resist. "Father himself complimented me on it." I can't help envying the greater leeway Zio Roberto gives her. Only a few other young ladies have dared to wear such bold looks; most of us are clad in whites and pale pastels cut up to our necks. Gianna's photo will be everywhere tomorrow, and she knows it. "No offense," she says, "but you look rather uncomfortable in your gown."

I won't complain about its scratchiness or its propensity to dig into my ribs and constrict my breathing. "It's fine."

Her smile grows at my forced stoicism. "You should really allow me to help you with your wardrobe. You've never had a knack for that sort of thing. Remember when it would get hot in the summer and you'd strip down to your…you know." As if it's so scandalous she can't bear to mention the specifics. It's a good thing I can't easily sigh in this dress. Why doesn't she go stand with her city friends if I'm so backwards? But this time she sticks to my side like glue. "I hear Enoch Royse received permission to court you. Why didn't you tell me?"

The one blessing of my inappropriate behavior on our date is that it is as embarrassing to Enoch as it is to me, so we're both motivated to keep the incident quiet. Which makes me wonder how Burke and Ereni knew about it. I certainly haven't spoken about it to anyone outside my family.

I lower my eyes in simulated modesty. "Oh, I didn't want anyone to get the wrong idea."

But Gianna already has the wrong idea and will not be deterred. She claps her gloved hands with excitement. "Has he proposed? Will it be a fast wedding? I wondered when Mother told me you wouldn't be coming with us to Fidelium after all." Poor Gianna isn't sure whether to be jealous about my theoretical marriage or smug that she's going on yet another trip I'll miss.

I glance around to see if anyone has overheard us. Ears are everywhere at events like this. "No, no," I say loudly enough to turn a few heads. Then I lower my voice. "We had an initial meeting, but my parents decided a match within Neopolitan would be preferable."

Her face falls. "Oh, that's too bad. He seems kind of mysterious, don't you think? With his little accent?" She sighs. "Not that *I* could ever marry a foreigner, of course. It's out of the question." I don't point out the double standard of wanting a match for me that would be completely unacceptable for her. I don't remind her that her father wouldn't be Doge had it not been for my own father's support and hard work persuading other key Senators and Assemblymen. I don't mention the unspoken agreement between our two fathers that her own father will step down at the end of this term and give my father his own chance to lead our country.

Does that mean soon I'll be as boring and perfect as Gianna is now? Maybe my lack of measuring up is why my parents have been so eager to arrange a match that will distance me from the political playing field. To them I will never be more than a potential liability.

"So why aren't you coming to Fidelium then?" Gianna asks, a gleam in her eye. "It's so sad you've never managed to go."

I mumble an excuse about Father deciding it isn't appropriate for me while she pretends to be sympathetic.

Gianna is the worst.

WHEN ERENI GLIDES up to us later in the evening, all eyes follow her. She manages the almost impossible feat of making her gauzy ivory gown look comfortable, but more importantly, the gown accentuates her beauty rather than drawing attention to itself. She's everything Gianna aspires to be.

"May I borrow Sienna for a moment?" Gianna's face falls when she realizes Ereni has come to speak to me, not her. "We won't be long." Ereni is using the same fake nice voice Gianna and I use with each other. She learns fast.

"She's a bit dull, isn't she?" Ereni whispers this as we make our way across the crowded room.

"My mother wishes I were just like her," I whisper back.

"Your mother isn't exactly a party herself." Ereni pulls me into a small alcove where we have relative privacy. "You're certainly hemmed in by a lot of rules."

"They help us become our best selves." But the words ring hollow. After all, who would it hurt if I were allowed to openly compete in the speeder bike races? The pride of any man I was able to beat?

Ereni makes a polite noise as if she knows I don't believe my own words. "Do the rules involve dumping pudding on your rejected suitors' heads?"

I remember the look on Enoch's face, and I can't help shaking with silent laughter. "How did you hear about that?"

Ereni shrugs. "I have my sources. Besides, it's obvious how you feel about him. All I had to do was watch your face while you talked to him tonight."

"I was polite." But I can't help tensing; will I receive yet another parental scolding for my behavior?

"Oh, don't worry. To the average onlooker, your performance will have passed muster."

I'm not sure whether I feel more reassured or nervous that she's watching me so closely. But I'm definitely jealous of her ability to read people. "What gave me away?"

"You were leaning slightly away from him while you talked. Your cheek muscles weren't engaged in your smile. And you only met his eyes once, and very briefly. You're going to have to do better with eye contact if you want to fool people into thinking you like them. They may not notice the lean, but they'll definitely notice you looking at anything but them."

"Thanks for the tip, but I'm pretty sure Enoch Royse already knows I don't like him." It comes out more acerbic than I mean it.

"Of course, but other people don't, and I assume you want to keep it that way. For now, at least."

"You really want Enoch Royse sent home?" I ask.

Ereni shrugs. "Along with the rest of his family, most notably his father. Yes. That would suit our interests. Providence is more conservative than Neopolitan, and less interested in what we have to offer. It would be a shame if they convinced your country to follow their lead."

"I want them gone," I whisper. "I want everything to go back to normal."

"Then we want the same things." She leans closer to me. "It might even be possible to have a doctor see your mother before we've finished cutting through all the bureaucratic nonsense around our clinics."

My last qualm crumbles away. "I don't want my father's reputation to suffer." I peer out at him and Mother laughing with Zio Roberto and Zia Sylvia across the room.

"I can work with that. He doesn't need to be involved."

"None of my family," I insist. "I don't want them hurt, and they can never know."

Ereni arches a perfect eyebrow. "Not even Leo? I didn't know twins kept secrets from one another."

I think about how Leo has been struggling ever since the racing accident. I want to protect him. "Especially not Leo."

"No one will know," Ereni says. "Not on my end either. The more people know a secret, the harder it is to keep."

"Very well. I'll see what I can do."

"Do you have anything for me right now?"

I shake my head. "My father is careful. He doesn't talk about sensitive matters, and he conducts much of his business outside the house. But I'll watch for anything interesting."

"I appreciate your cooperation." She follows my gaze to where my parents stand talking. "But you may have to do more than just watch if you want to eradicate your problem." She pauses to allow the implications to sink in. "Have you been enjoying the books I lent you?"

Finally a topic I can be entirely enthusiastic about. "Yes, I finished reading the history of Satori's founding just today. It's funny that a country that diverges from Neopolitan in so many ways could have anything in common with us, and yet it does, doesn't it? So many of the things your ancestors said they wanted could have been said by my own."

"It takes a certain type of person to become a galactic colonist. As one of my teachers liked to say, we're all dreamers at heart. People following a vision."

But the reading has taught me the Satori vision is completely at odds with the Sanctum one. They don't have churches or any organized religion that I can discern. Their system of government is non-hierarchical, and it seems like no one worries much about money, which I don't understand at all. If I've understood correctly, the women no longer even bear their own children; they have artificial environments for growing fetuses to term. It sounds as alien as if we were from two different species altogether, branching from the same distant ancestors.

Ereni drifts back into the crowd, dazzling smile turned to full wattage. A hint of honeysuckle scent is the only sign she ever stood next to me at all. She charms the room one person at a time, continuously leaning towards guests, tilting her head, her arms comfortable at her sides, her gestures mirroring those of her conversational partners. She smiles, she laughs, she looks like there's no place she'd rather be, spreading her own particular brand of charisma. I have so much to learn.

"She's really something, isn't she?" Burke's low voice makes me jump.

"She excels at what she does." I don't bother to hide the admiration in my voice.

"She's the star of the embassy."

He doesn't sound happy about it, and I laugh. "Sibling rivalry?"

He blinks. "What's that?"

I draw farther into the alcove so nobody notices we're talking. "You know, when you don't get along with your sibling even though you love them. When you feel like you're in a kind of competition with them."

"Is that how you are with your brother?" he asks.

"Not usually," I admit. "But lately…."

"You've been fighting?"

"No, not fighting. Just…there's been a lot going on. Things are complicated."

"And you're a better racer." He gives me a wink.

I laugh in spite of myself. As if Leo cares about that. "See? You understand more than you think."

"I understand rivalry, full stop. And you do too. I've seen you with Gianna."

Just hearing her name makes me want to roll my eyes. "I don't care about her."

Burke shakes his head. "Then why does she irritate you so much? You may not know yourself as well as you think."

Father has crossed the room without Mother and is in deep conversation with Enoch's father. Given how poorly Enoch's and my courtship went, I would have expected Father to give him a wide berth. But as I watch, they both burst into laughter. I cross my arms, my dress digging into my ribs. "So you think you know me better than I know myself?"

"Not at all. I apologize if I misspoke. I'm simply curious. I wonder what you do care about. Forgive me for saying so, but you seem a bit…restricted."

I toss my head in impatience. "I don't want to be Gianna. Her life is just as boring as mine."

"Then who do you want to be?"

I don't even have to think about it. "My brother. He gets to do everything."

Burke reaches out as if he's going to touch one of my fake curls. "I guess that explains your little show the other day."

I hate that he thinks he knows. How can he know anything? He's only just arrived. "He asked me to pose as him," I protest. "He practically begged me."

"I believe you." His lips quirk. "And you agreed."

"Of course. I will always help my brother."

His smile grows. "And how many people do you know who pretend to be their siblings to help them? Is that this sibling rivalry you've been telling me about?"

"Everything's a big joke to you, isn't it?" But his words make me uneasy. I know I didn't create this situation for Leo, but have I been too quick to capitalize on it? My motives are not as pure as I'd like.

But then I remember the race and how close I came to winning, and I can't regret anything.

"I'm merely trying to remind you that you're special," Burke says. "That you have the courage to do things others do not."

"Or the stupidity," I mutter.

"You know that's not what it is." His voice is low and warm, and I have to look away from the expression in his eyes. " Let's escape this place together, Sienna. For a little while, at least. Let me take you on an adventure."

"Excuse me?" I can't help remembering the way his hand had felt when he took mine back in the garage, and I blush.

"Sounds like you could use a little fun."

I back further into the shadows, not wanting him to see my reddened cheeks. "My mother won't let me go anywhere without her."

He laughs down at me. "Are you telling me you can't figure out how to slip away? The girl who raced with a passel of boys without a single soul suspecting?"

"You could tell," I counter.

"But it's not me you have to fool." He leans in and whispers in my ear. "Meet me a week from Sunday. The rose garden behind my house. You remember where. Just before sunset."

He walks away before I have a chance to tell him it's impossible.

It *is* impossible. But the more confined I feel, the more I'm tempted by impossible things.

CHAPTER 13

The following night, I am alone in the house. Leo disappeared without telling me where he was going. Father and Mother are at a social function.

And I have important things to do in Father's study.

Father always says you should have impeccable electronic security practices, but if you really want to keep something safe, you should keep a hard copy. Hard copies cannot be hacked. Hard copies require someone to physically break into your space to obtain. Hard copies are easy to destroy. And Father keeps all his hard copies at home in a safe in his study.

I don't know how to get into the safe, but there's no time like the present to take a look. There's also always a chance he's left something interesting lying around. I have to find something to give Ereni if I want her to get rid of Enoch for good.

I wait until mid-evening when most of the servants will be relaxing in their own quarters. I print out a document I can tell a servant I'm returning if I get caught. It wouldn't fool Father; he has no interest in a paper I wrote last year—unread and ungraded, of course—on the ethical ramifications of charity work. But he and Mother shouldn't be home for another few hours at least.

I stand listening at the top of the stairs and then race down, quiet in my house slippers. I slink around the corner and down the hall, and open the study door. I close it behind me and let out a big sigh. I've made it.

The room is dark except for a small amount of light filtering in through the French doors. I move forward carefully but still bang my shin against a chair leg. When I reach the desk, I switch its small lamp on. I take a photo of the safe built into the wall, hidden behind an innocuous painting of fruit, but I already know it's no good. I can see the retinal scanner built into it, and there's no way to beat something like that.

But I don't want to leave empty-handed. The desktop is completely clear aside from the straight line of clocks, not a speck of dust anywhere. I begin to go through the drawers. Pens and pencils, a few blurry photographs of him and Mother from when they were first married, and one of him and Zio Roberto, both young with more hair and goofier smiles. Some personal tax papers he's partway through filling out. Some handwritten cards, thanking him for gifts, for his attendance at an event, for mentoring somebody's son. One of the Doge's special seals, which is a bit odd. And a…key? Why does Father have a key floating around in the back of his drawer? Hardly anybody uses keys. I only know what it is because of the symbolic Key to the City ceremony we have every autumn.

I'm staring at the key, wondering what it could open, when I hear sounds from the hallway. It only takes me a couple seconds to switch off the lamp, drop the key back where I found it, and slide under the desk. I barely make it before the big overhead chandelier flares on. "Thanks for meeting me at home," Father is saying. Who does he have over? Why is he home so early? I'm surrounded by the wood of the desk so I can't see anything.

"It's my pleasure." I don't recognize his voice. It's not Leo. It's not Uncle Roberto. "I'm sorry I had to interrupt you at the function." No accent, so it's probably a fellow Neopolitan.

"It's not of any consequence." Oh no, is Father going to walk around the desk? Is he going to *sit* at the desk? I can't think of a single convincing excuse for why I'd be hiding under here.

Which is when I realize I don't have the paper I printed as my excuse for being here in the first place. Where did I leave it? I force myself to think through my sudden sickening surge of panic. Did I stick it in a drawer? I can see it's nowhere on the floor.

No. On the desk. I left it on the desk. The beautiful pristine desk where it will be immediately obvious. *Cazzo.*

"Would you like a drink?" Father asks. I relax a little. The drinks cart is on the other side of the room, by the leather wingback chairs where he sits with those in his inner circle.

Glass clinks and I know Father is pouring. Moving as slowly as I dare, I reach my hand up and feel the top of the desk. No paper, no paper, aha! There it is. I snatch the document and whisk it under the desk. Then I freeze and wait. Did either of them see me?

"Thanks, Senator." They clink glasses, and I let out my breath. I'm in the clear. For now.

"This new clique of Assemblymen are such bores," Father drawls. "They don't know a fine vintage from rotten grapes. And their ideas about the vote!"

"The Senate will keep them in check."

"Indubitably. That's what we're here for. But I have to ask myself, how in Heaven's name did four of these *cogliones* manage to get elected last cycle?" A pause, the musical jostling of ice cubes in glasses. "They'll need a firmer hand than Roberto has given them thus far."

"Astute as always, Senator." Ugh. This man is just saying what my Father wants to hear.

"Now what's so urgent you had to pull me out of that dull affair? You have documents that require my signature, yes?"

"I do, Senator, but that's not the only reason we're here."

My interest heightens, and I press the record button on my qualpad.

"I suspected as much. What do you have for me?"

"It's regarding some things Roberto—the Doge—has said and done. Nothing obvious, and it might not come to anything, but I thought—"

"Tell me." Father's voice is so calm, so in control, like the leader he is.

"He might be considering vying for a third term."

Silence. The old grandfather clock has never ticked so loudly. I count the seconds of no response from Father. Nine, ten, eleven, twelve....

"I see," he says. His voice is flat, emotionless. If you didn't know, as I do, that Zio Roberto had promised to sit the traditional two terms and no more before helping Father take his place, you might think he didn't care about this news at all.

"It's only been little things," his companion rushes to say. "He hasn't actually come out and said it. But he's watching his polls more closely than he needs to, given his incipient retirement, and he's hired a new image specialist. He talks about issues as if he'll have more time to influence them than the remainder of his term. It could just be a manner of speaking...."

"You did the right thing, bringing me this information." Father's voice remains flat. "We've always had a good working relationship, and I'm sure it will only get closer after I become Doge."

"Of course, Senator. That is my hope as well." A glass is set down heavily. "Oh, and can I get you to sign these documents?"

"By all means. Let me take a look." Father sounds so upbeat. Have I misunderstood? Did his best friend not just deliver him a crippling blow? Maybe Father doesn't mind waiting one more term for his turn.

Or maybe he's an excellent actor.

Father and his companion exchange various opaque comments about the documents he's reading before he signs and ushers the man to the door. I hold my breath, hoping Father will leave too, but once the door closes, I hear a huge sigh and footsteps. They come closer to me, and I brace myself. Being discovered now would be even worse than earlier. Now I've been eavesdropping as well as poking around where I shouldn't. I shrink back as far as I can.

But he keeps walking, stopping in front of the French doors. He stands there, back to me, hands in his pockets, for a long time. His head is bowed and he doesn't make a sound. Finally he turns and walks away. The door clicks shut behind him.

Later, in the safety of my room, I open a secret account on the net and upload the recording there, creating an easy shortcut to automatically upload recordings and photos in the future. I'm not going to tell Ereni I have it. It will be a private repository for my secrets. Just in case.

I SPEND the week establishing the pattern of going to Gianna's house every day. It is the only place Mother allows me to go without her direct supervision. She thinks Gianna is a good influence on me and because of her indifferent health, she's relieved to have me under someone else's supervision.

More strangely, Gianna seems happy to have me around. She even mentions the change. "The aborted courtship with Signor Royse seems to have made quite an impression on you." She looks away delicately. "Did you develop…feelings for him?"

I suppress my laughter and deny everything. She doesn't know about the hatred I feel, but in a way, she's right. Trying to avoid this match has led me to do things I'd never have otherwise considered.

Either word gets out about my renewed friendship with Gianna or Ereni is diligent about maintaining her social contacts, because she pays a call on Gianna toward the end of the week. Gianna's glance at me when Ereni's name is announced makes me suspect the former.

But Ereni covers well. "Gianna, I'm so glad to find you at home. I barely got to speak to you at the reception, and it's been an age since then." She turns to me. "And Sienna! What a pleasant surprise. How is your mother?"

"She is well, thank you." We both know I'm lying.

We chat about boring and inconsequential things like the good girls we are, or are at least pretending to be, until Gianna mentions a new gown and Ereni insists she can't possibly wait to see it. As soon as Gianna leaves the room, she becomes all business. "You must be desperate to escape your house to come here, my dear."

"She's not so bad." I can't believe I'm stooping to defending Gianna. "And yes, time away from my mother is in short supply these days."

"You're not forgiven then?"

"Not yet. Whenever Leo mentions his upcoming trip to Fidelium, it reminds Mother of exactly why it is I'm not going with everyone else." I shake my head. "It's not the happiest house at present."

"I can imagine." She leans closer to me. "Do you have anything for me?"

Am I really going to tell her what I've learned? It doesn't directly relate to Providence, after all, and I want to keep Father's disappointment private. But I know the intricate web of politics means this information could be vital for crafting the right plan to sour the Neopolitan-Providence alliance. I stall for time. "I examined his safe, but there's no way I can get in. It has a retinal scanner."

She frowns. "All right, I'll see what I can do."

I raise my eyebrows. Maybe she hasn't heard me correctly. "It's a *retinal scanner*," I repeat. "And there's no way he's going to open it for me, so...."

She just nods. "That's good to know. You think there could be valuable information in that safe?"

I shrug. "If he has any sensitive documents, that's where they'd be."

She makes a noncommittal sound. "Anything else?"

I take a deep breath. "The Doge is thinking of running for another term." I try to say the words nonchalantly, as if they don't really matter to me or my family, as if they're just another piece of gossip.

"I thought he and your father had an arrangement."

She certainly knows a lot about our politics for someone from another planet who's only been here a few weeks. "I'm just telling you what I heard."

"What did you hear?" Gianna strides in, her new gown held carefully in her arms to keep the skirt from trailing on the floor. "Did I miss something?"

"Sienna heard a lot of compliments about your dress at the reception. Isn't that right, Sienna?"

I want to glare at Ereni, but I have better self-control than that. Instead I smile sweetly. "I heard several compliments, it's true."

Gianna beams, and my lie tastes bitter in my mouth.

AFTER ERENI LEAVES, I do my best to be noncommittal while Gianna gushes about her newfound fashion prowess. It helps that her little sister Isabel is there rolling her eyes while she practices her penmanship. It helps even more when Zio Roberto interrupts us, wandering into the room with an absentminded expression.

If you saw Zio Roberto out on the streets, you wouldn't realize he's the most powerful man in Neopolitan. He's a round little ball of a man with a kind word for everyone, full of energy and curiosity for everything around him. He's been balding since I was born, and he's inordinately proud of his beard, which he keeps trimmed and waxed to a precise point. If his posture is slightly more erect and his face slightly more pinched now that he's Doge, it would only be apparent to the people who know him best.

The truth is Father chose to push Zio Roberto's candidacy first because Zio Roberto is so easy to love. The Senators and Assemblymen eat from Father's hand now, but Zio Roberto is beloved by the people too. It had been a while since we'd had a Doge with that kind of popular support, and while those people didn't have a direct hand in him being elected, it did make him a more appealing candidate. Zio Roberto has a warm charisma Father lacks, while Father can play the deep political game better than anyone. They've made a good team...until now.

"Ah, Gigi! And Isabel!" Zio Roberto beams with affection for his daughters. "And I thought I heard your voice, Sienna." Maybe not so absentminded after all. "Have you seen my special seal? I seem to have misplaced it again."

The Doge has a special seal he uses for all physical correspondence that only he is allowed to use. Well, him and Father, apparently, since Father has a copy in his desk. He waves his hands and makes a show of peering around, but I know it's an act. He has an entire staff to keep track of his seal for him.

"It's not here, Father," Gianna says in a bored voice. "It's probably in your study."

"I'm sure you're right." He smiles good-naturedly at his two daughters, and I like him in spite of myself. It's actually surprising how long he and Father have worked together as a team without any conflict, but even so, I thought it would go on forever. "And how are you doing, Sienna? It's good to have you here more often." He smiles benignly on the three of us. "You're all grown up now, aren't you? I still remember you staying at our country house and urging Gigi here to forage for blackberries. You looked like two wild things when you came home, faces smeared with sticky berry stains, arms covered with scratches." He shakes his head. "Those were good days, weren't they?"

"I remember," I say. I'd urged Gianna to follow my hoyden ways, and we'd all had a lot more fun than we do now.

Gianna tosses her head. "Don't remind me. I can't believe the things you convinced me to do, Sienna. It's embarrassing!"

It's not embarrassing. It's the foundation our friendship is built upon. It's why I don't write her off entirely, even though she's become so insufferable. Because I know underneath all the properness and pretense there's the little girl who was my best friend. The one who secretly wanted to go blackberrying even more than I did.

"I saw you talking to the new Satori ambassador's children at the reception." Zio Roberto strolls over to the window. "They seem fond of you."

I try my best not to look as guilty as I feel. He's obviously here in order to talk to me, and I have no idea what he already knows, or what he wants. "I don't know them very well," I say. "But they seem nice."

"Sienna took Ereni to the Mask Maker's Festival," Gianna chimes in.

"That was kind of her." He stares out the window, his hands

behind his back. "What do you think of them, Sienna? What are your initial impressions?"

Another "nice" comment isn't going to cut it. "I think it's very different where they come from," I say honestly. "But I think they mean well. They seem to genuinely want to help us and share their knowledge. It sounds like their understanding of medicine is far more advanced than ours. And their expertise regarding interstellar travel goes without saying." We've all stayed firmly on the planet since the Founding Families arrived.

"That is the case." He turns his head suddenly and looks straight into my eyes. "You're inclined to trust them then?"

"I'm inclined to listen to what they have to say," I hedge. "And learn from them. They say they might be able to help Mother. She almost died, you know. And she still has attacks from time to time."

I can only say this because it's Zio Roberto. We never discussed the details with any outsiders. "It's a family matter," Mother would say.

"I know it's been hard, Sienna." He's one of the few who does. But Gianna looks shocked, and Isabel starts writing again as if she's been caught listening to something she shouldn't. "I've spoken at length with Arum and Irisa Lhasa about what they can offer us, and what we might give in exchange."

This is a surprise. "You met with *both* of them?" I ask.

"Yes, they insisted." He shakes his head. "Irisa is a fount of hard data, as it turns out. And a shrewd negotiator." He turns back to staring out the window. "Perhaps it's time for a change."

"What do you mean, Father?" Gianna asks. I want to know too. Is he talking about advancing our technologies? Or something more? And what are the Satori asking for in exchange?

But Zio Roberto laughs it off. "It's nothing important," he says. "I've interrupted you girls' day long enough. Duty calls!" He nods to me. "Good to see you, Sienna. You're always welcome here."

Once he closes the door behind him, Isabel heaves a great sigh. "He's been acting so strange lately," she complains.

Gianna is looking at me oddly. "I didn't realize how ill your mother was," she says. "When was this?

"A while ago. Back around the first election. When you'd moved here and Leo and I were still in the country." It feels like ages ago. "You knew she was unwell."

But Gianna isn't going to let up. "I knew she was ill and it was affecting your father's campaign, but there's a big difference between being unwell and almost dying."

I shrug. Mother hadn't wanted everyone to know the true gravity of her situation. She'd said it was a private matter, and she'd been embarrassed to have to admit to any ill health at all. She had even told me her fears of gossip about how soon Father would remarry if people were to know the truth.

"I wish I'd known." Gianna bites her lip before gesturing me over. "Here, let me show you a new stitch I just learned. It's all the rage in Fidelium right now, I hear." And because I want to remain welcome here and continue the façade of friendship, I accept her peace offering and move to sit beside her. Our two heads bend over her frame, and I can't help noticing how soft and delicate her hand is, a shade lighter than my own. She doesn't belong in this world of intrigue and backstabbing any more than I do. "I'm glad your mother got better," she says softly.

This is the most substantive exchange we've had in years, and I find myself missing the way things used to be between us.

CHAPTER 14

On the day of my rendezvous with Burke, I tell Mother I'm going to Gianna's house, and she makes no protests. My meekness and efforts to please have lulled her into a false sense of security. She's satisfied I'm once more doing my best to be a model daughter, even if my best is not quite in line with her hopes.

I take the amphicar straight to the Lhasas' residence, delete the car's log entry, and hope Mother's newfound trust means she won't bother to check it. I have the car drop me at the side of the residence so I can scurry around to the back unobserved.

Dusk is settling over the garden as I dart from tree to tree, not certain if our meeting is a secret from Burke's family. Agreeing to help Ereni has made me paranoid. I make it to the rose garden without incident, the flowers appearing gray and blue in the dying light. The scent is heady, or maybe it's just my excitement about meeting Burke alone. What we are doing is forbidden, and not even Leo knows where I am.

I find the spot where Burke and I first me, the sundial dull now in the twilight, but after ten minutes of anxious waiting, I'm beginning to wonder if I misunderstood him. A cool breeze pushes through the bushes, and I shiver in spite of my many layers. Did I get the time wrong? Is this some kind of cruel Satori joke?

I'm rubbing my arms and thinking about going to Gianna's house after all when Burke finally emerges from the bushes. His hair is falling in his face as usual, and he looks unaccustomedly solemn, at least until he sees me waiting for him. The moment he smiles, all my anxieties fall away. We are both where we are supposed to be. He reaches out and takes my hand, and I can feel the heat through my glove. "Come."

That's all he has to say. He leads me through the garden, careful to avoid the thorny branches, pointing out obstacles along the path. "Careful of this hole" and "There's a step here, mind you don't trip." The light is failing fast now.

We come to a medium-sized truck, and this is where we stop. Its door opens for him, and I give him a questioning look. "Where are we going?" This is the first thing I've said to him.

'Do you trust me?" he asks.

His face looks strange in the shadows. I don't know him at all; he was born many millions of kilometers from here. But I don't want this moment to end. I step into the truck. There is a wall separating the passenger area from the cargo area in back. I sit and watch as he punches in a destination.

The engine gives a low purr, and the truck pulls out into the unknown. Music plays, voices singing in multiple parts, weaving in and out of each other, a low drone wheezing in the background. I can't make out any words. I've never heard anything like it. "Is this music from home?" I ask.

He nods. "I sang with this group before my assignment."

He's a musician? I can't imagine him singing this odd music. "Do you miss it?"

"I loved it." He taps his finger on the armrest that divides us. "But I have no regrets. I worked all my life for an assignment like this. I knew if I succeeded, it would mean leaving things behind."

"And people?" I ask in a low voice. Had he been in love back on his home world?

"And people," he agrees. He looks over at me. "You know, we're going somewhere private. You can get comfortable if you want."

I look down at my voluminous skirts and restrictive bodice. My wig is made of real hair, heavy and hot, and pulls on my neck. I glance over at him, and he gives me an encouraging nod. That's all I need to begin unpinning, unfastening, and shedding some of my many layers. A few minutes later, I'm dressed in pantaloons and chemise, my stockings pushed down into my boots. My wig perches on top of my pile of clothing, looking like a forlorn animal.

Burke takes my hand again, and I suddenly feel embarrassed. "How can you want to be with me?" I ask. "I look ugly."

"No," he says, and his eyes bore twin holes into my heart. "You look like Sienna." He waves his free hand at my discards. "That stuff is imposed upon you by a world that's not ready for the beauty of who you really are."

His words are like a punch in the gut. "You don't really think that."

He pauses as if to consider my words. "I'm only saying what I think is true."

Unexpected pain squeezes my chest. "No one would agree with you. If anyone else saw me like this and realized who I am, they would be disgusted." Because the racing, the haircut, it just proves what I've known all along: that something is wrong with me.

"Doesn't mean they're right." His grip on my hand tightens. "There's a whole big universe out there, Sienna. What people think in this one tiny country isn't what everyone thinks."

"It is when you're stuck here," I mutter.

He doesn't reply. We stare out the windows as the lights begin to show at more infrequent intervals. We're leaving the city. "You never said where we're going," I finally say.

"Somewhere where everyone is just you and me."

For some reason, his words make me want to cry.

~

WHEN THE TRUCK finally stops and I hop out, we really are in the middle of nowhere. The only light comes from the truck and the three moons, showing a scruffy, already golden mixture of grass and weeds, along with an occasional scrappy shrub. "Scenic," I say. I'm trying to resume control of myself.

"Wait till you see what we have in the back," he replies. He pushes a button and the truck door rolls up while a ramp descends. Another button and the lights inside turn on. Cocooned in special cubes for transportation are two shiny speeder bikes. I gasp and run up the ramp, eager to get a closer look. Burke chuckles. "I thought you'd be happy."

I haven't even pulled the bike from its cube before I realize it's a similar model to the one I raced a few weeks ago, only designed for longer distances. I'm sure Burke did this on purpose, plus it means he's learning his bikes, and my grin grows even wider. "I've missed you," I whisper to the bike, stroking its side.

Burke hands me a helmet. Not gold this time, but a sleek navy. "Wanna take it for a spin? I'll race you."

I look out at the desolate landscape around us. "There aren't any force fields out here." It's been a long time since Leo and I rode our bikes in the country, and the speeder bikes' high maximum speeds make them dangerous to drive off-track. But my fingers itch to squeeze the controls, and I want to go so fast I forget everything else.

"You afraid?" Burke smiles to soften it, but it's a taunt all the same. He guides his bike down the ramp and puts on his helmet.

"I'm practical," I retort. "If we're racing, neither of us should exceed a hundred kilometers per hour. Not in unknown terrain." I shove on my own helmet.

"Deal." He puts down his visor and straddles his bike. I hop onto my own and start the engine. Light floods from the headlight, showing nothing but overgrown grass stretching in front of us. The bike vibrates between my legs as I pull it up to a hovering position. Burke holds up his hand with three fingers, then two, then one.

My bike bucks forward as I accelerate, and I squeeze it more tightly with my thighs and hunch over, trying to force my body to become a streamlined part of its design. I pull up higher, relishing the breeze pressing against me, knowing I won't have to worry about crushed and tangled helmet hair later. My bare arms develop goose bumps, but I don't mind. They make me feel more alive. I whoop into my helmet, relishing the knowledge that no one will hear me and no one will judge what they cannot understand.

I'm vaguely aware of Burke on his bike a bit behind me and to my right, but all I care about is the ride. I can really open up the engine and go for it; only scrub and brush stretch as far as my headlight shines. I push faster and then even a little more, and when I glance at the speedometer display, I'm already going a hundred fifteen

And it isn't enough. The faster I go, the more at one I feel with my bike, the more possible it feels that I can leave all my worries behind me and be free. I crank my throttle, determined to go faster than I've ever gone before. The bike's hum barely increases, but the air sounds louder whooshing past my helmet, like I'm in my own personal wind tunnel.

I could keep going forever.

But suddenly my headlight illuminates a grove of trees up ahead. I can't slow down in time and they're too tall for me to go over, so I have to bank hard to the left. My bike leans almost parallel to the ground, and I swear I feel some leaves brush my foot. I bleed off speed and pull to a stop to make sure Burke's okay. I don't know how much experience he has driving vehicles like these.

I needn't have worried; he's way behind me. He executes a gentler curve away from the trees and slows to stop beside me. We both lift our visors. "No more than a hundred, huh?" he asks.

He's laughing at me, and I can't help joining in. "You're just mad you couldn't keep up."

"Not mad at all. Impressed. Although give me a few more chances on one of these and we'll see who's faster."

I gape at him. "Was this your first time?"

"We have similar bikes at home, but you know how it is. They don't handle the same way." I don't know how it is, but I nod as if I do. "Still, what a ride!"

His smile transforms his face. "You don't like it here much, do you?" I ask.

"Is it that obvious?" He takes off his helmet and runs his fingers through his hair, which is now longer than mine. He dismounts the bike and looks up into the night sky. "This isn't what I was expecting."

I take off my own helmet and go stand beside him. "Are we so difficult then?" I add a teasing edge to my voice.

He doesn't laugh. "I thought I knew what I was getting into, accepting this assignment. But I didn't expect it to become the Ereni Show. They're not giving me anything important to do. How can I contribute when they won't take a chance on me?"

I wonder how Leo feels about me placing fourth in that race, so much better than he's ever done, and guilt hammers in my brain. "But you're at least a little happy for her, right? I mean, she's your sister."

Burke snorts. "No, she's not."

I try for sympathy. "Did you two have a fight?"

"No, I'm serious. She's not my sister. We were raised at the same crèche is all. But she's several years older than me, so it's not like we spent any time together."

I blink. "But I thought…when you were introduced…what about your parents?"

He sighs. "Also from the same crèche, back in the day, but no, they're not my parents. Not Ereni's either. It's all just a polite fiction to make you more comfortable. We don't have family units the way you do."

"Oh." I'm so taken aback I don't know what to say. They don't have families in Satori? And yet they all live together even though they aren't related? I try to keep cool. "So then you're just…colleagues?"

"You could say that. It's hard to explain. And it's…complicated, keeping up the pretense all the time. I never thought I'd be assigned to a mission like this one. And Ereni…." He shakes his head. "She's so ambitious, she doesn't leave any space for me, you know? I know she's been waiting for this chance longer than I have, but"—he makes a face—"you'd think her extra years of training would make her less of a nightmare to work with."

I think uneasily of my arrangement with her. At least now I know she's kept her word and not said anything to Burke. "She's really that bad?"

"Yes." I step back at his vehemence, and he runs a hand through his hair. "No. She has her good points. But she's so dismissive of me. So maybe I'm not the best person to ask." He stares up at the sky for another minute as if it will give him the advice he needs. Then, with a huge sigh, he turns to me. "Enough about Ereni. We're here now, and no one can touch us. Not Ereni, not your parents, not your favorite suitor, Enoch Royse. Let's take advantage of it while we can."

He turns back to his bike and messes with the windscreen, and music starts to play. It doesn't sound familiar, and it's not the choral group he played in the truck. It's slow with a pulsing beat, a combination of keyboards and strings and drums with a female singer crooning in a language I don't know. "More Satori music?" I ask.

He nods. "This is a Pliaedes group." At my look of confusion, "One of our collectives. They live a great distance from where I grew up. This group became popular all over the planet." He pauses. "At least, it was when we left." We both take a beat remembering how much time has passed in his country since then. "It's dance music." He holds out his hand. "Will you do me the honor?"

I feel suddenly shy. "I don't know how to dance the way you do." I have no idea how the Satori dance at all. But given the music, it must be nothing like our own formalized sets.

"Well, it would take me years to learn your dances, so I figured this was my best shot." He gives me a questioning look. "I promise it's easy to learn. But only if you want to."

His offer of his hand means this dancing would involve the two of us touching. It's strictly forbidden for men and women to touch during Neopolitan dances. If it were to happen by accident, it would be deeply embarrassing for both parties. If it happened on purpose, people would be talking about it for weeks. But we'd already been holding hands in the truck, and that didn't seem so wrong. I take a deep breath. "Show me."

Very gently he takes my right hand. It feels cool against the heat of him. He steps closer to me and carefully puts his free hand around my waist. "Put your hand on my shoulder," he instructs. After I do as he's said, he pauses, waits, looks down at me. "Okay?" he asks.

I swallow and give my heart a chance to slow down. His pine scent fills my nose with every breath. His hand presses lightly against my chemise; it might as well be bare skin as far as my heart is concerned. But nothing happens. Neither of us spontaneously combust into flame. Neither of us drop dead from the indignity of our actions. I don't feel scared. I want to know more. "Okay."

"Follow my lead." His voice is low and brings heat to my cheeks. He steps to one side, and I copy him. Then back the other way. It's simple enough I can follow his movements.

He looks into his eyes, his face so close above mine, his hand still firmly holding me right above my waist. "*Ragazza d'Oro*," he whispers. I feel a strange shiver deep inside my rib cage. I'm not used to being seen for who I am.

"They all think it's Leo," I tell him. When I'd agreed to take Leo's place, first for his test and then for the race, I'd been focused on both the necessity and the rare novelty of it. What I hadn't expected is the ache from having to hide in plain sight. I want to shout my achievements from the rooftops, and instead I have to keep quiet as though they're a shameful secret.

Burke pulls me slightly closer to him. "But we both know the truth," he says. And in this moment, it almost feels like enough.

We move from side to side for the rest of the song, and then after the next one begins to play, he moves more, first leaning, then spinning me. I begin to understand his movements better, and once I get used to so much touching, I'm even having fun. I've always enjoyed dancing, but this is so relaxed. No one is standing at my shoulder to criticize my posture or make me run through the same sixteen move figure again and again until I can perform it flawlessly.

At the end of this song, he sweeps me down into a deep dip. His arms are around me, making sure I don't fall, and I love the feeling of speed and weightlessness. It makes my stomach plummet just the way riding a speeder bike does. "Do it again!" I sound as breathless as I feel.

He pulls me up and then drops me back down, and I giggle. I am still laughing when he bends down and brushes my lips with his.

My breath stops as a thrill races through me, and the sudden silence sounds as loud as thunder. I look up into his gray eyes, aware of the earth some centimeters below my head, of his arms supporting me, of my own arms that have inexplicably wrapped around his neck. To hold myself up, and then I wonder why I need such a defensive thought even in the privacy of my own mind.

He begins to pull back, and sudden panic shoots through me as I realize this moment is going to end, in spite of how much I want it to continue. He's no longer meeting my eyes either. I tug downwards on his neck, not wanting him to go, not wanting this moment of my first kiss to end in horrible awkwardness. He overbalances and we both end up sprawled on the dirt.

He's already scrambling off me, apologizing with that slight burr of his, and I remember that in spite of his seriousness and ambition, in spite of his traveling so far from his home planet, he can't be much older than I am. He might have almost as little idea of what he's doing as me.

He's rolled off me, lying on his back staring up at the sky. It's too dark to see the expression on his face. The music continues playing, its soft crooning helping me imagine we're in another place entirely, maybe even Satori. Somewhere me being alone with this man in the dark wouldn't be a scandal. Where it would just be…normal. Is that even possible?

I wish the answer were yes, and this might be my only chance. I roll over onto my side and lean in for a second kiss.

It is even better than the first, slow but heated. I pay attention to what he's doing and try to copy it, not wanting to embarrass myself with my lack of experience. I'm surprised by how soft his lips are, by how rough the small amount of stubble on his cheeks feels against my skin. He tastes subtly of spearmint, and I wonder what I taste like. What was the last thing I ate? I can't remember.

And then he's kissing me more fervently and any chance of

thinking about anything else vanishes. His hand cups my cheek as if I'm something precious to him. He moves his mouth, flicking my ear with his tongue, startling me, before he kisses down my neck, making shivers run through my body. And then his hand slips underneath my chemise.

Everything I've been raised to believe kicks in all at once, and I jerk away from him. I want to slap him across the face for being so forward, but he looks so confused. For him this isn't a defiance of his family's expectations of him. He doesn't even have any family. Maybe this is normal behavior on Satori. I'm stunned by the suddenness of remembering the wide gap that exists between us.

"We should get back," I say. I rub my bare arms, suddenly cold.

"Is everything all right?" I don't have the courage to tell him the truth. That this is my first kiss, that we are moving too quickly, that I don't know how this all works, that I don't want to become one of "those girls" Mother is always going on about, and I don't know how to avoid that. The gulf between our two worlds feels unbridgeable.

"It's fine." I tug my chemise down to hide my skin. "It's just, the longer we're gone, the more likely I'll be caught. I never stay late at Gianna's."

He doesn't argue, just stands up and holds a hand to help me. "When will I see you again?" he asks.

The correct answer is never, but I can't bring myself to say it. "I don't know."

"Then I'm going to hope for soon." He pulls me in for one final kiss. I wish it could last forever. "First one back to the truck gets the prize of their choice," he teases.

I'm the first one back, but I don't claim my prize. I have no idea what I want to ask for.

CHAPTER 15

Mother is struck down by another of her headaches. Whenever one hits, she stays in her darkened bedroom for a few days until it passes, seeing no one except Lizabetta, who brings her weak tea, broth, and cold compresses. It is a sign of my degenerate character that this bout of Mother's illness lifts my spirits. I've been feeling more suffocated as the days pass. Leo has been busy making masks now that his finger has healed, and Ereni continues to be disappointed by my failure to deliver relevant information.

And then there's Burke. I don't know how many times it's possible for me to replay our kiss out under the open night sky, but it must number in the thousands. I wonder what he's doing. I wonder what he thinks of me. I wonder what would happen if we were ever to be alone again. I lift my fingers to my face, and it's as if I can feel the light burn of his stubble on my cheeks, my nose, and my lips all over again.

I need to get out. So that night I remove my wig, dress in my boys' clothes, and scamper from the house before anyone can stop me.

I stay out later than I should, walking the bridges of my city, staring up at the twinkling lights strung between buildings, and skipping stones across quiet canals. I keep delaying my return another five minutes, another five minutes, and by the time I finally bow to reality, it's almost midnight.

I'm making my way across the back garden, having determined the easiest way to return indoors is to climb into my old bedroom window. I'm almost through the azalea bushes and to the herb garden when I see movement from the house. The glass doors to Father's study swing open, and a dark figure steps outside. I crouch behind one of the bushes, cursing my luck. What a night for one of Father's aides to be making a run to the Council Hall.

The person pauses for a moment as though checking for observers before tilting his hat to shade his face further and hurrying into the gardens. Luckily he chooses a route that won't lead him directly by my hiding place, such as it is, but I can't risk moving until he's out of sight. So I'm frozen in place when the ringtone breaks the surrounding silence.

At first I think it's my own qualpad and curse my stupidity, but after my initial shock, I recognize it's Father's, not mine. He pauses and fumbles in his coat pocket for a long moment before it falls quiet. Sloppy. Ereni would give him a good scolding.

I blush that I've had such a disrespectful thought.

He stands still again, as if waiting for someone to reveal themselves. My thighs begin to burn staying in this crouched position. Nothing happens for so long I wonder if he's just getting some fresh air when he begins to move again, looking behind his shoulder. I've never seen Father look so…furtive.

Of course I have to follow him.

It's not very difficult near the house. He stops looking behind him and picks up speed, but there's no way he'll outpace me. But once we reach a more commercial district he begins turning abruptly into alleyway after alleyway. He's afraid he's being followed, he must be, and his strategy almost works. But once we reach a certain neighborhood I make an educated guess about where he's going, and then it doesn't matter how many false turns he takes. I trail behind him, both in case I'm wrong in my assumption and because I don't want to beat him to his destination: the old law firm where he used to work when he was first starting out, before Leo and I were born. Or, as it turns out, the small public square directly across from it.

A man sits on a bench to one side of the square, and he stands as Father approaches. I can't see his face clearly; the only light comes from the small twinkling lights garlanding the square. I work my way around the edges, hidden by the ornamental hedge that borders it. My thighs ache from having to move while crouched so low.

The man holds up a hand as I creep around the corner and come up beside them, and I freeze, holding my breath. They both listen. My body shakes from the effort of staying so still. An amphicar rumbles several blocks away. An insect chirps. A breeze blows a food wrapper across the square. No one else is here.

If I get caught I'm going to be in the biggest trouble of my life.

"Matteo." The man pronounces Father's name with a slightly incorrect emphasis on the first syllable.

"Josias." Father clasps the man's outstretched hand, and then I realize who this is: Enoch's father, the Providential Ambassador. I hit the record and upload shortcut on my qualpad.

"Thank you for agreeing to this meeting," the Ambassador says.

"It's my pleasure."

"You've had a chance to consider what I said?"

"I'm very interested in strengthening our two nations' bond of friendship." I know why Father is so interested. He's spoken more than once of his concern that Providence will turn greedy and seek to expand beyond its current borders. Because the Providential settlers arrived on Sanctum several years after the original colonization efforts began, they didn't get the most favorable land selection, and resentment has grown in the generations since. None of the other nations fully trusts the "late" Providentials. Father hopes they'll choose to push expansion in a southeastern direction instead of towards us, but the Providential question has been one of some anxiety ever since I can remember.

"I trust you noticed the Consul slipped in an executive order this week pertaining to divorce. Women are to be allowed to initiate the proceedings, and for a whole host of ridiculous reasons! The Church will not stand for it."

Father shakes his head. "Roberto's been very careful to cultivate the Church. You think Bishop Greco has forgotten who appointed him? They'll let it slide, you wait and see."

One of the reasons the Providentials had been accepted as much as they had was their eagerness to be part of the Church—the same Church they had believed in back on Earth. Having a shared faith had convinced the earlier colonists the Providentials espoused the same values and would be able to meaningfully contribute to the new world they were creating.

"Did he run this…innovation by you before implementing it?"

There is a pause. "He did not." That would have never happened in the old days. The schism between Father and Zio Roberto must be widening.

"And the Satori?"

"Roberto does listen to them, you were right. I didn't realize how often he'd been meeting with them until you brought it to my attention."

"He didn't want you to realize." Josias Royse shakes his head. "He knows you're the real deal: a true patriot, one willing to do anything for your country."

"He and I were both that, once."

Josias Royse gives a condescending shake of his head, and Father's neck stiffens. "Things change, my friend. It is regrettable, but impossible to prevent. What we can do is make sure the rot doesn't spread."

"He's seen the polls. He knows the Satori and their ideas are hugely unpopular among the voting class. Your opinion pieces have been a big help there, by the way."

"We do what we can." Josias glances around, and I try to make myself even smaller. "We've heard your Doge intends to give a speech next week in support of the Satori. That he's going to discuss some of their medical advances in order to turn the tide of voter opinion. I think you'll agree this cannot be allowed to happen."

Father shoves his hands in his coat pockets. Did he already know about Zio Roberto's speech? His tone when he speaks is wry instead of angry. "You didn't get that piece of information from me."

"We have more than one source. Naturally." Father nods, showing no surprise. After all, they're both professionals. "I think we can agree the Doge cannot be allowed to generate sympathy for the Satori cause."

"Yes." Father heaves a sigh. "I'll take care of it." Josias reaches into his coat and pulls out an envelope. Father takes it and tucks it into his own coat without looking at it, patting it as if to reassure himself it's there. "Thank you for sharing your information."

"Just making sure you understand who the Satori really are and what ideas they wish to spread. We're in this together. If they get a foothold here in Neopolitan, that would leave them entirely too close to Providence for the Supreme Leader's liking. After all, who knows what other advanced technology they may have brought with them."

"We're looking into that," Father says.

"As are we." The two men shake hands again, and Father walks away.

I stay planted where I am. What have I just heard? I knew Father was friendly with Enoch's father, but I'd never imagined he would actually conspire against his country. Or against his best friend. The choice of meeting spot outside the law firm where Father and Zio Roberto made their start together so many years before feels twisted. Wrong. This all feels wrong.

If there has been one true thing in my life up until this point, it's that Father is never wrong. Not when it comes to politics. Not when it comes to his loyalty to his country.

I've given information to Ereni in order to chill this alliance between Neopolitan and Providence, but if Father is risking clandestine meetings with their Ambassador, it's not an alliance that will be easily broken. And Father is always playing a deep game. Who knows how the Providentials fit into the picture?

I have stumbled into something completely out of my depth. I can't tell Ereni about this meeting. There's too much I don't yet know.

∽

WHEN I GET HOME, Leo is waiting for me in my old room. He sits on the bed staring at me as I tumble over the windowsill, breathing heavily from climbing so quickly up the tree. He folds his arms and glares at me. "What do you think you're doing?"

I brush off my boys' clothes, ignoring his scowl. "What does it look like? Escaping the mausoleum for a sanity break."

"I've been waiting for you for hours. It's two o'clock in the morning. And you can't just pretend to be me without my permission."

"I'm not pretending to be you," I say with exaggerated patience. "No one even saw me, okay? You don't know what it's like, having your every move monitored, having Mother say no to everything."

"You have to be more careful." He sticks out his lower lip stubbornly. "You know how much trouble there'll be if they ever find out."

I can't argue with that. But I don't think he fully grasps how restrictive my life is right now. "You know how boring my house arrest is. Sometimes I feel like if I don't get out I'll suffocate to death."

"It's hardly house arrest when you're dashing off to see Gianna every chance you get." He's never been a big Gianna fan.

"Yes, I can hardly contain myself waiting for the next time I get to honor myself with her presence." I pause, and then we both crack up. "I have to see her almost every day, Leo, and can I confess it's the absolute worst?"

He shakes his head. "I don't understand how she can be so oblivious to how much you dislike her."

"Well, we used to be friends." I slip on my house robe to hide my outfit and begin putting on my wig. I'm too afraid to enter my new bedroom in Mother and Father's wing of the house without wearing it.

"That was a long time ago," he counters. "Anyway, listen, I need you to race for me again."

I pause with my wig partly affixed. "Are you serious? First you yell at me to be more careful and now you want my help?"

"I got worried, okay? I wanted to talk to you about the next race, and then I saw you were missing. I've been sitting here imagining all the things that could happen to a girl wandering alone in the city. You never used to be so…reckless, you know?"

"Because following the rules has worked out so well for me." I resume my wig ministrations. Thank goodness he doesn't know about the spying I've been doing for Ereni. Or the kissing with Burke. Or what I just overheard Father saying. It hasn't taken long for me to rack up a whole catalog of secrets.

"Well, I'm glad you think you're such a rebel, because I need your help again. The final race of the season is in two weeks. There's no way I can skip it and save face." He stands up. "This will be it, though, Si, I promise. Your last race, and then I'll announce I'm retiring from racing next season."

"You think Father will let *Ragazzo d'Oro* retire so easily?"

He ignores me. "Say you'll do it. Please."

Another chance on the track? Another chance to wipe that smug smile from Enoch's meaty face? Sign me up. But I'm worried about Leo. "Why don't you do the last race yourself? What's one race in the grand scheme of things?"

"They've started calling him the Invincible." I know he's talking about Enoch. "I can't do it, Sienna. I can't risk it." He holds out his hands. "I need these. I can't risk injuring them again, but Father will never understand. He'll say nothing is more important than our family's reputation."

The same line of argument he uses against me. "Fine, but you owe me." I smile to take the sting from my demand. "And you don't have to worry about me, Leo. I can take care of myself, I promise."

"I know you think you can, and that makes me worry even more."

For a second I waver. What would Leo think about the scene I just witnessed in the square? But the last thing I need is for Leo to insist on getting involved. My entire tower of secrets could topple so easily. "Everything will be fine, you'll see." I give him my most convincing smile.

He simply shakes his head.

CHAPTER 16

Once Mother recovers from her headache, she summons me to the sitting room. "You and Gianna should go on a shopping trip," she says. "On Saturday. I've prepared a list of shops for you to visit. And there's a new exclusive designer you both need to try."

"I haven't heard of anyone new." Normally Gianna would have talked my ear off about any such thing.

"Signora Bottelli has just arrived from Fidelium, and I managed to snag her first appointment," Mother says. "It's on Saturday at four o'clock. You and Gianna can use our amphicar for the day."

I don't understand where this generosity is coming from. "Are you sure you don't want the appointment yourself?"

Mother closes her eyes like she's summoning her patience. She takes a long slow breath and then picks up her needle, bending over her frame. "You might not have noticed, but there's been some tension between your father and Zio Roberto."

I can't believe she's actually telling me the truth. "Oh?"

"When two men work as long and closely as they have, there are bound to be a few rough patches." She squints at her fancywork before making another stitch. "That's why it's important you give this invitation to Gianna. This will be a special outing for the two of you, and it will remind everyone how close we are. Like family. Do you see?"

I do see. She's trying to remind the Rossi family of what they owe us. Father may not be able to sacrifice his pride to achieve this maneuver himself right now. It's so easy to forget Father married Mother for more than her delicate good looks, that she is formidable in her own right.

I'm not going to argue with an excuse to get out of the house, whatever the reason. Especially not when it's in service to the family. Saturday is Race Day, but Leo doesn't need me until the final race the following week, and Gianna refuses to run the Race Day charity booth without me. Suggesting a shopping trip instead is a peace offering of sorts. "I'll ask her."

Mother nods and continues her work. I take a breath. "Mother...."

"You should be working on your own piece." She nods at my abandoned frame, my clumsy stitches apparent even from a distance.

But I won't be deterred so easily. "Mother, the Satori brought doctors with them. I'm sure we could arrange a consultation. They might be able to help you."

"Certainly not." She bites off her thread with vehemence.

"But from what I understand, the Satori have superior doctors. They might even be able to cure you for good."

"It's out of the question." She glares at the needle she's trying and failing to thread, her hands shaking visibly. "I will never allow one of those godless men to examine me. Can you imagine? It wouldn't be proper."

"But you see Dr. Castello regularly," I argue.

"That is entirely different. Dr. Castello has a pristine reputation and is a member of the Church. Your father trusts him implicitly." She finally manages to push the thread through the eye of the needle. "I don't want to hear anything more about this, do you hear me, Sienna?" I force myself to nod. "Good. Now go invite Gianna on your little outing before you forget."

~

GIANNA SAYS AN ENTHUSIASTIC YES—NOTHING is more calculated to gain her enthusiasm than another opportunity to establish herself as a fashionista—and I spend Saturday in our amphicar with her, bustling from boutique to boutique. She's added a few stops to our list but is determined to make our appointment with the new designer, so our time is especially tight. I try to drown my worries in her inconsequential chatter.

As four o'clock draws closer, I begin to question my assumption that this shopping day would be better than staying at home. We leave another hat shop, me empty-handed and Gianna with two more hatboxes, and I sink into the amphicar's cushions with a sigh of relief. Maybe we can sit in silence for the short trip to the new designer.

But Gianna's not having it. "I can't believe your mother found out about this new designer before mine did," she says. "As the Doge's daughter, I have standards to uphold. This might be just the thing I need to stand out."

She never lets up. Why does everything have to be Doge's daughter this and Doge's daughter that? "I'm sure all your friends will discover her soon enough."

She shrugs. "It's inevitable. They're coming to my house tomorrow so I can put on a little fashion show. If I like what I see, of course."

Once again I've been excluded from a gathering. Gianna is only friends with me when it suits her, while I'm left swallowing her insults. "Why didn't you invite me?"

She dismisses my question with a careless hand gesture. "Oh, you're already going to see everything today. You'd be bored."

I'm so tired of the games we play. "All right, but why do you never invite me?"

She actually has the gall to look confused. "Sienna, I see you constantly. How many times did you visit my house last week?"

"When it's just the two of us, or with Isabel, sure. But you don't invite me to your little soirees or outings with your friends. Ashamed of my manners? I don't dress fashionably enough for you? Or do you just need a convenient time to laugh about me behind my back?"

She drew her mouth into an elegant little moue, which just made me angrier. "Goodness, Sienna, I never laugh at you. What gave you that idea? Some of my friends do, it's true, but they laugh at everyone. I'm sure they laugh at me when I'm not there too. That's just the way they are."

"Some friends." I can't contain my bitterness.

"Exactly." Her eyes widen. "I thought you understood. That's why I don't invite you. I'm protecting you. Those girls would eat you alive given half a chance. So I make sure they never get the opportunity. I make you sound so boring they want to leave you alone."

I don't believe her. "They think of me as a country bumpkin who doesn't have the correct social graces. And who do you think gave them that idea?"

"But you don't, do you? You're too likely to show your temper or say what you really think, and you were even worse when you first moved here. If I didn't protect you it would have been a bloodbath." She begins to look miffed. "I thought you knew. They didn't even give you a proper hazing like they did to me. And believe me, Sienna, you would have hated every second of it."

"A hazing?" This is new information.

She nods. "It got so bad, one night I went crying into Papa's office and begged him to resign as Doge. Anything to get those girls off my back." Her laugh sounds brittle. "What a silly little thing I was. I was so jealous of you, that you hadn't moved here yet, that you could afford to ignore those social connections. Father needed me to bolster his image, especially with no son to depend upon, but oh, how I hated it for the first year or so. Believe me, I'm doing you a favor by not inviting you tomorrow."

I sit blinking at Gianna and wonder how we've never shared any of this before. Could it be true? I can't think of any reason for her to lie about it. Does she actually think we're friends? *Are* we?

I sit in silence thinking over the ramifications of these revelations. Gianna sulks and looks out the window. The amphicar is just pulling up to new designer's office when my qualpad buzzes.

It's Father. Father never calls me.

"Sienna." There's a gravity to his voice that sends a thrum of fear through me. "You need to come home at once."

Gianna primps in preparation for exiting the vehicle. She'll never forgive me if we miss this appointment. "Can it wait?" I ask. "I can come home after our appointment. It shouldn't take long." Gianna raises her eyebrows at me. We both know I'm lying, but I wave her off.

"It's your brother," Father says.

"What happened?" My mind instantly jumps to worst-case scenarios. Today is Race Day. What if Leo decided to take my advice and race after all? What if there was an accident? Surely the force fields would have protected him. "Is he okay?"

"You need to come straight home." Father's tone brooks no argument, and I no longer want to give him one.

"Of course," I say. "Right away." He breaks the connection.

Gianna is already pouting. "I'm sorry," I tell her. "It's an emergency. I have to get home."

I expect her to try to change my mind, but to her credit, she doesn't. She pauses, pursing her lips, and then she nods with decision. "I'll get out here and keep the appointment."

Trust Gianna to care more about her clothes than my emergency. "Are you sure?" I ask. "With no chaperone? And how will you get home?"

"I don't need a chaperone with Signora Bottelli," she says firmly. "Surely a designer of her caliber is safe enough for my reputation. And I'll send for one of our amphicars right away."

I've already dismissed her from my mind. What matters right now is Leo, not Gianna's wardrobe plotting. "Fine, whatever you want."

"Maybe I can even find something you'd like. If you want, I can stop by your house on my way home."

I can't think straight until I see Leo. "That might not be a good idea." I can't keep up the pretense of not being upset.

Gianna reaches out and touches my gloved hand with her own. I flash to a night many years ago—we must have been only eight or so —when we slept overnight in an elaborate tent in the field behind my country house. Leo had been angry to be left out of our adventure and had made some ominous comments about wild animals, and I was terrified. Gianna and I slept hand in hand all night. "I hope everything's okay. It's not your mother again, is it?"

When I shake my head, she hesitates. I can tell she wants to ask more questions. But the moment passes, and as soon as she slides out of the amphicar, I head home as quickly as possible.

WHEN I RACE into the study, Father is sitting calmly behind his desk. He doesn't reprimand me for my abrupt entry. "Good, come in, come in." He beckons to me. "And close the door behind you."

I brace myself for the news that's coming. "What's happened to Leo? Is he hurt? Did he have an accident?"

Father chuckles, which only puts me further on edge. "No, no," he says. "You must have misunderstood me when I called. Leo isn't in any danger. Come sit down."

I'm torn between relief and anger. "I thought when you said I had to come home right away…." I slump into the chair across from him, and he doesn't even criticize my posture.

"I want to talk to you about your brother. Your mother and I have an important engagement in"—he checks the loudly ticking carriage clock on the mantle—"thirty minutes. I know you were out having fun, but family comes first."

He's daring me to complain about being torn away from my shopping trip, but I don't care about that. Something still feels off to me, but if it's a question of Leo, I'm there. I'll always be there.

"Of course," I say. "I'd do anything for Leo."

"I know you would." As my adrenaline dies down, I realize this is the first time I've spoken alone with Father since I spied on him conspiring with the Providential Ambassador. He seems exactly the same: his desk in perfect order, his cravat the precisely correct length, his beard well groomed. He doesn't shift his eyes from mine as if he's hiding a huge secret.

"To put it bluntly, I'm worried about Leo." Father leans forward.

"He mopes around the house, he's been missing his classes, he hasn't been going out with his friends. He hasn't raced since he succeeded in placing fourth, which I find puzzling. *Ragazzo d'Oro*, they used to call him, but now they don't call him anything because they never see him."

I know Leo's been spending a lot of time in his workroom creating new masks for Carnival, but I can't tell Father that. I stall for time. "He hasn't been going out with his friends?"

"Rarely. I don't have to tell you this isn't fitting behavior for my heir. I need you to intervene. You understand him in a way no one else does. We'll move you back to your old bedroom so you can get him back on track. Encourage him to get out more, that kind of thing."

I can't possibly get Leo to stop obsessing over his masks, but there's no point telling Father that. "I'll do my best," I promise. I want to return to my room. Maybe things can finally go back to normal between me and my parents.

But even as I think that, a sinking feeling in my chest makes me wonder if normal is even a possibility.

WHEN I COME into the playroom, Leo is watching some old show we've both seen a dozen times already. He mumbles a greeting as I look into my room. The servants have already moved my things back, and I breathe a sigh of relief before sitting beside Leo. "Guess you're stuck with me again," I say.

He gives a victory air punch but doesn't smile.

"Why aren't you in your workroom?" I venture.

"Father's concerned." Leo rolls his eyes. "He's having the servants 'keep an eye on me.' I'm going to have to do all my work in the middle of the night until he forgets about me again."

"What if he doesn't forget?"

Leo gives me a horrified look. "Don't even joke about that." But we both know the day is coming when Leo can no longer shirk the responsibilities Father wants him to assume. "I've been spending every spare moment working on my portfolio."

This is news to me. "A portfolio? I thought you were working on masks to sell at Carnival."

Leo shrugs. "I went to see Signor Gipetti." Signor Gipetti is one of the oldest and most celebrated mask makers, and a kind of mentor to my brother. "He said I needed a portfolio if I was ever going to make anything of myself as an artist."

I stare at him, and he doesn't meet my eyes. We both know what he's saying is absurd. You use a portfolio to get a master to accept you as an apprentice. And no master will ever risk accepting Leo as an apprentice, not when doing so would mean facing Father's wrath. Things have gotten worse than I thought.

I settle beside him on the couch as the news comes on, trying to figure out how to broach the subject. Leo is silent beside me during the lead items: a bit of speculation on Zio Roberto's upcoming public address, coverage on the artisans' guilds continued talks to combine into one large union for greater negotiating leverage, a move of questionable legality and a major point of contention between the Senate and the Assembly. I wonder if Leo's imagining one of his masterpieces in his head as we watch.

But he's jolted to attention by the Breaking News fanfare. Both of us sit up a little straighter as the camera focuses on Danny Trevino's grave face in the newsroom. "In a new scandal that could rock the highest echelons of our government, our sources confirm the Doge's teenage daughter Gianna Costa, a favorite amongst young people all over the country, was recorded in public today with an unidentified man, accepting and possibly even inviting untoward advances." Leo and I look at each other in shock, and I can tell we're thinking the same thing: that Gianna would never in a million years do such a thing. She cares way too much about what everyone thinks. "Saint Gianna, as she's affectionately known by the public, might not be such a saint after all. We invite you to watch the scandalous video clip."

They start the clip, and I recognize the turquoise building Gianna stands in front of as the new stylist's office. A tall man with a black beard stands close to her. They appear to be arguing, but the video doesn't have sound. Then he lunges forward, grabbing her arm, and pulls her into a deep kiss. It's hard to tell from the video, but right before it cuts off it looks like she might be whacking the man on the side of the head.

The news returns to Danny Trevino, who looks even more disapproving than usual. "Thus far we've been unable to identify the man in the video, but there's no question Gianna Costa has been caught red-handed in her licentious behavior. And now we have to ask ourselves: Is this the first such transgression or have there been others? And if our Doge doesn't have what it takes to keep his family living in virtue and harmony, does he have what it takes to govern our fair nation? More after the break."

"What a load of *cazzo*." I am shaking with indignation on Gianna's behalf. I think back to my rendezvous in the wilderness with Burke and thank God there's no video of *that* night. I'm the one who's reckless. Never Gianna. She must have been forced into that kiss.

Leo shrugs. "You know what people are going to say, though." He raises his voice to mimic one of Mother's friends. "'Did you see what she was wearing? I could see her entire collarbone. She's become so bold since her father was elected Doge.'" I know he's right. "Weren't you supposed to be shopping with her today? I'm glad you decided to stay home."

I collapse against his shoulder. "I did go shopping with her. But Father called and I left early." A horrible suspicion blooms as I say the words. Mother setting up a surprise designer visit, Father's manufactured emergency. The ramifications make my stomach queasy.

Leo continues on, oblivious. "Okay, but be honest, don't you feel satisfaction that Gianna's gotten what's coming to her? Maybe a tiny bit? She's been awful to you for years."

The terrible thing is, I do feel a pleasing sense of superiority that this happened to her and not me. That even Gianna can't succeed at perfection all the time. But that just makes me feel worse.

I can still feel the pressure of her gloved hand on mine as she asked after my mother. I have to do something. "She doesn't deserve this," I tell Leo. "It can't possibly be true. I was with her. She had no opportunity to plan some kind of sordid liaison, and I'm going to tell people so myself."

Leo scoffs. "You think Mother and Father would ever allow you to give a public statement in order to defend someone accused of impropriety? Gianna's on her own, whether you like it or not."

There's a new bitterness in his tone, a hardness around his eyes. "Well, I don't like it. What's wrong with you, anyway?" I want to shake him to make him wake up and go back to being his usual self. "We have to keep trying to do what's right, don't we?"

"What's wrong with *you*?" Leo shoots back. "Ever since I let you dress up as me, it's like you don't understand how the world works anymore. You're sneaking in and out of the house at all hours, you're spending loads of time with Gianna, who we both know you hate, and don't even get me started on your unhealthy fascination with Ereni and Burke Lhasa. They're going to chew you up, digest you, and then spit you right back out."

This is so unfair. I'm just making the best of an impossible situation. What does he want from me? "What about you and your portfolio that you didn't even tell me about? I'm not the only one with delusions here. Father will never allow you to accept an apprenticeship."

"Don't you think I know that? I know this portfolio won't get me anywhere. I know I'll show it to Signor Gipetti, and he'll nod and stroke his beard and make noncommittal noises and that will be it. But you're exactly the same. You know there's no future for you in racing or in diplomacy or with your fancy new friends. You never listen to me anymore."

Fury boils up inside me. "All I'm allowed to do is listen," I shout. "And I'm tired of it. I have things to say. I have things I want to do. You think I don't notice how small my life is? How little control I have over anything important? How nobody cares about me, how I have no real friends? Well, I do. Believe me, my inability to change anything is pathetically obvious. But I refuse to give up. I don't want to be dead on the inside just because of where I am on the outside."

We are both silent. Tears prick my eyes. "You're right." Leo's voice sounds creaky and strange, and my anger disappears as quickly as it arrived. "I'm just so frustrated there's nothing I can do to make things better for either of us. I try, but…it's like running into a brick wall, and it never gets any better. I hate it."

"You and me both, twin." We huddle on the couch together, watching the parade of commentators ripping Gianna's reputation to shreds. "You and me both."

CHAPTER 17

*L*eo is right. Father and Mother won't hear of me supporting Gianna in any way, adamant that I avoid all taint of association. "The public has to see you making the right decision," Mother tells me. Zio Roberto's public approval rating is as low as it's ever been.

I watch his planned address the following week with Mother. His speech is so bland and insipid, he might as well have not given it, and I remember Father's promise to the Providential ambassador that the speech wouldn't happen. *"Perhaps it's time for a change,"* Zio Roberto had told me. A distant hope had lurched awake inside me at his words, but apparently he's not willing to hurt his approval rating further by supporting the Satori.

"Why did you really organize a shopping trip for me and Gianna?" I ask Mother. My anger gnaws at my heart almost constantly now. I know she worked with Father to ruin Gianna's reputation.

But Mother won't engage with me. "What a bizarre question. You had much better turn your attention to your embroidery."

Gianna's disgrace is all my fault.

I NEED to talk to Ereni. After a few days of crippling guilt and boredom, I tell Mother I'm incapacitated by that time of the month, and unsupervised at last, I transform my appearance and sneak from the house.

Once out, I take my time, relishing the feeling of swinging my arms, skipping over bridges, and staring unabashedly at anything that captures my interest. The heat has coaxed a dank unsavory smell from the water, but nothing can dampen my spirits. The unaccustomed freedom has me bouncing on my toes and seeing the beauty in every little thing I pass.

I wind through the streets, stopping to check my qualpad from time to time to correct my course. Even people who live in San Marco their entire lives can get lost here. Amphicars glide by on the wider canals, leaving the few gondolas bobbing in their wake. As I walk, I watch the city gradually change, becoming poorer and more rundown, the streets changing from smooth paving to cobblestones not fit for amphicars, loud music blaring from open apartment windows superseding the dignified quiet, and the clothing of the people around me becoming simpler and more worn.

I make what feels like a wrong turn into a narrow alleyway. The rotten smell increases from the trash piled by the buildings' entrances. A pack of young boys race past me, kicking some kind of metal object, the air full of their shouts and swears. A few of them don't wear shoes. I realize my fancy qualpad makes me a target and slip it into my pocket.

It's cooler in the shadows, goose bumps forming on my arms. I walk a little faster, looking left and right, keeping one hand over the pocket with my qualpad inside. I think I hear footsteps behind me, but I don't dare look. A burning smell wafts down from above.

I turn another corner and recognize the street where the Lhasas live. When we'd visited before, I hadn't realized quite how unfashionable a neighborhood it was. This street has garbage collection at least, and fresh coats of paints have freshened the buildings. But I don't know anyone who lives near here, so close to what Mother would call "the Great Unwashed."

I straighten my cap and make sure my jacket is buttoned before I knock. Just like before, there is a painfully long pause before Ereni opens the door, giving me her usual dazzling smile. "Took you long enough." She doesn't bat an eyelash at my short hair and boys' clothing, reminding me she's not one of us.

She leads me through the increasingly cluttered foyer into a sparsely furnished music room. The walls, covered with candy-striped wallpaper, are bare of art, and aside from the grand piano in the center of the room, there are only two wooden music stands, a couple of simple chairs, and a black cabinet with closed doors. Ereni sits on the piano bench and pats the spot beside her. "I'm determined to learn how to play." She hits a key at random. "We don't have mechanical pianos in Satori. Did you know it took almost eleven months for your artisans to build this? Isn't that incredible? Do you know how to play?"

"A little," I admit. "But I don't practice."

She claps her hands. "You'll have to play me something. But first, tell me, what news?"

I ignore her invitation to share close quarters and sit in one of the chairs instead. "How is Burke?" I dream about him at night, his soft lips, his arms around me, the tremendous heat of his body. I miss him in spite of myself.

Ereni shrugs. "I don't know. The same as always." She is obviously completely uninterested in talking about her brother. No, her colleague. I have to continually correct the way I think about them.

"Burke says you're not his sister," I say. "And that you're much older than him. How old are you, anyway?" I'd spent all this time assuming she was my own age.

She pinches the top of her nose as if her head hurts. "Burke talks too much."

I'm not going to let her off so easily. "Why is this all so secret?"

"It's not secret. It's just simpler to allow you to believe what's already familiar to you instead of challenging you to understand too many differences at once. Diplomat to diplomat, you can see how that would work better, can't you?"

She's using flattery again, but this time it doesn't affect me. It feels like everyone I know—politicians, diplomats, and their network of wives and daughters that is my social circle—are playing some complicated deceitful game, and part of me wishes I could just escape it altogether. I can't, of course. I'm stuck here. There's a whole wide universe out there, and I won't be allowed to see any of it. "Tell me how old you are."

"I've lived twenty-six of your years."

Twenty-six? She's not the appropriate age for a friend at all, then. She's a matron, and not only that, but a spinster as well. My heart falls in disappointment. "Oh."

"It's not such a big deception when you think about it." Words trip from her honeyed tongue like she can reorganize the world at her whim. "I could have paired off with a fake husband, of course, the way Irisa did; my hands were going to be tied by my gender no matter what. But as a girl on the cusp of womanhood, everyone simultaneously underestimates me and is charmed by me. It's actually been very effective for making connections and gaining a practical understanding of how your society works. And I'm still very young in Satori terms. Irisa is seventy-three of your years, did you know that?"

I gape at her. That can't be right. Her mother—wait, no, her colleague—can't be older than her mid-forties, like Mother, and remarkably well-preserved for that age. But Ereni is nodding. "I told you our medical tech is better than yours. We have a much longer life span. That's just one of the advances we'd like to share with your people if we can develop a mutual understanding."

"But you lied about your family relationships," I persist. I'm used to a certain level of obfuscation, but she's taken it too far.

"I'm as annoyed with Burke as I would be if he were my little brother. Does that count?" When I don't laugh, she sighs. "You weren't ready for this yet. Why is it so hard for him to see that?"

Her condescension stings. "Maybe if you'd given me a chance, I would have surprised you. Perhaps in this instance, Burke is right and you're wrong." She thinks I care about the details, the fact that we're so different. But since the Satori first came here, I've been fascinated by all the ways they diverge from ourselves. No, what I'm upset about is the deception. If she's so reluctant to trust me with the truth, then maybe our two cultures aren't so different after all. And that's the most disappointing possibility of all.

If I'm a source of information to her and nothing more, then fine, I'll behave like that. I interrupt her before she has a chance to do more than offer a token apology. "Father is conspiring with the Providentials, just as you said. I saw him meeting with their Ambassador in secret. They talked about manipulating the contents of the Doge's speech. And my father orchestrated Gianna's disgrace. He used me to do it."

"That speech was a great disappointment." Ereni is back to being all business. "It's too bad you were so easily managed."

Her words are like a slap. She may have lied about her age, but Father and Mother lied to ruin a reputation. How much of my anger really comes from being their dupe?

"Did you get a recording of your father and the Providential ambassador?" I hesitate, then nod. "Good. I've been collecting evidence of the collusion between them. The Doge must be informed so he can act to defend his position. Although how he continues in ignorance is beyond me." She doesn't know Zio Roberto like I do: Father was always the political mastermind behind the pair. She hands me a small flash drive. "I want you to add your own evidence to this data, and then find a way to personally hand it to the Doge."

I stare at the tiny piece of plastic and metal as if it were poisonous. "You're asking me to betray my own father."

"You think he wouldn't do the same to you?" She begins to pace in front of the fireplace. "Wake up, Sienna! He might have already married you off to that human refuse pile if you hadn't thrown some gears into the works. He doesn't have your best interests at heart."

"You wouldn't understand." I glare at her. "You don't know what it's like to have parents. To have a family."

She pauses. "You're right," she finally says. "But I have to say, from observing your experience, I'm relieved not to know. I'm better off without parents like yours. I'm better off being free." She holds out the drive. "And you could be too."

"That's impossible, and you know it." Longing lances through me, a throbbing ache I wish I could ignore. "You're not from here. You can leave on your fancy ships whenever you want. You don't know what you're asking."

Ereni sighs. "We know the Doge is less tradition-bound than many of your politicians. In his talks with us, he's evinced an interest in improving conditions for his people and in allowing us to assist. I know this is hard, Sienna, but the stakes are high. With the Doge's support, we can save thousands of lives, and improve the quality of living for countless more. This is your chance to do something that really matters. Isn't that what you've always wanted? To be a hero? To make history?" She takes a step closer. The drive lays inert in her outstretched hand. "Will you join us?"

I never should have let her get to know me this well. "If my father ever finds out, he'll never forgive me."

"He won't find out." Her confidence stands absolute, and I can't help wondering if she's ever had a choice of this magnitude to make.

I take the flash drive and stare at it, a tiny black bug of a thing. I could crush it in the palm of my hand. I could flush it down the toilet.

I slip it into my pocket. A flash of relief crosses Ereni's face. "Good girl," she says.

If I deliver this drive, I'll never be a good girl again.

CHAPTER 18

I'm having breakfast with Mother a few mornings later, the flash drive hidden safely under my mattress while I decide what to do with it, when our housekeeper Teresa scurries in and whispers something into her ear. Mother inhales sharply and drops her spoon with a loud clang. I'm about to ask if she's feeling well when she orders the screen to turn on. Headlines scroll across the bottom, but I can't comprehend them until Mother says the devastating news out loud: "The Doge has been murdered." That's when I realize the small sound that had been bothering me for the past few minutes is sobbing. The staff found out before we did, and they've already begun to mourn.

Mother begins to pray, clasping her hands devotedly in front of her, but I'm in too much shock to join her. Numbness spreads over me as the live report plays on the screen in front of me, explaining how the Doge had been found slumped over his desk in his home study. Not by the housekeeper or one of the maids, as might be expected, but by Gianna, bringing an early morning cup of tea to her hardworking father. She'd dropped the cup and saucer, and my mind keeps replaying versions of that moment, shards of china spraying across the hardwood floor, the pool of still steaming tea spreading slowly, seeping into the grain of the wood, Gianna's confusion turning into a horrifying shock.

Zio Roberto had been poisoned, and from what the reporters keep saying, it was a quick but painful death. "A national tragedy," they keep saying. "The whole nation mourns."

Father appears onscreen to give a brief statement. Words come from his mouth, but they don't make sense to me. "A cowardly weapon," he says at one point. "Poison is the preserve of muling women and weak foreigners." We all know weak foreigner is code for the Satori. "I feel like I've lost my own brother," he says at another point. He does not cry; that would not befit a man of his stature. But he does look undeniably shaken and angry.

I watch this unfold without saying a word, my breakfast egg unbroken in front of me, and I feel nothing. Nothing at all.

At some point I stand and say, "I should go to Gianna." My sudden sense of urgency makes me feel better. I want to do something besides stare at my egg.

But Mother shakes her head. "This is a time for family," she says. "Right now they are at the cathedral praying. I'll send flowers and we can offer our condolences at the funeral."

I sit again. My heart feels like a cold dead thing. I don't know what I'm supposed to do. How can Zio Roberto be dead? I keep wondering if there's been a mistake, but the ongoing news reminds me it's all too real.

I GET UP EARLY the day of the funeral. Lizabetta helps me into a modest black dress with tiny buttons going from my waist all the way to my neck. "It's such a tragedy," she whispers, even though no one can hear us. "For such a beloved man to be snatched away in such a fashion. My sisters can't stop crying." I still can't believe it's real. I fasten the traditional black armband myself.

The cathedral is packed, a crowd thronging outside the huge double doors in the plaza to pay their respects. They all wear armbands too. The Doge may have been struggling with his dipping approval ratings, but in death he is beloved.

Because of Father, my family sits in the second pew directly behind Gianna's family, who aren't yet present. As I wait for the service to begin, my eyes keep returning to the black lacquered coffin sitting on the dais. Zio Roberto is in that box. No, not Zio Roberto. Just whatever's left of him.

That's when it really sinks in that someone deliberately put him there. Father has stayed tightlipped about the investigation, merely saying it's in good hands. No suspects have been announced. One person struck down in an act of violence, and look at all the chaos that has ensued. Could it have been a political opponent? Or maybe a foreign operative? A spike of fear wedges itself in my already shaky heart.

Zio Roberto's family enters at the last minute, one girl on each side of their mother. All three of them wear heavy black veils that hide their faces, and they walk strangely, as if they're carrying something heavy. I can't make eye contact with Gianna, not through that veil. I wonder if that's why she's wearing it, to hide from the world.

The service drags on, and I watch the back of Gianna's head the entire time, but she never turns around. She stands and kneels on cue, and she reaches behind her veil to dab her face with her handkerchief again and again as the priest drones on. I look over at Father, head bowed and hands gripped into tight fists at his sides. Does he regret plotting against his friend now that he's gone? I'm glad I never delivered that flash drive. At least the Doge died not knowing of Father's betrayal.

After one last lengthy prayer, we all stand to parade by the coffin. The casket is open in spite of rumors the poison discolored the Doge's face. When I peek inside, my whole body tightens. I thought it would look like he was sleeping, but even though his face is a normal color and only slightly puffy, he doesn't look peaceful. There is something uncanny in his stillness. His arms are crossed over his chest, and his hands in their gloves look too small for the rest of his body.

But it's his beard that gets to me. It's perfectly waxed as always, and I can't help thinking it will never need to be waxed again. This is it. Zio Roberto is really dead. But tears don't come. Instead I feel vaguely nauseous. I've known him all my life. But now I'll never see him again. I stare until Mother takes my arm and pulls me away.

Gianna and her family leave directly after the service. The actual burial is private, but we attend a reception in the evening. I follow Father and Mother into the Costas' sitting room to offer our sympathies. A single camerafly hovers in the corner, making a discrete record of our actions. Her mother and sister have removed their veils, but Gianna still wears hers, and it dwarfs her within its voluminous folds. Mother leans heavily on Father's arm. Father says all the right things, and Mother offers any assistance the family might need, but their words sound empty.

When it's my turn, I understand why. There's nothing I can say that will remove this awful pain. "I'm so very sorry." It comes out almost a whisper. I can't tell if Gianna is looking at me, and she doesn't say a word. It's her mother who thanks me for coming, who tells me how fond Zio Roberto always was of me. Her politician's wife veneer stands up to this latest tragedy, and I feel guilty she's the one comforting me instead of the other way around.

And then our turn is over. A line of well-wishers waits behind us to offer their own flimsy words. Father joins a whispering group of fellow Senators, and Mother goes across the room to join a similar group of Senators' wives. After a long pause, Leo drifts over to talk to Enzo by the table of hors d'oeuvres. I don't want to talk to anyone.

I cover my upset by getting myself a glass of punch. If it weren't for all the black armbands and somber colors, we could be at a garden party. The volume level is only slightly lower, the conversations still breaking into occasional laughter. I ladle the pink-colored liquid into my glass, wishing I could be anywhere else.

"A rather grim affair." Burke slips beside me and gets his own glass of punch. He takes a sip and grimaces. "I want something stronger."

"There isn't anything stronger, not today. This is a solemn occasion." Another burst of laughter gives the lie to my words.

He looks out with me over the select group of well-connected Neopolitans. They may be clad in dark colors and wear the appropriate armbands, but I wonder how many of them are actually sad Zio Roberto is gone. Today is a chance for the men to jockey for position given this sudden vacuum of power.

Burke gestures at the strategic groupings of guests. "In Satori, we celebrate the life of whoever has passed on. There's a service where someone tells the person's life story, and then we stay up all night, drinking and dancing and honoring the person's contribution to our lives." He takes another sip. "It is sad, yes, but bittersweet, not without comfort."

His words are a reminder of how backward he must find us, and embarrassment tinges my grief. Even my emotions are wrong, not only here in the country of my birth but in Satori as well. "I imagine it's easier to take a sanguine view of death when you live so many more years than we do."

He doesn't bat an eye at the bitterness in my voice, and he doesn't apologize. "It is different, yes. We see life as a cycle, and its end isn't something we find inherently tragic. Although it is undeniably shocking when that cycle has been interrupted by violence." He takes a step towards me as if wanting to comfort me, but then shakes his head. It's impossible while we're in public. "Sienna, I'm so sorry."

"I'm going to miss him so much," I burst out. I'm having trouble imagining life without Zio Roberto in it. True, I'd rarely seen him since he became the Doge, but his benevolent care had remained laced through every moment, his presence at the head of our country a reassuring reminder that everything was likely to work out for the best.

"Your families were close, yes?"

I'm sure he's been briefed about it already, but I'm still grateful for the question. "I've known him my whole life." I swallow against the tightening in my throat. "To the country he is a great leader, but to me he's like family. He's my godfather, you know."

"I didn't." Burke reaches for me again, then checks himself. "It's a great loss. He struck me as a man of integrity. I know Irisa thought highly of him, which is quite a compliment."

Nothing he says can make me feel better. But I appreciate that he's trying.

"I'm surprised you don't take more precautions against this kind of thing," he continues. "Bodyguards, security logs, tighter screening. This seems like an avoidable tragedy."

The thought that Zio Roberto's death might have been avoidable disrupts the little composure I have left. I swallow the remainder of my punch and escape onto the balcony, Burke following behind. A chilly wind blows, keeping most guests inside, but I don't care if I'm cold. I lean on the railing, looking down to the canal below. White petals fall from the surrounding trees and drift lazily by. I take several deep, slow breaths, pushing my tears into the deepest recesses inside me.

Burke slouches next to me. "About the other day…."

That's all it takes to send me back to the way his tongue tasted, the softness of his lips, the feeling of his fingertips brushing against skin. But I'm supposed to be sad right now. And I haven't heard from him since, not that there have been any opportunities. Usually when a boy courts you, you have some guarantee of his seriousness, but that's not the case with Burke.

He leans closer to my ear. "It's been too long since I've seen you. I missed you," he whispers. A shiver runs through my body. "Did you miss me?"

I can't possibly admit to something like that. "I'm with you right now."

"It isn't quite the same though, is it?" He balls his hands into fists and releases them again. "I want to be able to hold you. To comfort you properly. To not be able to touch you at a time like this…it feels so unnatural."

I allow myself to imagine what it would feel like to relax into his arms, the relief of being cared for by another person and not having to stifle my feelings. "We could meet again," he suggests. His slightly slanted eyebrows give his face a devilish cast, but I don't want to refuse the solace he's offering me.

"When?"

"Soon." He moves his hand closer to mine on the railing. "I like you, Sienna. There's something about you"—he shakes his head—"I don't know what it is, but I want to spend more time with you. I like who I am when I'm around you."

I'm not used to such frank conversation, and I snort in disbelief. "Are you sure you haven't had anything stronger to drink?"

"Nobody ever tells you anything good about yourself, do they." It's a statement, not a question, and his gray eyes look sad. "Tell me when you can meet."

I stare at the single light smudge on the back of my glove, not knowing how to answer. I'm glad when a commotion breaks out inside, giving me an excuse not to. A cadre of uniformed police officers are making their way through the crowded room, and eventually they get close enough for me to hear what they're saying. "Burke Lhasa, we're looking for Signor Burke Lhasa." Someone inside gestures towards the balcony. Towards us.

Burke straightens beside me, but he looks completely calm. "Don't worry," he says. "I'm sure it's nothing, and besides, I have diplomatic immunity on my side." He winks at me before turning to the lead officer just emerging from indoors. "Officer, I'm Burke Lhasa. How may I be of assistance?"

The officer gestures to two of his compatriots, who circle on either side of us. "Signore, it is my duty to inform you that you are under arrest."

Burke looks more amused than afraid. "Oh really? And what are the charges? I can assure you, it's been at least a week since my last joyride." He gives me a knowing look, and I blush.

"You stand accused of the murder of Doge Roberto Costa of Neopolitan. Per the arrangements of the Satori's international treaty with Sanctum, you will be immediately transported to Fidelium, until such time as legal proceedings can be pursued against you." The two officers flanking us move in, while another steps forward to pull me out of the way.

"This is absurd." Burke's eyes have grown wide. "I haven't done anything." But the police officers ignore him, and one of them pushes a hypospray against his neck. He goes instantly limp, falling into their ready arms. The group of officers form up around him and drag him away, while all the important people in San Marco watch.

I sink onto the nearest bench, unable to process what's happened. Why would they think Burke of all people had killed Zio Roberto? It didn't make any sense. One moment he'd been murmuring sweet compliments to me, and the next the entire world had shifted.

Could this be true? Could Burke have done it? He's certainly resourceful enough. He could have slipped into the Doge's house that night, secure in his knowledge of our lax security protocols, and put the poison into the Doge's drink or shot it straight into his bloodstream. But the scenario makes no sense, and I have trouble picturing it. Why would Burke do something so vicious?

The Satori have been disappointed by the Doge's address. They've been stymied by our government's lack of cooperation and by the rapidly warming relations between us and Providence. They haven't been achieving their goals, and they've traveled such a long way to get here. Ereni doesn't seem to have qualms about her methods. But assassination?

Has Burke been a trained killer this whole time?

My hands grow cold in my gloves as I sit there, only a portion of my attention directed toward the chaos swirling inside the party. I don't believe it. I can't. Burke wouldn't do something like this.

But a shadow of doubt casts a growing pall over me. How well do I actually know Burke? The tension in my stomach increases as I imagine a shadowy figure sneaking into my own house to quietly dispatch Father. As the queasy feeling intensifies, the chaos inside the house blurs. I lurch to my feet and retch into the potted plant next to the bench, the bitter bile burning my throat.

I can feel Burke's hand clasped around mine in the truck that night. It had felt like freedom, but now it feels like a brand. What if the ensuing investigation uncovers my indiscretion? I hate myself for worrying about that when the threat to Burke is so much larger, but I can't stop the fear coursing through me. My reputation would never survive intact. I retch again.

Later that night, safe at home, I sit at my dressing table and stare at myself in the mirror. I've become a stranger to myself. What did I think I was doing, dabbling with forbidden love, something bound to end in tragedy? Emotions are not meant to be embraced, not unless you're prepared to face a heart-cleaving disappointment. It's so easy to be broken by the world. My disgust at my own weakness becomes so overpowering I think I'm going to choke.

I pick up a heavy jar of face cream and throw it into the glass. It shatters with a loud cracking sound, the same sound my heart is making inside my chest.

I no longer know who I am.

CHAPTER 19

Burke's arrest is all over the news for the next several days. Somebody from the police lets slip that the poison used to kill the Doge was pentobarbital, commonly used by Satori doctors in cases of assisted suicide, a barbaric practice the Bishop himself has condemned. The detectives verified the Satori brought a supply of this drug to Sanctum. In other words, Burke had access to it.

My anger is a slow burning in the pit of my stomach. I can't express it in any way. No one can ever know I cared about Burke Lhasa, the foreign assassin who killed our beloved Doge. I don't know where to direct my anger. At Burke, who I still can't believe would have done such a thing? At the detectives for not presenting any alternate theories? At the shadowy figure of the actual killer? I stay awake nights worrying about Burke's trial, when I'm not terrified Burke will talk about our rendezvous and give me away.

Gianna and her family go into the deep retreat of mourning. I'm no longer allowed to spend time with Ereni, the sister of a murderer. I'm surprised the Satori embassy stays in San Marco at all; they no longer have any friends here, and any hope they had of achieving their purported agenda has turned to dust. Meanwhile Father and Mother have entered full political mode. The country is grieving, but soon we'll need a new Doge, and it's Father's turn. Everyone knows he was the Doge's trusted confidante, and if the Doge could depend on him, why not the entire nation?

The routine of my life smothers me: the needlework; the dance lessons; the English lessons; receiving visits with Mother, looking the right way and saying the right things even though I'm bored out of my mind. I know I won't be allowed to restart the charity booth at Race Day, but when I ask about becoming involved in different charity work, my parents exchange glances and tell me to be patient.

My only outlets are preparing for Leo's final race and slipping down the tree late at night and exploring the city incognito in my boys' clothes. I steal time between my obligations practicing for the race in VR, and when I get home after my midnight prowls, I watch all the footage I can find of Enoch's past races. I don't know what I'll do when I don't have a race to practice for, but I try to shut that thought from my mind. I want to perform as well as possible, and that means being able to maintain an indomitable focus, even in the face of the worst Enoch can throw at me.

The day of the race, Leo doesn't emerge from his workroom. In the wake of the tragedy, he's retreated even deeper into his art, and I miss him. I wear a turtleneck under the racing suit this time to hide my lack of an Adam's apple. But when I stare in the mirror, every difference between Leo's face and my own screams out at me.

When I go downstairs, Father catches me in the foyer, clapping me so hard on the shoulder I stagger. The possibility of Father catching us in our deception is almost enough to make me start hyperventilating. "Make me proud, son." His fingers feel like they're carving indentations into my shoulder. "Our family can use all the positive press we can get right now, and I know you won't let me down."

Father seems so tall looming over me like this, and the pressure of his hand feels like it's compressing me, making me even shorter. I get so caught up in how hard it is to be me, I sometimes forget Leo's struggles. To avoid disappointing Father, he has to wear his achievements like badges of honor, with no quarter if his efforts don't measure up.

I'm too afraid to mimic Leo's voice so I just nod. That seems to satisfy Father, who releases my shoulder, thumps me on the back a few times, and retreats to his study. I roll my shoulder with a slight grimace. I can shake off the physical pain, but the expectations weigh heavier. I don't want Leo to have to face Father if I fail in his place.

This time I know the drill. I plan to keep my helmet on no matter what happens. In Leo's flashy racing suit, sturdy boots, and thick gloves, my disguise feels impenetrable. I arrive earlier at the garage so I can check my bike thoroughly, but I show up at the starting line late, just like last time. Not only does it mean less chance of my cover being blown, but it gives me a better shot at maintaining focus and keeping my nerves in check.

But this time I have a superior starting position…right next to Enoch. He lifts his visor and sneers at me. "You think nobody's noticed you haven't had the balls to race me again?" he asks. "I get it, you know you can't beat me, and you don't want to smear your daddy's name. You shouldn't be here, a coward like you."

He's trying to get under my skin, but it's not working the way he intends. Sure, I'm angry, but I'm not ashamed. I would have been out here racing him in a heartbeat if Mother hadn't been keeping such a close eye on me. And my failure to win first place wouldn't hurt Father's political chances in the slightest. Not when the people love their *Ragazzo d'Oro* so much. I can hear them chanting my name in the stands. They haven't forgotten.

"I've had better things to do," I say. "But I'm here now."

"Think you can play with the big boys?" He stands too close to me, trying to intimidate me with his size before he looks up and waves to the crowd. Their noise swells in response.

I stand my ground and wave too. Size isn't everything. And in a race, my smaller body is a distinct advantage, something every real racer knows.

Enoch shoulder checks me as he walks away, right into the shoulder Father already mauled. "You won't make it to the end of this race," he says under his breath. "Amateur."

He must feel threatened by me to give me such a hard time. I can't let him into my head. We're all amateurs here, and while I don't technically have the right to race, that's not due to any lack of ability. I flip down my visor and mount my bike. This might be my last chance to show the world exactly what I can do.

I look over at Enoch. He's revving his engine like he's got something to prove, even though he's won every race since he got here. It will never be enough for him. He's one of those people who stays empty no matter how much he consumes.

I'm as ready as I'll ever be.

The red light in front of us blinks as the announcer counts down. The instant it flips to green I'm squeezing the throttle and jumping forward. My bike purrs underneath me like a living thing as I coax it to speed around the first curve. Enoch is ahead of me, but I'm happy for him to crow over his superiority. I won't let him rush me.

I glance in my mirror, checking the position of the other racers. Two are right on my tail, the one closest inching downwards. He's going to try to sneak underneath me. I don't want to bob too much to prevent it, draining off speed in the process, so instead I prepare myself. And sure enough, after the next curve, he makes his move, but I veer downwards, blocking his way too quickly, and he has to brake or run right into me. He chooses the former and falls a bit further behind.

Enoch is still ahead of me, but he hasn't been able to widen the gap. I've studied his races enough to know I don't want to get past him, not yet. Every time he's been passed, the racer in question has ended up crashing. Every single time. I don't want to pass him till the last minute, when he won't have enough time to respond. But I have to keep pace with him to give myself that opportunity.

Which is why it's especially bad when the other bike that's been on top of me this whole time suddenly veers right and gets around me. I have to adjust my optimal angle into the next turn to avoid crashing into him. I feel myself losing control of my bike, the ground coming towards me way too fast. Failure stares me into the face just before I manage to pull up enough to continue.

But now I'm a distant third with the fourth too close for comfort.

My heart quakes in my chest from my near miss with the ground, and for a moment I consider coasting to the end. I can place in the top five, no problem, just by continuing to do what I'm doing. Top five is great placement for Leo, given his track record. Father won't be disappointed. Leo will be happy, probably more so than if I place higher. And Enoch will have no reason to harass my family. Well, no new reason.

The temptation thrums through me harder than my bike's vibrations. Why not do what everyone expects? Make everyone happy? Isn't that what I've been raised to do?

I set my jaw. I'm going to do this for me, not for anyone else. My anonymity means for once I can do exactly as I please.

And I want to win.

By the time I get back into my rhythm, we have a few laps to go, and Antonio Pantaleo, the second-place rider, zooms past Enoch. He must not have done his homework. I ready myself to avoid the inevitable slaughter, and it doesn't take long. Enoch cuts into the inside of Antonio's curve, and Antonio adjusts, but not in time. He and his bike bounce off the force shield and skid across the track. He's out of the race.

If he hadn't adjusted, both he and Enoch would have been out. Enoch's strategy of expecting his fellow racers to do all the work to avoid a collision leaves a sour taste in my mouth, even though it's obviously effective in our little circle. I can feel my lips pulling back in a fierce snarl.

Enoch lost a little speed with his maneuver, so now he's only half a bike length ahead of me, my head parallel to his knee. One lap left. He's going so fast, making no mistakes, using his booster on every straightaway. The high curving walls of the track begin to feel claustrophobic, even though they're transparent. I'm going to place second. There's no besting him.

My hatred of him pulses through my body like a drum beat. His horrible insinuations at dinner. The punishment I've endured since then. The trouble he's caused Leo. His entire attitude, justified by his performance on the track. I'd do anything to take him out.

Fine, I'll use his own dirty tactics against him and see what happens. I've got nothing to lose.

I time my pass attempt at the beginning of the next curve. I've never tried this before, but I've watched Enoch do it enough times on video to feel confident I can replicate it. I wedge the front of my bike into the inside of his turn, waiting to see if he responds the way all his victims have: by avoiding the collision and losing control of his bike.

He doesn't. Instead he continues to steer right into my nose. We both smash against the wall's force field and careen across the track. A terrible shattering sound echoes in my ears, and we're moving so fast my vision blurs. All I can do is brake and hope nobody behind us drives into us and makes things worse. We bounce off the force field on the opposite wall and slow to a stop mid-track, cushioned by the ground's force field. The lack of motion is a huge relief, even as my whole body shakes and I fight the urge to be sick.

Okay, I'm in one piece. I flex my fingers, feel if my helmet is intact (it is), remind myself not to stand up and be hit by other racers who might be driving overhead. I blink and try to assess my surroundings. I was thrown from my bike at some point (when, I'm not quite sure), and it lies forlornly on its side about a meter in front of me. Its nose is crooked and it has a huge dent. The bike's brokenness gives me physical pain and only increases my anger at Enoch.

I try to push myself up a little and wince at the stiffness of joints and soreness of muscle. I hurt. Leo's uniform is slightly scuffed but it looks like the force fields have done their job. I'm bruised but nothing more serious.

I turn my head to see Enoch sprawled out behind me. He doesn't move, and I wonder if he's been knocked out or if he's quietly seething. I know I am. He's been winning race after race by forcing the frontrunner into spinning out of control for his benefit, but with the tables turned he proved he's more ruthless than any of us. I didn't realize it was possible for my dislike of him to become any more pronounced.

Reality begins to sink in. I didn't win. I didn't even place. Father *will* be disappointed. Everyone will. I'd been so sure I'd show everyone how wrong they'd been, and instead here I lie on the ground, my body one giant pulse of pain. The graphics above me indicate the race is over, but I don't care who won. It's all I can do to push myself up slowly. I squint from all the bright lights, looking for the closest exit so I can be alone in my defeat.

But then someone in a bright blue racer suit barrels into me, nearly knocking me off my feet. "Ouch!" My muscles protest this rough treatment.

He steadies me, and I see it's Leo's friend Dante sans helmet. "You're a hero, Leo!" He shouts so close to my ear I hear ringing. "You did the impossible! You took out the Invincible! I didn't think it could be done."

He slaps me gently on the back, and I cough as I lift up my visor. I take a gulp of unfiltered air, and a trickle of sweat rolls down the side of my face. I am so confused. "But I didn't win."

Dante laughs and shakes his head like I'm too much. "Who cares? You stole the win from that blasted foreigner for the first time since he got here."

I'm about to answer that I care, thank you very much, when I'm surrounded by my fellow racers. All of them want to congratulate me and eventually Dante gets down on his knees, they push me onto his shoulders, and he heaves me up into the air.

That's when I hear it. I've been ignoring the crowd, so disappointed by my loss that I didn't want to hear them cheer for someone else. I still don't know who won. But it dawns on me they're chanting *my* name. "*Ragazzo d'Oro! Ragazzo d'Oro!*" They seem as excited about what I did as my fellow racers.

I raise my arm to wave and the crowd screams its approval. Eventually some of the other racers boost up Stefano Palermo, the actual winner, and he takes my hand and raises our joined fists into the air. The noise gets so loud it feels like it could knock me over. I can't see what's happened to Enoch. He must have escaped the way I initially intended.

I relax then and let the adulation wash over me. I may not have won, but I've earned this one moment. I've done something worth celebrating after all.

CHAPTER 20

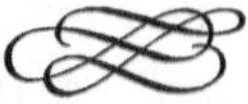

By the time everyone is ready to leave the track, my legs are shaking and I'm covered with sweat. I make my apologies, promise to attend parties where I won't dare show my face, and retreat to my garage, which I open for the official truck to deposit my poor broken bike. The comforting smells of grease and oil greet me. The bike delivered, the door rolls down behind me, and I collapse with a huge sigh onto a hard wooden chair, finally able to remove my helmet and rub my hair, which is now itching like mad.

A slow clap echoes through the space, and Ereni emerges from behind the work bench, blond hair shining against her sober gown. "I watched the whole thing. Nicely done. You've inspired a lot of patriotism today."

I roll my eyes at her. "You mean I've taken the Providentials down a peg." I remember the slack look on Burke's face as the detectives drugged him and took him away. "Our arrangement is over," I continue as calmly as I can manage. "I can't take the risk of being seen helping you. And Zio Roberto...." My voice shakes in spite of myself. "He was like family."

Ereni spreads her hands. "You must understand, Sienna, we had nothing to do with his death. Such an action would be against every-thing we stand for."

My chair makes a screeching sound when I stand up. "Maybe, maybe not. But regardless, the risk is too great. Everything has changed." Father will become the new Doge. He won't need to marry me to Enoch, not anymore.

"Burke's innocent." Ereni speaks with conviction, exactly the way she's been trained to do. I harden my heart against her words. "He had nothing to do with the Doge's death. He's being framed, Sienna. Surely you can see that."

I glare at her. "I know that's what you'd tell me, and I'm not saying I don't believe you. But there's nothing I can do about it. It sounds like they're building quite a case against him, what with the pentobarbital they found."

She begins to run her fingers through the bottom of her hair, the first sign of nervousness I've ever seen in her. "The pentobarbital proves the culprit wanted to blame the Satori, nothing more. Think, Sienna. Who benefits? It's not us. We'll never achieve our objectives with your people now. Our mission to this entire world has been compromised. And the Doge's death was a major blow to our agenda even before these false accusations."

To her, this is part of a political puzzle. But for me, Zio Roberto's death is personal. "Who do you think did it?"

Ereni shrugs. "I can only speculate. Maybe a Providential agent? Providence stands to gain the most from this upheaval in the status quo. But with all the focus on Burke, we might never find out. Don't you want justice for the deceased Doge?"

Of course I do. But she's using that fact to turn the conversation around. "I don't trust you."

"It would be ridiculous if you did." She grins. "But as long as we have the same goals, we can continue to work together."

I'm so hot I can hardly think straight. I turn away, unzip my suit partway down, and begin peeling off my heavy riding gloves. "I don't know what you want from me. I'm no detective. And I might not like the Providentials, but that doesn't matter anymore. Father's given up on the match between me and Enoch Royse."

"Are you sure about that?" Ereni runs her fingers over the dented nose of my bike, her words worming into the heart of my worries. Because I'm not sure. Father will only reveal his intentions when he's ready to do so. "I want you to break into your father's safe for me."

Just when I think she can't get any more outrageous. "You can't be serious." But she's not smiling. "I already told you, there's no way I can get into that safe."

"I have a present for you." She takes a small envelope out of a pocket hidden by the huge amount of fabric used to make her skirt.

I stare at it in distaste. "What is it?"

"Contact lenses." I look at her blankly. "Small discs you can put in your eye to change your retinal imprint." She says it matter-of-factly, as if she's in the habit of discussing spy craft in dimly lit bike garages. For all I know, she is. "These have your father's retinal imprint, to be precise. There are two sets in this envelope so you can practice getting them in your eyes."

I stare at the envelope, shocked she would ask this of me. "Why would I do this for you?"

"How's your mother's health?" I take in a sharp breath, but Ereni keeps going. "Did you know one of the Doge's last acts before his death was to get our medical clinics in San Marco approved? We can still give your mother the treatment she needs, Sienna. It's not too late."

I shake my head. "She'll never agree to go."

Ereni refuses to be daunted. "And think, there might be information in that safe that can prove the Providentials were involved in the Doge's assassination."

"My father would hand over anything relevant to the case."

"Do you think so? Even if it would incriminate him?" I hesitate, and she goes in for the kill. "We can protect your father if we have to, Sienna. Make the evidence seem like it has a different origin. But if we don't find something, Burke may be executed. Is that what you want?"

I wince. When she puts it like that…. "What would I be looking for?"

"Anything related to Providence. Deals that have been made or that are being considered. Background information on the parties in question. Blackmail material. Whatever you find. I'm sure your father has been thorough."

I give her a warning look. "My father's reputation has to remain pristine."

"Ah yes, our future Doge. Your family is to be congratulated on the happy news."

I can't get Zio Roberto's lifeless face out of my mind. "There's nothing happy about it."

"I'm not sure everyone would agree."

I'm so tired of her double entendre. "Perhaps not. Just everyone who matters." I take the envelope from her and slip it inside my suit before crouching beside my damaged bike—no, *Leo*'s damaged bike—and running my hand over it. "I'll let you know what I find out," I say. I can hold back anything that implicates my father in this whole Providential business. If I'm the one who looks, I can control the information.

"You do that."

I pretend not to watch as she tucks all that blonde hair into a dark snood, also retrieved from her pocket. She returns to her former hiding place and pulls out a long black hooded cloak, much too heavy for the weather, and wraps it around herself. I shake my head. She looks suspicious wearing something so out of season, but at least she doesn't look like herself.

She pauses with her hand on the door. "Be careful," she says. "The stakes of this game have become higher. We all need to watch our steps."

I stare at the door after she closes it behind her. There's a killer amongst us. That's what she didn't say. Someone in this whole tangled mess is willing to take a life to get their desired outcome. If it turns out to be Burke after all, well, he's in custody and we're all safe. But what if my gut feeling is right? What if Burke is innocent?

Then whoever's responsible for the Doge's murder is still out there, free and able to act as they please.

~

I'M lucky when I get home; my parents are nowhere in the vicinity and I'm able to head directly upstairs to my room, peel myself out of Leo's suit, and take a long hot shower.

When I return to my room, rubbing my short hair with a towel, Leo is sitting on my bed. He's holding my suit across his lap, and he's just staring into space, no qualpad I sight. Everything's quiet. He's put on a little weight recently, and we look less alike than I'm comfortable with.

"I watched the race," he says.

The last remaining adrenaline still courses through my veins. Finally I'm with someone safe, someone I can talk to about how I really feel. "Wasn't it amazing? Did you see what I did?"

"Yes." There is a distinct lack of enthusiasm in his voice.

"Did you see how I cut him off? Just the way he's been doing to everyone else this season? Some of the guys are talking about trading off next season to do the same maneuver to him every race so he can't dominate anymore."

"Some of the guys?"

I give him a questioning look. It's a brilliant idea, and I can't take any credit for it.

He flops backwards. "You're better at being Leo than I ever was."

I pull my robe's tie tighter. We neither of us fit into the role we're supposed to have. "It's okay, Leo," I tell him. "We make each other better. We don't have to be good at the same things."

"You don't have to comfort me." I know he means it. "I'm proud of you, Si, really. It's just…how are you ever going to go back to the way it was before? How are *we*?"

I lie down beside him and stare up at the blank ceiling. When we first moved here, I'd lay awake for hours, trying to find interesting patterns the way I had in the wooden whorls in my ceiling back home. But I've never succeeded. "I don't know. Maybe it will be better when I'm married." As long as it's not to Enoch.

But Leo is shaking his head. "You've never been happier than these last few months, pretending to be me. You really think being a wife will satisfy you?"

No. Sometimes it's easier to lie to myself than it is to lie to him. I want more, and I'm beginning to be afraid I'll always want more. I touch my short hair. "I have to try," I whisper. "I don't want to be… unnatural." That's exactly the word for what I am. The hatred the public had for Gianna after her kissing scandal would pale in comparison to what they'd feel for me were the truth to come out.

"You're not unnatural," Leo whispers back. "Twin pact. I'd tell you if you were."

"You're not either." There are tears in my eyes. "Twin pact."

We sit together in silence for a long time.

It is the middle of the night, two fifteen in the morning. I sent Leo off to bed and tried to sleep for a few hours, an alarm set to wake me at the proper time, but I couldn't get comfortable. I ended up perched at my window, pressing my nose against the cool glass and looking out into the dark.

When my alarm starts beeping, I spring into action. I spend a few minutes putting on my wig and robe before delving into Ereni's envelope. I practiced putting the soft discs in my eyes earlier, but it still takes me several minutes of blinking and tearing before I get them in. I feel like my eyes should look different, but the faint line around my pupils is almost unnoticeable.

Burke's life hangs in the balance. I know I'm doing the right thing.

I have to be doing the right thing.

My stomach gurgles with tension. I stare into my mirror to give myself a pep talk, but its jagged fault lines remind me of my doubts in the wake of Zio Roberto's murder. I can only see certain triangles of my face: my left eye, my right forehead, my chin. Like I'm not a whole person. Maybe that's why I feel so empty.

I take a breath, then another one, grab my qualpad so I can take photographs, and creep downstairs. The climate control hums, and the house is dark except for a slight glow from the baseboards. I pause in the playroom, listening for any sounds from Leo's room, and after a moment I hear the low rasp of his snore. Good. He's not going to interfere.

I take the stairs carefully, feeling for each step with my foot in the dim lighting. I don't want to risk alerting the servants to my presence by turning more lights on. If I'm caught, I'll tell them I'm hungry, but then this opportunity to check the safe will be lost.

The study door creaks when I open it, making me wince. The chaos surrounding the Doge's murder means our house isn't as well-oiled as usual. I pray no one's awake to hear it. I risk turning on the small desk lamp and immediately move to uncover the safe. I look into the sensors and hold my breath. A red light blinks once, twice, three times, and then turns green. The safe door swings open.

The safe is deep and contains neat stacks of folders reaching all the way to its ceiling. It's going to take me forever to go through all this paperwork. The only other thing inside is a small metal strong-box. I pull it out and try to open it, but it's locked. I frown at it, wondering if I should set it aside. It's probably just Father's cash on hand.

But when I set the box down on the desk, I remember the key, the strange one I found in Father's drawer when I'd been snooping. I fumble for it, and yes, here it is, and it's the correct size. I insert it carefully into the lock and turn it, and the box pops open.

About half the box is filled with stacks of paper money, as I expected. There are also a few bars of platinum in the back. But what catches my attention are three vials of clear liquid. I take a few photos of the box and upload them from my qualpad before pulling a vial out and squinting at the tiny writing on the label. "Pentobarbital," it reads. "10 g."

Pentobarbital? It can't be. There has to be some kind of mistake.

I take a close-up shot of the vial and am still staring at it stupidly when the door to the study swings open. Father towers in the door-way, a scowl on his face and a gun in his hand. His eyes narrow when he sees me standing behind the desk with the strongbox open in front of me and the small bottle in my hand.

"Father." I slip the bottle into the cuff of my robe and push the record and upload button on my qualpad. The pentobarbital here in his safe can't mean what I think it means. It can't possibly…. I have to think of an excuse for being here, and fast. But what can I possibly tell him? And how did he know I was here?

Father stares at me for another moment, his gaze moving from my face to the strongbox to the open safe on the wall. He lowers his gun and shuts the door behind him. "Sienna." There is a world of disappointment in his voice. "I didn't think it would be you."

CHAPTER 21

The only things I can think to say are clichés from Leo's action movies I'm not supposed to watch, so I stay silent, wilting underneath Father's gaze. "My own flesh and blood. A servant, well, those can be bribed, but my daughter?" He shakes his head. "I'm strict with Leo, but I've always had a soft spot for you. A daughter is meant to be coddled. After all, she can't control her weaker impulses. But now we see what my leniency has wrought."

My legs shake underneath me. "I'm just making sure I never need to marry Enoch Royse. That's all I'm doing, I swear. Father—"

"Silence! I'm not interested in your paltry justifications." He examines the open safe and comes beside me to look inside the strongbox. He runs his fingers over the stacks of money, the platinum bars, and stops when he reaches the vials. "I really wish you hadn't opened this," he says.

"It's just money." I'm beginning to feel frantic now. "I haven't taken any, I wasn't going to take any."

"Sienna." His voice is so even, so reasonable. "Show me your hands."

I slowly reveal my palms, the vial secure in my sleeve, pushed past the elastic. This can't be happening. Any minute now I'm going to wake up and find it's a bad dream.

Father checks my robe's pockets before beginning to pat me down, beginning at my shoulders. The unaccustomed physical contact makes me cringe. It doesn't take long before he finds the vial. "Give it to me."

I do as he says. What choice do I have? He holds the vial in front of my face. "Do you know what this is?"

The trembling in my legs grows stronger. I shake my head. He slaps me hard across the face so suddenly I yelp. "Did I teach you to be a liar as well as a sneak?"

I shake my head again, pain blossoming across my cheek, hating myself for the tears beginning to well in my eyes. Father doesn't like it when I cry. He says it's manipulative. I try to think about something else, to ignore the fear coursing through me, but the tears spill in spite of my best efforts, running down my throbbing cheek.

"Do you think tears will make me go softer on you?" Father's silky whisper scares me more than the slap. It's the kind of thing that could slither around your neck and squeeze you dead. Like an undetected drop of poison in a drink. "Do you think you're ill-treated?" He pushes my chin up sharply, forcing me to meet his eyes. "You do know what your actions tonight would be called by the High Magistrate, don't you? Treason."

I flinch at the strong word. "It's not," I insist, even though I know it will do me no favors to argue. "I would never do anything to hurt you or Neopolitan. Please." I don't even know what I'm begging for.

"If you don't want to betray me or Neopolitan"—Father takes hold of both my shoulders and punctuates each word with a hard shake—"then you. Must. Learn. To. Obey."

The way he never must, he means. I'm still as terrified as ever, but my anger coils up from my core, hot and sweet and noxious. "I'm not the only traitor here, Father." I spit out the words with a defiance I didn't know I was capable of expressing. Not to Father. Not when I've been caught clearly in the wrong.

But which is worse? Trying to discourage the undue influence of a foreign power on your own government? Or murdering the person in charge of your government—oh, and the person who happens to be your closest friend—so you can take their place? Compared to Father, my hands are bleached clean.

Father's fingers feel like claws sunk into my shoulders. "You ungrateful little…" He pauses as if he can't think of a word bad enough to describe me. "You have no idea the sacrifices I've made for this family."

"And Zio Roberto? What about him? What about *his* family?"

"You're talking about things you don't understand." But I can tell I've hit a nerve from the way he's stopped meeting my eyes.

"You want to explain murder to me? By all means. Maybe that's what's missing from my upbringing."

But nothing I say will have any effect on him. "Your Zio Roberto betrayed me," Father says. "And he betrayed the founding principles of this country. He let power make him complacent. He had the hubris to believe he should be the one to lead us to change from our traditional ways. That's never what we've stood for. That's never what we talked about when we planned how things would go."

"People change."

He's holding my gaze steadily again, a fervent look in his eyes. "They do. And Zio Roberto changed for the worse. I did what I had to do for my country."

I snort. "Doesn't hurt you'll get to be Doge in his place."

I brace myself for another slap, but he simply puts the vial back in the strongbox and locks it. "You didn't turn out the way I'd hoped," he says, and it's worse than any slap he could have delivered.

"Neither did you," I whisper.

He rounds on me. "Now tell me who helped you break into the safe. Was it your Satori friend? What is her name, Evelina?"

I consider lying, but who else can I blame? "Ereni," I say instead. "Her name is Ereni."

"We should never have given those people permission to land their ships here. They've been nothing but trouble since the moment they arrived." He grabs my arm, not bothering to be gentle. "Come." He half-drags me around the desk and out of the study.

"Where are we going?" I try to project a bravery I don't feel.

"Your new home."

I slip my hand in my pocket to turn the qualpad off.

MY NEW HOME turns out to be my father's dressing room, a spare windowless space smelling of dust, wool, and cedar. Racks of Father's clothes line the walls, ordered meticulously by season and color and level of formality. Drawers hold his cravats and socks and cufflinks. A single hard chair sits off to one side, and another door leads to Father's luxurious bathroom. Father escorts me inside, his grip around my elbow unnecessarily tight.

He takes my qualpad before he goes, but he doesn't ask me to unlock it so he can check it. He doesn't have that much faith in my abilities. "I'm going to give you some time, Sienna." His rich voice is full of fake sorrow. He used the same tone with Zio Roberto's wife when he was paying his condolences. "Think about what you've done and consider the future. I will not allow you to bring our family to ruin."

The door closes behind him with a decisive click, and then the lock turns. I check the outside bathroom door, but it's locked as well. The bathroom, all black tile with gold specks, has a single narrow window high up. I could never fit through it even if I could reach it.

Besides, where do I have to go? Sneaking out and roaming around the city is one thing, but I always come back before daybreak. I am a Tascioni through and through. Without my family, who would I be?

I hated Burke when I thought he might have killed Zio Roberto. I hated him even though I care for him, even though he's the best taste of freedom I've had. If he'd done what he was accused of, I would have been glad for him to rot away in a cell for the rest of his life.

But it was Father who killed Zio Roberto. It was Father all the time. I've been hating him without even knowing it.

Did he really do it for the greater good? For all of us, for everything Neopolitan and our Founding Families stand for?

And if I can't find a way to believe in him and his choices, what will I do?

There must be something deeply wrong with me. Most women don't seem discontented with their lot. Mother loves being a politician's wife, from the hosting duties to the social maneuvering to giving Father support behind the scenes. She's never longed to wander around the city unaccompanied, to compete in male sports, or to make her own mark on the world. Neither has Gianna. She'd be shocked if she learned half of what I've done.

Father thinks he's given me too much freedom, but even that isn't enough. Nothing will be enough for me. Maybe I've been looking for change on the outside where none is possible. Maybe what needs to change is something essential about me.

I spend the rest of the night sitting on the hard chair, staring at Father's rows of suits and wishing I were the person I'm supposed to be.

I AM LEFT ALONE. Day after day after day. Father brings me meals himself. If he's out, I go hungry. I see nobody else. I hear nobody else. On the first full day, Father locks me into the bathroom for a few hours, and when I'm let back into the dressing room, there is a cot and a Bible, and some of his clothing is missing. After that everything stays the same. Even the food is the same. Day after day after day.

He won't speak to me. At first I don't talk either, but after a few days I start feeling desperate. I ask him what's going on outside, but he won't tell me. I ask about Leo, but he won't tell me. I ask when I can leave, but he won't tell me.

I begin to think he'll never let me go.

I spend a lot of time in the bathroom watching the light change through the window. It gives me the reassuring sense that time is passing. I listen to the birdsong. I take long hot baths. I do ridiculous calisthenics. It's not like anyone is watching.

Father comes and goes at different times. I only take my wig off in the bathroom with the door locked. I know he won't interrupt me if he thinks I'm not decent. What would he do if he knew about this other secret? Just thinking about it makes me shiver. My short hair is proof there's something wrong with me, a badge of shame. I don't want him to see it. I don't want anyone to see it. When I let Burke see it, was he secretly disgusted by what he saw? I can't imagine him feeling any other way.

Nothing is ever going to change, I see that now. Ereni was a mirage, an invasive species from another world. Maybe things are different in Satori, but what does it matter? I will always be in this closet.

I have always been in this closet. I just didn't realize it until now.

I hope Leo's okay.

I take happiness where I can. I spend time cuddling with Father's hand knit sweaters, the ones that were gifts he never wears. I give them names and treat them like pets. There's Cynthia, the soft gray sweater who holds herself a bit aloof, and Mario, the loud black and red sweater who will never shut up, and Luisa, the shapeless blue sweater who disappears easily into the background. It occurs to me I might be losing my grasp on reality, but if so, I'd rather do it with my sweater friends.

I begin to eat less and sleep more. All I want to do is sleep. Sometimes I dream, and when I can remember my dreams, I play them over and over in my mind.

I don't cry, not since that first night. I know I am weak. I'm supposed to cry, even though it would make Father angry. That's what women do. But it feels too much like another loss, and I've already given so much.

Maybe I was confused about what I saw. I could have misread the label on that vial. Or maybe Father confiscated the rest of the Satori supply so they couldn't use it to hurt anyone else. Maybe it was an accident. Or Zio Roberto did something I don't know about, something so bad this was truly the only way. When my thoughts begin to spiral like this, I have to pinch myself until I bruise to keep a clear head.

I know the truth. I feel it reverberating in every cell of my body, and when I try to believe something else, it just vibrates harder.

Think of who has something to gain, Ereni said. Father wanted to be Doge. Zio Roberto wasn't going to step down on schedule.

Father murdered Zio Roberto. He planned it, and then he struck. So much for the importance of leading a virtuous life.

But I guess that rule only applies to me because I'm a girl, and I don't matter.

I've never felt the truth of my insignificance more, as day after day after day passes, and nobody comes.

CHAPTER 22

*A*lmost three weeks have gone by when Father finally speaks to me. I'm sitting on the chair when he comes in, ankles demurely crossed, eyes downcast, hands lying like limp rags in my lap. I've restyled my wig. I've washed my nightgown in the bathtub. I no longer look like a wild thing.

Let him think he's broken me. Let him think that.

Maybe he has broken me. Maybe I've been broken all along. Here I sit, still desperate for his approval. As if nothing has changed.

Father approaches me one slow step at a time, his shoes slapping against the hard floor. I've made up my cot. I've trimmed my nails. I've buttoned my robe all the way to the collar.

I can see his feet in his immaculate shoes, but I resist the urge to look up, to meet his eyes, to show my defiance in any way. I cannot be myself. I've buried her way, way down until it's safe for her to come out.

(Will it ever be safe? I wonder.)

Father's voice, when it comes, is a deep growl. I can never look at him the same way. I can't look at him at all. "Will you be a good girl and do as you're told?" he asks.

I stare at my carefully shaped nails. "Yes, sir." I speak softly but not too softly. I know how to be perfect. This is what I've been trained for.

"*Everything* you're told?"

"Yes, sir."

"Enoch Royse will resume his courtship of you."

He waits. I hate Enoch. I catch myself beginning to curl my fingers, wanting to claw, wanting to dig my nails into my palms, wanting to object to this arrangement, wanting to scream and never stop.

This is a test.

"Yes, sir." I do not look up. I relax my hands. I pretend they belong to someone else.

"The two of you will appear in public together at my inauguration in three days' time. You will look happy. You will smile and wave. You will take his arm."

A lump forms in my throat. To be so publicly linked…that means an impending engagement. Father means to go through with it then. Even knowing how I feel. A quick engagement, an elaborate wedding, and then Enoch will be summoned back to Providence, and I will go with him. Followed by a chain of excuses, reasons why I can't come home, no time for a visit this year, too much of importance happening in Providence, or Father and Mother are too busy, and then I will be too encumbered bearing Enoch's children. In Providence, I've heard, the families are large. Enoch is the oldest of six.

This is Father's way of getting rid of me.

"Yes, sir."

"You will say nothing of substance to anyone. If you're asked about the previous Doge, you'll call his death a tragedy. If you're asked about me, you'll talk about my clear commitment to my patriotic duty. If you're asked about Enoch Royse, you will blush prettily and let someone else speak. Do you understand?"

And what if I don't, Father? What if I mar the illusion of your ideal family? What then?

Will you kill me too?

"Yes, sir."

I've been in these rooms for so long, they've forced me to confront the truth. I am a coward. I don't want to die. And I don't want to know what Father is capable of. My entire life has been built on a hollow carapace, and I don't know where to place my feet. The only sure way is absolute obedience.

And maybe, a tiny voice whispers, in the space obedience wins me, I'll get my chance.

But I don't really believe it.

~

Mother behaves as if nothing has changed. In the weeks I've been locked up, she's lost more weight. She walks slowly and carefully, as if each step pains her. I wonder if her dizziness has returned as well, but I know she won't answer any of my inquiries. Just as she wouldn't intervene in my punishment.

I still sleep locked in Father's closet every night, and I am never left unattended. Lizabetta hasn't told them about my hair and the wig, but she's no longer left alone with me. Father has hired a new chaperone for me, a battleaxe named Signora Bartelli, dressed all in the grays and blacks of mourning. Even her face looks gray. She still wears a wedding band on her finger, and I get the feeling her mourning will last the rest of her life.

All I wanted was to get out of that horrible closet, but now my attention wanders and I have trouble listening to what Mother says. It doesn't matter since all she talks about is the Inauguration. It's being held the day before Carnival begins, giving the populace a five-day celebration of my father's ascension. The hubris of this decision would make me sick if I were capable of feeling anything at all.

I am Mother's puppet. She feeds me, she dresses me in different outfits, she makes Lizabetta try hairstyle after hairstyle. I pose, I smile, and then the same activities repeat.

When Mother is otherwise occupied, I sit by the window and stare out at the garden. I seem to have developed a taste for doing nothing. If I actually cared enough to do something, I think my numbness might fail me.

At first I think Leo is avoiding me, like I have a plague that's catching. But then I realize he's not here at our home. They don't tell me where he is.

～

THE MORNING OF THE INAUGURATION, Signora Bartelli and Lizabetta take three hours to prepare me. Mother has dressed me in a gown of the palest pink that shimmers in the light and makes me look taller than I am. My wig is styled with tiny matching rosettes and crystals, my gloves are white and starched and crisp, my face is painted just so. When Lizabetta walks me to the full-length mirror to show me the end result, we meet eyes, but there's nothing either of us can do to halt the inexorable tide of what's coming next. I stare into the face of a younger version of Mother. The black mourning badge around my arm contrasts starkly with the apple blossom into which Mother has transformed me.

Yes, this should make the people happy. Much more than the truth.

When I walk down the stairs, stiff as a mannequin, I see Leo for the first time since my punishment, pacing back and forth in the foyer in his own formalwear. He doesn't say anything, but he doesn't have to. His worry and relief are written all over his face.

Mother is regal in plum silk, slipping into the role she's been waiting for. I wonder if she knows the price Father paid. She can't know, can she? But I'm no longer sure of anything.

She stumbles as we leave the house, and Leo has to catch her and hold her up. Beads of sweat appear on her forehead before she can wipe them away with a handkerchief. The lump in my throat gets larger. "Please, Mother," I whisper, "go see a Satori doctor. I'll help you. No one needs to know. Please." But she turns her head away and pretends I haven't said a word.

We are silent for the short distance to the Council Hall, where we will be meeting Father. I expect Mother to begin rattling on about the countless Inauguration details she's been instrumental in organizing and reminding us of all the rules of protocol, but after tapping at her qualpad for a few minutes, she stashes it into her reticule and looks straight ahead with a grim expression.

The Council Hall sits right on the Esplanade, the biggest canal in the city. People are jammed into the square so tightly I wonder how they can move, and they spill down the stairs all the way to the waterway, a path through them held clear by guards in their signature black and blue. Mother takes a handful of pills and washes them down with water. When we emerge from the amphicar, the crowd erupts in cheers, and I hear a few chants of *"Ragazzo d'Oro!"* That last race feels like a lifetime ago, but they still remember what I did. The knowledge warms the vestiges of my former self.

Leo dutifully waves and pumps his fist in the air, but I don't miss the sour look he tries to hide. All of this show and pomp, but what happens behind closed doors in our family remains a secret. We're trapped into acting out this masquerade.

The ceremony is to take place in the huge hall between the Senate Chambers and the Assembly Chambers. But we are led now to a smaller reception area where Father and a few of his top supporters are waiting, including Enoch and his family. It's so exclusive, I don't notice any cameraflies in the vicinity. Just seeing Enoch's face, his apple cheeks, the mole on his chin, makes me feel nauseous. I guess I'm not as numb as I thought.

Mother rushes off to see to some critical detail, and Father calls Leo over before returning to his conversation with a circle of important men. I stand awkwardly alone where I can overhear Father and his cronies.

"You'll be traveling to Fidelium soon then?" someone asks him.

"Indeed." Father adjusts the lapels of his jacket. "It is of the utmost importance to us as a nation, and to me personally, to see this young Satori upstart brought to justice."

They're talking about Burke. I can't afford to care about him anymore, but I linger to hear what they say next.

"In fact," Father continues, "I plan to leave tomorrow. His trial is set to start soon, and I want to make sure the other Founding Nations are clear on our position and what's at stake. The Satori are a corrupting influence, that much is clear. We should have never granted them permission to land and disrupt the status quo."

"Hear, hear," a portly gentleman says. I think he's a high-ranking justice.

"I always thought the Sanctum Unity Council's decision was a mistake," another senior senator declares.

A few men frown, but no one contradicts Father. "They cannot be allowed to interfere with our affairs," Father says. "We need to demand their immediate departure."

"And what about the boy?" It's Bernard Romano, a former Assemblyman. He's never been one of Father's big supporters, but his is one of the most respected voices in Neopolitan, so of course he's here today.

Father shrugs. "Justice must be done." That's all he says, but he exchanges a look with two of his fellow senators, and I know he'll press for the harshest punishment possible. He might want the Satori gone, but my guess is if he gets his way, Burke won't be going with them.

But none of this is my concern anymore. I'm here as the beautiful model daughter of the next Doge of Neopolitan. If I pass this test of obedience, I'll survive to see tomorrow.

I am one of the only women in the room. I move as quietly as I can toward the corner, hoping to remain invisible. But I realize Enoch is following me, and I hesitate, wishing I could run away. Leo drifts closer to me. He'll protect me if he can.

Enoch approaches me with a wide grin, surveying me as if I'm a particularly delicious meal. "Well, well, don't you look lovely today." My numbness falters again at his voice, at how much bigger than me he is.

No one is paying attention to us, unless you count Leo skulking nearby. "Signor Royse." I incline my head. "As always, you are too kind."

"I might not be as kind as you think," he says. He grabs my arm roughly and tucks it under his own.

I struggle against him and the embarrassing physical contact.

"Enoch," I hiss, "you know this isn't appropriate. On the dais, as a show for the people, but not till then."

He sneers down at me, and I can see pleasure at my humiliation in his eyes. "Do you see anyone stopping me?"

He's right. Everyone is very conveniently not looking at us. Even Leo is staring uncomfortably at his boots, unsure of how to intervene. My cheeks burn, and I stop trying to retrieve my arm. Father has made sure there'll be no coming back for me from all this.

"Don't worry, Sienna. Both you and your brother may have repeatedly insulted me, but I know it's not your fault. You haven't been taught your place, but I intend to correct that oversight." He leers at me, and I look past him at Leo, a look of pained indecision on his face. Enoch is behaving this way with Father's tacit approval, and we all know who holds the power in this room. "I'm going to enjoy getting you in line. In Providence, you'll find things are very different from what you're used to." He squeezes my arm too tightly. "You should have taken me up on my earlier offer. Remember, any favors you choose to give me now might affect your position once I take you home." He winks crudely at me, and I shudder and look away.

He leans in so close I can feel his hot breath on my ear. "You'll even learn to like it."

That's it. My anger reaches a quick boil, and I yank my arm away so fast I've escaped his grip before he can react. My chest heaves as I raise my hand, whether to slap him or punch him I never find out. Because Father is there, pulling it back down to my side. Leo hovers behind him, his unhappy shadow.

"Look at the happy couple," Father says in carrying tones. A camerafly zooms in from out of nowhere, recording his words for posterity. "Sienna didn't want anything to detract from the Inauguration today, but I can't keep the happy news a secret any longer. My dear daughter is engaged to be married to this fine young man."

The room erupts into applause, and Father gives me a warning look. I swallow and look down. My hands shake. I want to lash out so badly the well-wishers blur in my vision. Enoch reclaims my arm, and there's nothing I can do, not after that announcement. Not with everyone staring and discussing us. Not with the camerafly broad-casting the news across the entire country and beyond. Between the two of them, Enoch and Father have managed to decimate my comfortable numbness in the space of five minutes. I didn't realize it was possible to hate Enoch more than I already did.

And Father? He's snapped my family loyalty in half like the twisted thing it's always been. Until this moment I still thought he might be bluffing, that he wouldn't go through with this, that maybe he really was doing everything for my own good. I know I'm difficult. I know I'm not everything a good girl should be. I've tried to keep it hidden, but it always wriggles into the open to bring me fresh shame. Maybe drastic measures were called for.

But now I'm going to be sent away to a foreign country where I'll never belong, and I'll never see my family again. That Father would be willing to murder his best friend to gain power shocked and appalled me, but that he's willing to exile me, his own daughter? The Tascionis are lost to me. And if they don't owe me anything, well then, I guess I don't owe them anything either.

It's the height of irony that right now, when I'm losing what little control of my life I have left, I also feel the most free.

CHAPTER 23

The Inauguration goes without a hitch. Father looks properly Doge-like as he's sworn into office on the copy of our family bible, brought from Earth by our Tascioni ancestors. During the formal receiving line afterwards, my neck gets sore with so much deferential nodding. Every family of any importance in Neopolitan has come to pay their respects and try to get into Father's good graces.

Every family except the Costas. They're still in deep mourning. Were she to know about my situation, I wouldn't get any sympathy from Gianna. But I still find myself wishing she were here.

Afterwards I circulate around the party with Mother. She doesn't leave me alone for a second. People gather in small clumps, whispering excitedly, but as Mother and I draw near, they fall quiet or approach to congratulate us again. The fancy hors d'oeuvres taste slightly rancid, I'm dizzy from all the strong perfumes, and I wish I knew what time it is.

Father spends a great portion of the evening with a small group of Senators and Assemblymen. A few are old allies with whom we've socialized many times, but there are several less familiar faces who I recognize as hardliners, politicians Zio Roberto had worked hard to appease but hadn't been closely aligned with. Times are changing with Father. No wonder the gossip at this party is at a fever pitch.

I've half-formulated a plan to talk with Ereni alone, but she and the other Satori diplomats aren't present. I saw her at the Inauguration earlier, staring at the other ambassadors and diplomats from my spot on the dais until I spotted her and her "family" at the very back. Ereni was wearing the gold glass necklace I'd given her the day of the Mask Maker's Festival. She must have worn it on purpose, but I'm not sure what message she was trying to send. I wonder if they already have a plan in place for saving Burke. I hope so.

We leave while the party is still in full swing, Father a shining figure in its midst. Signora Bartelli watches impassively as Lizabetta helps me out of my dress, removes the makeup from my face, undoes my hair. I look like a pale shadow of the girl I've been masquerading as all day.

And then I'm locked up in the closet like nothing has changed.

I DON'T SEE Father again before he leaves for Fidelium the next day. For a few hours I hold out hope his departure will result in less stringent security measures, but Signora Bartelli continues her hawk-like vigilance, and I'm locked in the closet as usual right after dinner.

I'm staring at the bathroom window, wondering how much weight I'd have to lose to squeeze through it, when I hear the lock being turned, a sound to which I've become hyper-attuned. Did Signora Bartelli forget something? Has Mother had second thoughts? I rush into the closet, only to see Leo standing in his oversized pajamas, a small knapsack slung over his shoulder, looking around the small room with a dubious expression.

I stop short. Then I run to him and fling myself in his arms. "Leo! What are you doing here? Won't you get in trouble?"

He squeezes me too tight, my lungs collapsing in protest, but I don't care. "I'm so sorry," he breathes into my ear. "Father sent me on a sudden mission to Providence a few weeks ago, and I had no idea what was happening to you. I wondered why you weren't answering my calls, but…I don't know, I thought you were busy helping Mother plan the Inauguration or something. I was an idiot, but you have to believe me, I didn't know."

It's funny, with all that dead time to torture myself with my own thoughts, I never doubted Leo. I didn't know where he was, what had happened to him, why he couldn't help me, but those were all details. We have a twin pact, and it's the only thing I know I can count on. Even now.

He must feel the same because he hasn't let me go. "I heard what that *stronzo* said to you before the Inauguration," he says.

I quell the urge to break into hysterical laughter, but I can't resist sarcasm. "Hasn't Father chosen me an exemplary life partner?"

"You can't marry him." He says it with a conviction I don't expect. "I saw what things are like in Providence, and Sienna, you can't live there. It would kill you."

"What choice do I have?"

Leo pulls back from me, meets my eyes so I can see he's serious. "You can run." He tosses the knapsack onto my cot. "Your boys' clothes are in there. Your qualpad. A little bit of money. And travel supplies. I wish I had more to give you."

I don't know where to go, but I know I can't stay here. "He killed Zio Roberto, Leo. Father killed him." It's such a relief to say the words out loud. "And I have proof. That's why—" I gesture around the closet. The mother-of-pearl cabinet inlays and hardwood floor give it a touch of luxury, but it's a prison all the same.

Leo goes so pale I can see freckles on his cheekbones I didn't know were there. A second later he's rushing into the bathroom and retching into the toilet. I look through the knapsack: the clothes, the spare socks, some nutrition bars, a water bottle. When he comes back out, I'm staring at a simple black half-mask, wondering why he included it. "It's the first night of Carnival," he says. "If you wear that mask, you should be able to sneak through the revels unnoticed, get to the track, and take one of the bikes. Travel a far enough distance no one will be able to find you."

I guess we're not going to discuss Father's perfidy further. And after all, what is there to say? "Won't you come with me?" I ask.

He shakes his head. "I'm safe enough. Besides, I might be able to bear some influence if things go wrong." If I get caught, he doesn't say.

"I'll stay in touch with you. Let you know where I am, how things are going."

But he's shaking his head. "We can't communicate at all, Sienna, don't you see? I can't guarantee he won't find a way to intercept our messages. It's better if I don't know anything." If Father gets angry enough to return from Fidelium, Leo's right to be afraid. There's no telling how far Father would go, not anymore.

I kiss him on the cheek. Who knows when I'll see him again? His familiar citrus scent fills my nose. "Thank you," I whisper. "I won't forget what you've done for me."

"Twin pact. You'd do the same for me."

He hugs me, and for a moment I let myself relax in the false security of his arms. I don't want to let him go. But eventually I have to. "Be safe," he says. And then he leaves the room, the door gaping open behind him.

Now I have bigger things to worry about. Like where to go. I can't imagine staying in Neopolitan. As Doge, Father will have unlimited resources to find me. I'll have to be clever and try to disappear altogether.

But I can't help thinking of Burke, standing trial for a crime he didn't commit. A crime Father pinned on him and for which he will be shown no mercy. It's not my fault. I'm not responsible for him. I didn't tell him to leave his planet and come here.

So why do I feel so responsible? Why can't I get his face out of my mind?

With a sinking heart I know exactly where I'm going.

I'm going to Fidelium.

CHAPTER 24

I'm in over my head, and I know who I need: Ereni. Always so cool and collected, she could hatch a convoluted plot every day before breakfast. She can help me get to Fidelium, and she'll know what to do once we're there. If there's anyone who can figure out a way to clear Burke from the crime Father committed, it's Ereni.

I'll worry about the future later.

I change into my boy's clothes, wrapping my breasts as quickly as I can, and hurry down the stairs, mask dangling from my fingers. I rummage through the knapsack as I go, fingering the strands of my wig, which I've hidden underneath a change of clothes. How much money has Leo given me? Will it be enough?

And that's why I'm distracted enough to run smack into Enoch in the foyer, making a high-pitched shriek of surprise. My forehead throbs where it hit Enoch in the shoulder.

"You're as hardheaded as I'd expect, Tascioni." Enoch draws himself up to his full height, but he's also rubbing his shoulder, ruining the effect. "Don't go thinking this will be my only payback."

I clear my throat and pitch my voice as low as it will go. "Is that a threat or a promise?" I try a boyish swagger.

He growls deep in his throat. "Wouldn't you like to know."

Well, no one says it takes wit to become an ambassador's son. I look around for the servant who let him in and will doubtless be returning any moment. The sooner I can leave, the better.

"Be a pal and go fetch your sister before you go," Enoch says. "I want to give her a little pre-conjugal visit, if you know what I mean."

Surely he doesn't think he can get away with something like that. Not in my own house. But as he lurches closer, I smell the alcohol on his breath. "What, you don't want to play the field while you still can?" I try to say it neutrally, the way Leo might, deflecting instead of giving into my temper.

"Who says I can't do both?" He winks at me, and I kindly decide not to throw up all over his shoes. Instead I place the mask on my face and tie the ribbon firmly in the back. I feel safer when I can hide like this.

He looks me up and down. "So you're out slumming it with the revelers tonight, I take it?"

I shrug. Let him think whatever he wants about Leo. I'll be gone soon enough, no longer leaving messes for Leo to clean in my wake.

I'm unprepared when Enoch suddenly darts forward and grabs me. I struggle with him, trying to knee him in the crotch or force my arms free, but before I can put up much of a fight, he's pulled up my shirt, revealing the overly loose wrapping underneath. Enoch hoots in triumph and I take advantage of his distraction to slam him in the neck with my hand. He falls back, coughing and grabbing at his neck. "Son of a bitch," he swears. "I knew it the moment I heard that shriek. Been carrying on a bit of a double life, have you, *Sienna*? Maybe we'll have more fun than I thought."

"Stay away from me." But we both know who is stronger.

Enoch rubs his throat and continues to give me some space, but he's undressing me with his eyes. He pulls something out of his shirt, a pendant in the same shape as the yellow sigil on his racing suit. "Do you know what this stands for, Sienna? My dearest?" He practically purrs the words.

"No, and I don't care." But I stare at the pendant between his fingers as if it's a weapon.

"Purity above all." He says it with a fanaticism that makes me back up a step. "But you haven't been very pure, have you, Sienna?" He stuffs the necklace back into his shirt. "I can help you. I can purify you." He leans forward, his eyes narrow. "I'll *burn* it into you if that's what I have to do. And someday you'll thank me for it."

The full depth of Father's betrayal in giving me to this man hits me harder than any punch. This isn't going to be my future. Not if I have anything to do with it. I run, taking Enoch by surprise. He thought I would surrender.

He doesn't know the first thing about me.

I fling myself at the front door, escaping through it only a few arm's lengths ahead of Enoch. We race down the stairs and out the front yard into the city. He has longer legs, but I'm faster.

Barely.

I run across the nearest bridge and into the dense warren of pedestrian streets and alleys that make up the heart of San Marco. I've gotten to know them better during my nocturnal outings masquerading as Leo. Surely I know them better than Enoch?

But it is the first night of Carnival, and the dense crowds prevent me from running. I push and squeeze through the masked throng, glancing over my shoulder to spot Enoch, obvious due to his height and lack of mask, always behind me. Someone steps hard on my foot, and I push forward, limping. Music blares from all directions, people singing along, oblivious to my danger. Vendors shout in front of their carts, the smells of hot nuts and sweet icing thick in the air. The colorful lanterns and strings of light I usually find so charming distort the scene around me, casting grotesque shadows.

I'm terrified I'll accidentally trap myself in a dead-end. With so many people it's hard to tell where I'm going, and I've gotten turned around in the labyrinth of streets. I think about hiding in a shop, but what if Enoch corners me inside? Masks menace me from all sides. I finally come to a square I recognize, too far south. I adjust my route, all the while watching Enoch elbow his way after me.

The crowds thin closer to the Satori embassy's unfashionable neighborhood. I spot a dark corner where I might be able to hide, only to find an amorous couple already there. I keep hoping Enoch will get tired and decide I'm not worth the trouble, but there he is, still keeping pace with me, even though I've been able to widen the distance between us substantially. I can move faster now, but I have to be careful. I don't know this neighborhood well, and the danger of getting trapped by a canal with no bridge to cross is ever-present. If I have to jump in the water, I'll need medical treatment or I'll fall sick from all the contaminants. Either way I can kiss my escape plans goodbye.

Only a few blocks from the Satori embassy, the streets clear out completely. It must be past two in the morning, and the poorer families who live here went to sleep a long time ago. The three moons shine brightly above us, and Enoch is too close behind for me to have any chance of hiding. "Sienna!" he shouts. I keep running. "You have nowhere to go," he taunts me. "No one cares what happens to you. You're all mine."

But I remember Ereni wearing the necklace I gave her at the Inauguration, and I don't give up. I'm running as fast as I can, my footfalls sounding thunderous in my own ears, my breathing rhythmic but too fast. I'm getting tired. My foot throbs. On the stairs of the last bridge, I stumble and almost fall, but I push myself up, the force jarring through my arms. There it is, the familiar Embassy house, and I practically throw myself at the door, pounding on it with both hands.

Enoch laughs behind me. "It's the middle of the night," he says. He slows down, taking pleasure in my obvious panic. "They're not going to let you in."

I pound again, breath heaving through my lungs as though they're filled with gravel. Enoch strolls toward me slowly, like he has all the time in the world. I push myself back into the door. He's so much bigger than me.

He pulls back his fist, and I know he's going to hit me. I brace myself for the impact. And then the door behind me opens, and I fall inside.

~

Ereni catches me. I rip off my mask and look desperately up into her face. She whispers something I don't hear and draws me behind her. A small pulse of hope returns to life in my chest.

Enoch pushes through the door after me. "That girl is my responsibility." His voice reverberates through the narrow space. "You must return her to me at once."

Ereni makes a little noise that almost sounds like a laugh. She's fully dressed even though it's the middle of the night. "I will do no such thing." Her voice sounds like a whisper compared to his, and he leans forward as if to hear her better. "I suggest you calm down."

"She belongs to me by law," he rasps out, and I stumble backwards. "Her father and I have already signed an agreement. As her fiancé I've become her guardian."

Ereni merely looks at him. "Do I need to remind you you're now on the sovereign soil of Satori? Your laws and agreements hold no sway here." He opens his mouth to argue, but she holds up her hand. "I'll need to consult with my colleagues. You may wait." She nods at the open door leading into the music room.

They stare at each other for a long moment, and I think Enoch will object and drag me out with brute force if necessary. But then he gives a long-suffering sigh and heads through the door.

"Please make yourself comfortable," Ereni says after him. Then she takes my hand and leads me into the house and up the stairs. No one is stirring even after Enoch's bellowing, which should have been enough to wake the entire household.

It's only after she's shut the door behind me that I realize we must be in her bedroom. It's a fairly small room, with a narrow bed, a small rosewood writing desk, and a vanity table not unlike my own. The walls are bare, painted a rich amber color. Besides the cosmetics and fragrance bottles lining the vanity, the only personal item on display is a large photograph by the bed of five grinning teenagers. None of them look demonstrably like Ereni until I examine their smiles. I pick her out, voluptuous and sturdy, tight brown curls clustered around her head. This must be how Ereni used to look back on Satori. The smile is the only thing that's the same.

"Now what are we going to do about you?" She surveys me from head to toe and shakes her head. "Excuse me for saying so, but you don't look so good. And you need a haircut. Unless you're growing it out?"

I touch my hair self-consciously. Leo would never be allowed to let his hair grow this long, but I've been too closely monitored to do anything about it. "My father caught me in his study."

She clicks her tongue. "Ah. I wondered."

She doesn't ask what he did after that, for which I am grateful. She saw me at the Inauguration, arm in arm with Enoch. She can guess. "I'm going to Fidelium, and I want you to come with me," I say.

She goes to look out her window. "I can't leave right now. Plenty of our people are in Fidelium helping with the trial. I'm needed here to oversee the opening of our first clinic."

She must not understand the urgency. "My father has traveled to Fidelium. I know he plans to argue for no clemency for Burke."

"What a surprise." Her tone is as dry as I've ever heard it.

"Burke needs you there. Don't you want to help him?"

Ereni turns back toward me. "He wouldn't want me to abandon our mission. Our time table's been moved up considerably."

"But...."

"Believe me, Burke isn't taking it personally that I'm not there to hold his hand."

"Don't you care about him?" I don't understand her indifference. "How can you stand by doing nothing?"

"Who said I was doing nothing?" Ereni's eyebrow crooks in that suggestive way of hers. "Be careful what assumptions you're making."

I take a deep breath. "I can prove it. I can prove it wasn't Burke who killed the Doge." I pull my qualpad from the knapsack and connect to my secret account. I pull up the photo of the Pentobarbital vials. I hesitate before playing the audio recording of Father's and my conversation that night. But then I push the button. At least one person in our family can do the right thing.

Ereni is paying attention now. I don't doubt she's recording this entire conversation herself. There's no turning back for me now. I hate the way I sound in the recording. So surprised, so helpless. But

Ereni gives me an approving nod. "I'm glad you've decided to go to Fidelium. Evidence from the daughter of the new Doge himself? That's a source that will be hard to dispute."

"I need you there with me," I say. "I can't do it alone." Running away is one thing, but facing my father? That will take a whole different level of courage.

"You have to." She grasps both my hands. "Listen, Sienna, I'm doing important work here. It's possible we'll be withdrawn from Sanctum any time now, and it's imperative I accomplish as much as I can before then. Do you understand? Can you do this without me?"

"I don't know how to make them listen to me." I hate having to admit this to someone who seems to get everything she wants just by smiling. "I've never been to Fidelium. I won't even know where to go."

But she dismisses my concerns. "Go the courthouse. It's impossible to miss that monolith. I'll have someone meet you there. We'll make sure you get to testify." She squeezes my hands. "I know it's hard, but you have to make them hear you. Do you think you can do that?"

She looks at me with such intensity, I can't bear to disappoint her. Of course I can't do that. No one has any interest in hearing what I have to say. What must it be like to take for granted that your voice matters?

"Burke is depending on you," she says.

I remember dancing with him at the edge of the forest. Our hands touching, both of us spinning, the way I felt when he dipped me. The way he didn't make a fuss when I became too frightened. "I'll do my best."

But then I remember Enoch seething downstairs, waiting to take ownership of me. "What about Enoch?" I can't suppress a shudder at what he had planned for this evening. "He'll never let me testify. And now he knows I've been dressing up as Leo. The scandal...." I trail off. I don't know if there's any way to explain to Ereni how bad it could get.

"You leave him to me. You think I haven't found all kinds of dirt on him?" Her smile is cold. I wouldn't want to be her enemy.

She leads me down the back staircase and into the kitchen, which has another exit. But she stops me before I go. "You're doing the right thing."

"I know." It doesn't dissolve the lump in my throat when I think of telling the truth about what Father has done. But it still helps to hear.

"About Burke." She clears her throat, looks uncomfortable.

"Yes?"

"You understand the best outcome is that he leaves Sanctum with the rest of us." She plays with her cuffs.

"Of course." I know she's trying to be kind by setting my expectations, but I don't need her to tell me there's no future for the two of us together. I haven't gone to such lengths to avoid marriage to Enoch just to get married to someone else, however much I might like him. "If you're still opening the clinic...."

"Yes?"

"Do you...do you think you could treat my mother?"

Her face twists up for a second, and there is pity in her eyes. "You really haven't figured it out?"

My heart sinks. I'm so tired of the endless torrent of bad news. "Figured what out?"

Ereni rests her hand on her forehead as if, after everything we've discussed today, this is the thing that breaks her heart. "It's not real," she finally says. "Your mother's illness. She's been faking it the entire time."

Finally Ereni has gotten something wrong. "No, you don't understand, she's been sick for years. The doctor thought she was going to die. The treatments made her so sick she had to wear a wig, and she's never been the same since then."

Ereni shakes her head. "I didn't realize the truth for the longest time. Your mother plays a convincing invalid when it suits her. But... you deserve to know the truth. It's all lies. Your mother is fine. She's always been fine. I swear it."

"But that means...." The force of the betrayal freezes me in place, my brain spinning between unlikely explanations that will prove Ereni wrong. "But Father...." Father must have known. And I remember all the positive press during his campaign about his devotion to civic duty even during Mother's illness, about her bravery in carrying on in spite of everything. The wonderful optics of having her look so pale and wasted. Makeup and a strict diet? Is that all it had been, in order to win that first campaign? And then whenever it was convenient, whenever I was stepping out of line, whenever I needed an extra dose of fear to keep me performing as the dutiful daughter?

It had been entirely real to me, the threat of losing my mother hanging over me like a knife on a string.

A silent scream reverberates throughout every cavity of my body. I cannot live this way. I cannot. "Thanks for your help," I tell Ereni stiffly.

"I'm sorry, Sienna. I really am." As far as my parents are concerned, I'm just an insignificant pawn on the board, and that's all I'll ever be. I have trouble listening to the words she's saying to me. "Good luck. And hurry. The trial begins the day after tomorrow." She clasps my shoulder one last time, and as I leave, all I can think is that I never want to come back.

CHAPTER 25

I make it in time.

I visit Leo's garage and choose one of his sturdier speeder bikes with a lower top speed but a more rugged build and better handling for distance, and I ride all through the night, hunched over the handlebars, pushing myself to the limits of my endurance. When I absolutely can't keep my eyes open, sometime in the middle of the morning, I pull over by a vineyard, check to make sure most of its care is automated, and curl up on the ground behind a pump station. I wake up three hours later and keep going.

One more nap, and a few stops for snacks and water, and it's dawn again, the spires of Fidelium's skyscrapers rising in the distance like tiny needles against the purple sky. San Marco doesn't have any buildings so tall or so delicate, and I wonder how they avoid collapsing in on themselves. They look like they could be knocked over by a particularly strong gust of wind. San Marco's buildings are spread out, separated by the network of canals and bridges around which it's built, but Fidelium's skyscrapers are clustered tightly together, a dense profusion of metal and glass. The international courthouse is somewhere in the heart of all those spires.

From a distance, the newly risen sun reflecting on Fidelium's glass buildings makes it look like the jewel-encrusted crown of our planet. The reality up close is different. The city is barely controlled chaos, the streets a labyrinth of unexpected one-way roads and no left turns and the densest traffic I've ever seen. When I look up, I have trouble seeing the sky.

It feels like it takes me hours to find the courthouse. Unlike all the buildings around it, it matches the architectural style of San Marco: built of stone and marble, it's solid and squat, the only building in sight that doesn't look like it's in a competition to touch the sky. Its twelve famous columns greet me, one for each nation of this planet. The original settlers constructed it before the Providentials arrived, which is why there aren't thirteen. All thirteen flags fly in its front courtyard though, surrounding the Planetary Flag in the middle. We come here to resolve our differences with each other, and this is where Burke's case will be tried.

I don't know when exactly I'm needed, but urgency makes my heart pump faster as I hurry up the stairs and through the massive front doors, wearing one of Leo's more utilitarian racing suits. Once I pass through the security scanner, I emerge into an atrium with a tall golden dome of a ceiling. A huge staircase ascends and separates to the left and right. Hanging over the landing is the Founder's Seal, the circular symbol of unity from when Sanctum was first colonized. Neopolitan's slice of the circle is a deep royal purple. I hesitate, surrounded by people who all seem to know where they're going. More than anything I want to slink right back outside this building.

I take a deep breath and remind myself that, here and now, I am Leonardo Tascioni, and I belong just as much as anyone else. After all, as *Ragazzo d'Oro* I'm as gilded as the dome. I try to walk with purpose and authority. If Ereni can fake it, then so can I.

I'm exiting the heaviest flow of foot traffic when I hear someone clear her throat. I turn and see Gianna in full formal mourning: black dress, armband, dark gray gloves, and a black veil pushed back from her face combine in an unalleviated picture of bleakness. I blink. "What are you doing here?" I blurt out. I automatically use my fake lower voice, and the fact it is so easy now is both a disturbance and a relief.

Gianna's lips purse in her familiar disapproving look. "Hello to you, too, Leo. And yes, I have been having a difficult time, thanks for enquiring."

I cast down my eyes, uncomfortable speaking with her after everything that has happened. "I apologize."

"As to why I'm here, where else would you expect me to be? My mother is here as well. We intend to watch justice be served to my father's killer. We appreciate your family's support. Your father told us he came here on our behalf to plead for no clemency."

Her words fill me with guilt. "Actually, there's been a mistake. I know Burke isn't the one who killed your father." How will I be able to face her when she knows the truth? Nothing in our shared past can cushion that blow. "I intend to bring the true killer to justice."

I'm a coward. I can't tell her the whole truth, not like this, not right to her face. Let her find out with the rest of the courtroom.

I can't look away from her eyes, individual red veins visible in their whites, all the foundation in the world not enough to mask the dark smears underneath them. "I don't know what you're talking about. That Satori scum killed my father, everyone knows it. The case against him is solid."

How can I convince her? "New evidence has been uncovered."

"Why are you determined to upset me at a time like this?" She dabs at her eyes with a clean black handkerchief. "I just want this trial to go as planned, surely you must understand that. This isn't a joke, Leo, and it's not like you to be so insensitive."

I take a quick step back. Gianna grew up with us. If anyone could see through my façade, it's her. "My apologies." I overcompensate, making my voice a little extra deep, and it cracks. I push forward, hoping she won't notice. "Is there anything I can do for you?"

She narrows her eyes. "Wait a minute. Show me your left hand."

I flex my hand in its black glove. Leo has a nasty scar across his left palm, received when he retrieved Gianna's hat at a garden party many years before. "That wouldn't be appropriate. Not in public."

"Show me." Her eyes bore into mine, searching out my secrets. Mutely I shake my head. "Well, well, well. My mistake. What on earth have you done to yourself, Sienna?" She wrinkles her nose in disgust. "Your hair…it's freakish."

"I can explain." Panic rises in my chest. "I have a good reason, I promise."

She snorts. "We're not children anymore. This isn't some kind of game. When are you going to grow up and acknowledge your obligations?"

Her words sting. "Why else would I come? Do you think I want to be here right now?"

But Gianna's eyes narrow. "You've been sweet on that Satori boy ever since you met him, and don't try to deny it. I warn you, Sienna, don't interfere in things that are none of your concern. I don't have time for you, not after you betrayed me on that shopping trip, so you'd better stay out of my way." She turns on her heel and flounces away with a swishing of skirts.

Of all the people to know my secret, rule-abiding Gianna is one of the worst possibilities. I watch as she threads her way through the crowd and opens an unlabeled door. She assumes I had something to do with that stunt to discredit her on our shopping trip, and how can I blame her? She'll have more cause to hate me soon enough. I just hope she holds her tongue and doesn't spread any additional vicious gossip about me.

Then I realize how absurd that thought is. What harm will more gossip do once the world knows the truth about Father?

A tiny doubt blooms in my heart. This kind of scandal will render me and my family untouchable. The consequences won't fall on Father's head alone.

"Signor Tascioni." Irisa Lhasa hurries up to me, her skirts bunched awkwardly in her hands as if she's not used to handling them. A large wrinkle carves a line between her eyebrows, and her gloves look dingy. She plays the part of the befuddled Satori diplomat so well I wonder how much of it is true, and I'm surprised by how relieved I am to see her. "I've been expecting you. Won't you please come with me?"

IRISA LHASA TAKES me to a far less grand hallway lined by doors, many leading to the offices of judges and various court officials. I open my mouth to ask her about Burke, but she shakes her head at me. "Not yet."

She leads me into a small room at the end of the hall, strictly util-itarian, with a metal table, some chairs, and a screen high up in one corner. The walls are painted the green of lime gelato, the floor scuffed linoleum. It is ugly in a way that speaks of disrespect to its inhabitants. "This is the office assigned to us in the Halls of Justice." She gestures at the bare walls. "Isn't it inspiring?"

"I want to see Burke." I don't want to cry in front of this strange woman, but now that we're out of public view, I feel my knees start to shake.

"He's a little busy at the moment." She gives me an ironic smile. "Take a seat, won't you, please? Sienna?" She says the last hesitat-ingly, as if she can't quite believe the audacity of my charade. "We are so grateful you've come. Your courage and integrity in sharing this information with us, well…you are a most impressive young person. It is our pleasure to do everything within our power to make you comfortable while you're here in the Capitol."

I slide into the offered seat, but I don't know how to respond to what she's said. I'm betraying my own father. Any integrity I have left is a result of insufficient loyalty and unwomanly behavior. But she's Satori so she wouldn't understand.

"I'm sure once it can be arranged, Burke will wish to see you. And our legal team wants to speak with you as soon as possible, if I may alert them to your presence?"

"Do I have any choice?"

I try to make it into a joke, but it falls flat, and she merely shrugs. We both know the answer is no.

I SPEND several hours closeted with the Satori legal team in the increasingly uncomfortable room. There are five of them, three men and two women, and I'm too tired to keep their names straight. They go through my secret cloud repository of evidence and ask me questions until tears prick my eyes. I can't remember the last time I've slept a full night. Irisa Lhasa must notice because she insists on taking me somewhere to rest. They don't let me keep my qualpad. The entire team agrees I must be kept in seclusion until it's time for me to testify, for my own safety. I don't ask them if they think Father would kill me too. I don't want to hear the answer.

Signora Lhasa whisks me away to an elegant flat near the top of a nearby skyscraper. Normally I'd be excited to be in such a fast elevator, to see the view of Fidelium from so high. But not today. She shows me my bedroom and presents me with several gowns and a new wig. My chest constricts, and I feel like I'm not getting enough air. My breath comes out in fast frantic gasps. "I'm sorry, I'm so sorry." I flap my hands as if that will put my body back under my control.

She sits down beside me on the narrow bed and reaches toward me. I recoil from the pity in her sad eyes, and then she says, "Oh my poor sweet child, I'm so sorry for the things that have been done to you." I've been struggling so hard to keep it together, but these words break something inside of me. It should be my own mother saying this to me, but I'm stuck with this stranger from another planet who still somehow manages to understand me better than anyone at home. I sag into her, breaths rattling through my body, and she wraps her arm around me and strokes my back. I don't cry. I can't allow such a loss of control. Instead I sit there and shake.

"We'll protect you." I realize she's saying it over and over. I don't believe her, but it's nice of her to make the effort.

Eventually my breathing slows and I force myself to pull away, to stand up, to begin my transformation back into a proper young lady.

And then I do want to cry, because why does being a woman have to squeeze me so tightly? No matter what choices I make, it feels like everything remains out of my hands.

CHAPTER 26

The Satori keep their promise, and the next day at noon, Burke shuffles into the little lime-green room where I've been waiting. We look at each other for a long moment, and then I'm in his arms. I don't know how we bridge the gap between the two of us, I just know after everything that's happened, the captivity both of us have suffered, I want to feel him against me. I want the physical evidence that he's really here. My ears ring and we're not alone in the room and what we're doing is shocking but maybe I'm past the point of no return in that regard because I don't care as much as I should. He pulls back just enough to kiss me, and as his lips meet mine, so much emotion fills me I almost start crying.

He tastes of salt, he smells of harsh minty soap, these are both unfamiliar, but I don't care. His lips are still soft and his cheeks are still rough, just how I remember them. I want to wipe away all my memories with his kisses until he becomes my whole reality.

How could I have ever thought he was a murderer? I kiss him harder by way of apology. I shouldn't have doubted him.

Finally we come up for air, breathless. I look around, but whoever accompanied Burke has left, and the two of us are alone. "I thought they would lock you away." I touch his shoulders, his chin, his cheeks, as though I can lay claim to him through my fingers. "I didn't think they'd let us be alone."

"Being a diplomat has its privileges." He tucks a piece of my fake hair behind my ear. "Although they only reach so far. I sleep in a cell at night."

Because of Father. "I'm so sorry."

"Not your fault." He fingers the lace edging my neckline before running his hands down my arms and grasping my hands. "Is it true you rode a speeder bike here by yourself and made it in record time?"

"Well, I didn't want to be late."

There's something about Burke that makes me feel witty, like I'm a person who says things worth hearing. I like it. I like him. I might not want to marry him, but I also don't want him to leave.

But I know that's the best-case scenario, him leaving the planet forever. This is what I'm forced to hope for.

"Ereni said…." He pauses like it pains him to give Ereni credit for anything, even passing along information. "She said you might be able to help me. But we didn't know how long it would take for you to get here, and when you didn't show up right away…." He doesn't finish the sentence. He had doubted me, too, I can see it in his eyes, and I can't blame him.

"Might? I thought she had more faith in me than that." I force a laugh. "Don't worry, Burke. I have the evidence that should clear you."

He stares at me as if I'm too good to be true, then whoops and pulls me back into a tight hug. "Sienna to the rescue. I knew there was a reason I liked you."

His words make my insides thrum. "One of *many* reasons," I point out.

His laugh is slightly hysterical. "Of course. But if you help me get off this nightmare of a planet, you'll have my lifelong gratitude."

His words reverberate through me like a slap, even though I keep hugging him. He really hates it here that much? Stupid Sienna, of course he does. He's never pretended otherwise.

But given he's been framed for murder by my own father, how

can I blame him for wanting to leave and never think about Sanctum again?

Will he still think about me once he leaves?

I kiss him again. Now is the only time we have.

But he pulls away. "What is this new evidence? Because they found several bottles of Pentobarbital in my bedroom. Planted, of course, but it doesn't look good for me. And your father has testified I was in the Doge's residence that night. He's lying, of course, but I don't have an alibi."

I swallow. "I thought the legal team would have filled you in by now." I see why they've been looking so worried. Father's testimony has established the opportunity as well as the means for Burke to have murdered Zio Roberto. He's determined to make the Satori take the fall. And if I were doing as I was told, he'd be getting away with it too.

Burke shakes his head. "They told me to ask you."

I don't know whether to bless them or hate them. "I know who the real killer is."

Burke looks at me expectantly. "And? Who is it?" He shakes his head. "It would be Ereni who figured it out. It's always precious Ereni."

It wasn't Ereni. It was me. But I can't tell him what I know. Not yet. He'll never look at me the same way again. "It's someone in the Neopolitan government," I say instead. It's not a lie, after all. "And your lawyers say they have a strong case now that I'm here. That's what's important."

"You can say that again." He leans his forehead against mine. "You're my hero, Sienna. What would I do without you?"

I try not to melt at his tone of voice. "Die by lethal injection." I am both joking and not joking, trying to distract myself from these feelings I don't trust.

"You do realize you come from a completely barbaric civilization, don't you?" He's using a light tone as well, but he's not really joking either. I'm so close I can see the color variations in his irises, but our experiences are worlds apart.

"I'm sorry this happened to you." I wish I had a way to show him how much I mean it.

"Don't be. It's not your fault." He kisses me again. "I've missed you."

He wouldn't say that if he knew the truth. I wonder if I'll spend the rest of my life apologizing for Father.

~

It takes Father two days to find me.

Mother must have told him I'd disappeared, and Father knows everybody. He has the resources and power to grease the right palms. I'm surprised it takes him as long as it does. Even now I'm not his top priority. After all, he doesn't know what evidence I brought with me.

He doesn't knock. He walks right into the Satori's flat as if he owns the place, startling me from my place curled up on the window seat. Luckily I'm wearing my wig and a simple dress Irina has lent me. Even now I have my secrets.

Ever since I discovered the truth of his crimes, I've been watching him, looking for any little sign I'd missed, some flag that says "Murderer" in flashing letters. But I never find any. He's wearing a gray three-piece suit, a gold chain snaking from one pocket. His gloves are as spotless as usual, his beard as meticulously trimmed. He has the same worked leather bag slung over his shoulder. Maybe he's always had something terrible living inside him.

"Sienna." He says my name in a normal voice, as if he's happy to see me. "Sienna," he repeats, and he holds out his hand, "it's time to go."

But even Father can't erase history so easily. I draw back towards the window, tucking my feet further underneath me, feeling the coolness of the glass through my gloves. Am I about to die?

No. No, that's a terrible thought to have about my own father. He would never...but I don't bother to finish the sentence in my head. Because I'm no longer sure what he would never do and what he'd do all too readily.

What I do know is that right now, pressed against the window, I feel like prey.

So when two Satori burst into the room, I'm relieved. Father glances over his shoulder at them and pretends to be unconcerned, but he begins stroking his beard. They're breathing hard, as if they've been running, and one of them, a young man whose vest is halfway unbuttoned and isn't wearing any gloves, approaches me. "Is there anything you require, Signorina Tascioni?"

The other one sizes up Father. "Would you like us to escort your uninvited guest outside, Signorina?"

I'm tempted by her offer, I really am. But if I mean to testify against my own father in a court of law, surely I can handle one private conversation with him? When will I have another chance to get some answers from him? I take a deep breath. "It's okay. I'd like to talk to him."

The man nods at me. "We'll be nearby if you require assistance." He marches over to stand on the far side of the room, and the woman leaves by the front door, giving us the illusion of privacy.

Father smiles at me as though he's won a point. "Good girl."

I smile back at him, but it feels more like I'm baring my teeth. We both know I'm anything but.

"Why did you do it?" I cut right to the question that haunts me. I've run so many scenarios through my mind, but none of them make sense. Father loved Zio Roberto like a brother. I know he did. Their fates were linked right from the beginning. They rose together. And now they'll fall together, in spite of Father's best efforts.

"Sienna, these are adult affairs. Men's matters. You couldn't possibly understand." He's trying to brush me off. In his eyes I'll always be six years old.

My anger makes me strong. "Try me."

His sigh is patronizing, as if murder should be self-explanatory. As if he's disappointed in my lack of insight. "Sometimes, for matters of political expediency—"

I interrupt him. "Cut the *merda*. Why'd you do it? Zio Roberto would have taken a bullet for you."

"He would have done no such thing," Father says sharply, stung into something more closely resembling candor. "He was a disloyal, power-grabbing *testa di cazzo* who was in the process of betraying the ideals upon which Neopolitan was founded."

"So you're a patriot, is what you're saying."

"That's right." He clasps his hands behind his back. "Sometimes you must act for the greater good, even when doing so requires you to pay a high personal cost. I did what I had to do." He shakes his head at me. "I don't expect you to understand, Sienna. Duty and loyalty have never been your strong points."

I wait for his words to sting the way they once would have, but nothing happens. The angry fire in my belly is burning too hot. It incinerates his words before they have a chance to draw blood.

"Perhaps not." I fold my arms deliberately in front of me, shutting him out. "But if that's the case, it's only because I learned it from you. I don't think killing your best friend and political partner qualifies you to lecture me about loyalty."

Father shakes his head sadly. "You used to be such a sweet girl. These Satori are corrupting you, changing you into an entirely different person."

But I know the truth. It's not the Satori who changed me. It's him. "You were mad at Zio Roberto, weren't you? He wanted to experiment, to explore new ideas to improve conditions for more people. And you, you just wanted your chance to be Doge. A chance he no longer wanted to give you. When did he figure out how corrupt power had made you?"

"You don't know what you're talking about," he snaps. I've hit a nerve, and I relish his discomfort. "You're just a naïve little girl."

"Then why are you wasting your time talking to me?" I counter. "Oh, that's right, because I can prove you murdered a sitting Doge. What will everyone think of you when the truth comes out? Where will your precious reputation get you then? I'm not a naïve little girl. I'm the bomb that's going to blow your careful plans to bits."

Father gives me a pitying look. "You've never had a mind for politics."

As if Leo ever did any better. "I do okay."

Father glances at the man in the hallway, then steps forward.

"You're being manipulated, Sienna, can't you see that?" His voice is low, earnest, like he's suddenly decided to start taking me seriously. "This kid—what's his name, Brock? Barton?"

"Burke." As if he doesn't know.

"He knows how sheltered you are, how susceptible. He's playing on your emotions to get what he wants. You think you love him, don't you?" I hesitate, not knowing the answer to his question, or at least not wanting to admit it. Do I love Burke? The last time I saw him, I'd felt something almost painful deep in my chest. But these days my emotions are in such an uproar it's difficult to feel anything remotely resembling clarity.

Father takes another step forward, now close enough to reach out and put his hand on my arm. The man in the hallway is watching us, but he doesn't intervene. "Don't worry, Sienna, you can tell me. I'm your father. No one will look out for your best interests the way I will."

I stare at him incredulously. How can he still believe that, after the weeks in the closet, after the marriage match with Enoch, after the way Enoch chased me across San Marco intent on harming me? How can he think I'll ever be able to trust him again?

But even as I look up into his familiar brown eyes, I know why. Because he's my father, and I love him. And more than anything, I *want* to trust him. I want to defer to him. I want him to take care of me and tell me the right thing to do. I want to be as protected as I'd always expected to be. What I have now, this freedom, it's exhilarating, but it's also frightening and painfully lonely. I don't know what I'm doing. I'm seventeen years old, and I've left everything I know behind. The only person I trust here is Burke, a boy from another planet I've known for a matter of weeks. This is never what I would have chosen for myself.

"I trust him," I say stiffly. Whether I love him or not is irrelevant right now, and even if I knew, Father would simply see that as another sign of weakness.

But he doesn't relinquish the idea. "You're an inexperienced girl, Sienna. You may fancy yourself to be in love, but I can guarantee he doesn't love you back."

I've gotten the only answers I'm going to from him. "Okay. I think you should go now." I look over at the man in the hallway.

"You've been acting as Ereni Lhasa's asset, and Burke knew that. He was working with his…sister." His pregnant pause shows he's aware they're not actually siblings. "She gave him the task of romancing you, making you more motivated to work for the Satori's best interests."

Why does he have to twist everything? "That's not true. Burke had no idea what was going on. And I wasn't working as an asset." He's making me sound so cheap.

Father shrugs. "We can discuss your treasonous activities another time. You're lucky I'm the Doge." Implying my life is in his hands, as if it hasn't been all along. "But Sienna, think. What will happen if this young man is found innocent?"

"He'll be allowed to leave."

"Exactly. He'll leave you behind, and you'll never see him again. You do understand there's no future there, don't you? Or have you gone so far astray you no longer care about your virtue?"

My throat closes, and I wonder if it's possibly to physically gag on somebody else's words. "You're the one who doesn't value my virtue," I manage to get out. The terror of Enoch stalking me during the riotous Carnival celebrations comes back to me all in a rush. I never want to celebrate Carnival again. "You gave Enoch permission to… to…" I can't finish the sentence. I can't even look at him. Instead I turn to the window and look down at the dizzying drop.

"I'm only doing my best for you, making sure you're well situated." He's using his sweetest voice now, the one he uses with his political opponents. That's what I am now: his opponent. What a surprise for us both. "Let me help you, Sienna. It's not too late." He puts his hand on my shoulder, and I have to steel myself not to flinch. "You're still my daughter. Let me take you home."

I give myself a moment to believe him, to believe we can go back to the way things were before, only better. To imagine the four of us in our beautiful house in the country, once again a close-knit family. To be with Leo, to have Mother stop lying about her health, for Father to give me input into the identity of my future husband, to believe that together we can pick a man who will let me play a more interesting role in life, helping him from the shadows.

The problem is, I no longer want that life either, and it's a good thing I don't because it's lost to me. I want something else, something more expansive. I want a life outside of these strictures. If I could leave, I would.

But I'm also afraid to want. I wanted Burke, didn't I? And that's something I'm never going to get, my desire turned sour.

I let the fantasy slip away, and I make myself walk toward the man in the hall. Only when the Satori bodyguard is close enough to make me feel safe do I meet Father's eyes. "I'm testifying."

Father thinks I'm so weak, but I can show myself how to be strong. He killed Zio Roberto, and Burke did not. Those are the key facts here. Not that Burke is leaving me. Not what Father is offering me until he can snatch it away again.

"He's using you," Father says. "He's been toying with you this entire time. Him and Ereni both."

I do not let him see the cracks this conversation has spread throughout my body. "I hear you."

"Your mother has been getting sicker." He raises his voice. He's losing his cool. I have some power in this situation after all. Only a little, perhaps, but it's enough. "We didn't want to worry you, but it's serious."

Another betrayal that sears me to the bone. All the times I cried myself to sleep, and Mother was fine the whole time. "How many lies do you think I'll swallow? Just stop! I'm not a gullible child anymore. I know she's not sick."

He sighs, falling back on his role of long-suffering father. "The Satori have poisoned your mind, Sienna. Your mother needs you. We all do."

Once upon a time I would have given anything to hear those words, but it's far too late. "You know what's ironic? If you hadn't tried to arrange my marriage with someone as boorish and violent as Enoch, I would have never found out you murdered Zio Roberto. If you had put your family above your political interests, we wouldn't be here right now." I pause, the terrible truth squeezing me in the gut. "But that's just not who you are, is it?"

More than anything, I want this conversation to be over.

The man in the hallway has come to stand at my shoulder. I'm surprised he hasn't intervened until now. But he just looks at me as if waiting for orders.

"Sienna, you're hysterical. You don't know what you're saying."

There will always be a reason why I'm wrong. "Do you see me crying? Do you see me hyperventilating? I'd say I'm as clear-headed as I've ever been." I straighten myself, drop my arms, look Father straight in the eye. "And I'm testifying."

"You stupid little girl." Father's voice is loud and cutting, and it takes every bit of willpower in me not to instantly beg him for forgiveness. "You won't be testifying, do you hear me? You won't be allowed to take the stand. Do you think anyone will believe your word over mine? It would have been better for the entire Tascioni family if you had never been born." He takes a step toward me then, his hand raised, and I cower before the man steps between us.

"Signore, I'm going to have to ask you to leave." He puts a hand on Father's shoulder and propels him toward the door. The woman has reappeared from the hallway, looking ready for a fight.

Father shrugs off the man and turns to look me, rage distorting his face. I can finally believe him capable of killing Zio Roberto. He points a finger at me. "You'll regret the day you turned your back on this family. Don't come crawling back to us when the world devours you. This was your last chance." He storms out the door.

I stare at the space where he so recently stood. I'm shaking, and my nails have etched little red marks into my palms. "Are you okay, Signorina?" the man asks.

I nod. I have to go forward with the plan. No other option remains open to me.

I'm going to make sure Father can never hurt me again.

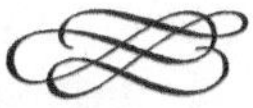

CHAPTER 27

On the day of my testimony, Signora Lhasa helps me get ready. "Are you sure I can't be Leo?" I shake out my wig, trying to make the locks fall more naturally. "Just this one last time?"

She shakes her head. "You'll be testifying under oath. Some things you have to do under your own name."

"They won't believe me." That is my worst fear, that this will all be for nothing. That Burke will still be convicted, that Father will go free, that even this simple execution of justice will go astray.

Signora Lhasa sighs and comes to stand behind me, resting her hands on my shoulders. I will never get used to the casualness with which the Satori touch one another. I know I'm supposed to feel reassured, but all I feel from her hands is a great weight. "We can't always determine outcomes, my dear. We do what we must, and then we move on from there."

I turn around to get a good look at her face. "Will you let Burke die if he's convicted? You know he's innocent."

I want her assurances that if all else fails—if *I* fail—there's a fallback position. But she won't give it to me. "We'll meet that challenge if it comes," is all she says. She watches with an unwavering gaze as I don my wig and become an outwardly perfect daughter of my people.

~

I AM TESTIFYING first this morning, so I don't have long to wait. Signora Lhasa sits on one side of me, and Tomas, one of the men who guards the flat, sits on the other. In the packed courtroom, every seat is taken and people stand shoulder-to-shoulder at the back of the room. The steady hum of gossip and speculation makes my head ache.

We're only a few rows from the front, and I stare at the back of Burke's head, wishing he'd turn around and acknowledge me. When I finally look away, I glimpse Father's hawk-nosed profile on the other side of the room. It's as if he can feel my eyes on him because he turns and shakes his head at me. I don't even need to hear him to know what he's saying. *Don't testify or you'll be sorry.*

The bailiff hits the huge gong and the hall gradually subsides into silence as the justices file in. They wear the black robes of their office, and they are old and sour. They must hate Burke, who is everything they aren't.

The Chief Justice bangs his gavel and instructs the defense to proceed. It is time. The lead Satori lawyer announces my name, and the room behind me erupts into mutters. Whispers follow me as I walk to the front of the room. I wish I was wearing Leo's clothes, Leo's name, anything to make me feel less exposed.

The justices lean forward from their higher elevation, scrutinizing me. None of them look particularly sympathetic. I do as I'm supposed to, laying my hand on the huge Bible and giving my oath to tell the truth. Not that any oath will save me.

The courtroom looks even more crowded from the witness box, and the seat is hard and unforgiving. My hands are so damp I'm afraid I'll sweat through my gloves. No one in the audience will meet my eyes.

Among all the faces, I pick out Father's. He looks collected and untroubled, like the powerful man he is. He doesn't look afraid, and a jolt of dread seizes my stomach. This isn't going to work. I'm ruining my reputation for no good reason. If he were at all concerned about my testimony, would he be here watching? He thinks he can get away with it.

And yet, even as I stare at the smug face that has caused me so much pain, I don't see the new Doge, as everyone else does, or the notorious murderer, which is who I hope to turn him into. I wish I did, but I've seen his face every day of my life.

He's my father, and I'll never get another.

The whole time I explain who I am and what I know, I watch Father. Every photograph admitted into evidence, every audio clip, I keep searching out his face. And as my testimony proceeds, exactly as I practiced, his face transforms. Gone is the confident, self-assured Doge. He scowls at me, his cheeks slightly mottled, his eyes narrowed. He looks like he wants to kill me. And I bet this time he wouldn't use poison either.

The people around him start to shift in their seats, casting small glances at him as the ramifications of my testimony sink in. Audible gasps punctuate the recordings. The justices' disapproval is no longer directed at me. I might be a girl, and a bad daughter at that, but the salacious story I'm telling is enough to distract from that. At least for now.

Father underestimated me.

But as the prosecuting attorney approaches me to cross, I know not to make the same mistake.

He gives a genial smile. "You're engaged to be married, isn't that right, Signorina Tascioni?"

I can't think of Enoch without shuddering. "That's correct."

"A match arranged for you by your father?"

"Yes."

"And what would your fiancé think of you coming here to testify?"

I don't want to talk about Enoch, and I don't know where this line of questioning is going. "He wouldn't like it."

"But even knowing that, you came?"

"I did." Murmurs from the audience. *This isn't making me look good.*

"Is it fair to say you aren't happy with your engagement?"

"I guess." *I'm bucking against convention by admitting this publicly, but I'm under oath. What else can I say?*

"Very good, Signorina Tascioni. Now forgive me, but I must ask you a question of a personal nature."

As if he hasn't already been doing that. I brace myself. "Yes?"

He walks up till he's right in front of me, then lowers his voice, but not so much that the entire room can't still hear him. "Is it true that right now, at this very moment, you are wearing a wig?"

More gasps from the spectators, and a sickening lurch of my stomach. *This man is out to destroy me. How did he find out, and how much does he know? Can I lie and get away with it?* I look over at the Satori legal team, but their faces are blank, offering me no clue as to how to proceed. "Yes."

"I'm sorry, Signorina, I couldn't hear that."

He's taunting me. Once the truth comes out, no respectable person will ever associate with me again, so I might as well face my downfall with dignity. "Yes, I am wearing a wig." It comes out loud and unapologetic.

"And why is that? Have you been ill?"

"No."

"An unfortunate beauty accident, perhaps?"

He's enjoying toying with me. "No, I'm wearing it because I cut my hair short."

He gives a pained look to the Justices, to the courtroom at large. "I see. I hate to ask you this, Signorina"—*you liar, you're loving every second*—"but why would you do such a thing?"

How much does he know? "I felt like it."

"You felt like it. Hmm." He says it to the audience, not to me, skepticism dripping. *Here it comes.* "And what would you say if I told you I have a witness willing to testify that the reason you keep your hair short is because you routinely flaunt all that is respectable and right by masquerading as a boy?"

The courtroom erupts into chaos. Voices tumble over one

another as people react to the shocking allegation. I hear *scandalous, abhorrent, unnatural,* along with a few references to the *corrupting Satori influence.* I've never felt so dirty. At the front of the room, Burke closes his eyes as if he can't bear to see what's happening to me.

The Chief Magistrate pounds his gavel repeatedly. "Order in the court," he shouts. "Order in the court, or we will close these proceedings to the public."

His threat does the trick, and people slowly sit down and lower their voices. The Chief Magistrate glares at me, his shaggy gray eyebrows drooping disapprovingly. "Well then, Signorina Tascioni. Answer the question, and remember you are under oath."

The justices scrutinize me from their higher elevation as if I've morphed into a particularly distasteful kind of parasite. The prosecutor, so serious when he faces the crowd, is leering up at me like he's already won. If I lie, does he actually have the witness he claims? If I tell the truth, how much will it discredit the rest of my testimony? Surely my recordings stand on their own.

If I tell the truth, there will be nowhere in this world I can go when all of this is over. I will be an infamous outcast forever, the unnatural Doge's daughter who had it all but threw it away, dressing as a boy and betraying her own father.

And then I see her across the aisle from Father: Gianna, sitting next to her mother. I'd been so focused on him I hadn't even noticed them. Gianna is staring straight ahead, a sick look on her face, and I don't need anyone to tell me she's the witness. She's the one who has ruined me. She must have told Father everything she knew, not knowing the truth of what he did.

I should have told her when I had the chance. I should have trusted her. And now here we are, caught in the grinding mechanisms of politics and justice neither of us can control.

"Are you sure everything you've told us today is true?" the prosecutor asks. I see what he's doing. He's giving me a chance to walk back my testimony, to claim to be confused or coerced, to say the recordings have been doctored, to turn on Burke in order to save my own skin. I won't escape without a strong taint no matter what I do, but I could spare myself the worst of it.

If I lie, I might still find a place here.

But Zio Roberto deserves better.

"Everything I've said is the complete truth." My defiance rings out across the room like a liberty bell. Let them shun me. Let them hate me. Lying has already gotten me into enough trouble. I won't regret this moment when I die.

The prosecutor bares his teeth and I know he's going in for the kill, even if it may no longer save his case. Out of spite, maybe, or from instructions from Father. It doesn't matter. "Is it also true, then, that you dress up as a boy?"

Silence can no longer save me. "It's true."

Two little words that strip me of so much. As I look out at the audience, staring back at me with such disgust, I feel something shrivel and die inside. It hurts more than being born.

AFTER MY TESTIMONY a group of Satori cluster around me and escort me from the courtroom. The aisle seems to stretch forever. A few people hiss as I pass, and a few more whisper "Tramp!" and "Slut!" My cheeks may be red, but I refuse to look down. I should be allowed to race. I should be allowed to make something of myself. Leo shouldn't be the only Tascioni sibling who matters. The anger may have nowhere to go, but it's the only thing keeping me whole.

The bailiff closes the courtroom doors behind us with a decisive slam, but right before he does, Gianna hurries through them, a sneer marring her face. "Well, you've finally done it. Ruined yourself completely and irrevocably. I hope you're happy."

I stare at her in incredulity. "I was trying to help you, you ninny," I say.

"In case you hadn't noticed, my father is *dead*, thanks to your traitorous family. Every one of you deserves to suffer for what you did to him." The venom in her voice is new; usually she's so careful to sound cordial and sweet. "You've never understood me, have you, Sienna? Always thought you were so much smarter. Well, welcome to my world. This is what it feels like to lose everything. Your image is even worse than mine now. People will forget to judge me, they'll be so busy hating you."

She's ready to ruin my reputation to save her own, and I have to admit, her betrayal hurts. "I can't believe you care about your image at a time like this."

"What else do I have left, pray tell? What else, after the chaos you and your family have left in your wake? Your father has been like an uncle to me. I thought I could trust him. That he could be capable of this...." She wavers, pain racing across her face to be replaced by sheer fury. "And who are you to look down on me? You betrayed me that day you lured me to that appointment and abandoned me to that man who assaulted me. How could you?" Her voice shakes, and a single tear rolls down her cheek. "But even after that, I couldn't do the same thing to you. It was Enoch Royse who told your father you've been dressing like a boy. Your secret was safe with me."

I had put Enoch entirely out of my mind, not wanting to think about our last terrifying encounter, but it made sense he'd do what-ever he could to make me pay for my rejection of him. Of course he'd contacted my father and told him. I should have guessed what was coming.

And for once Gianna was as innocent as she always pretended to be.

Tomas leans in and whispers in my ear. "Signorina, we need to get you someplace safe." The Satori have been concerned I may receive death threats after testifying, and now they're giving each other nervous looks.

"One minute." I turn back to Gianna. I need her to know the truth. "I didn't know anything about what they had planned for that shopping trip, I swear. My parents didn't tell me. They tricked us both."

"I don't believe you, and even if I did...where were you after-wards? Why weren't you there? I thought you were my best friend."

I should have snuck out to be with her. I should have made a statement to the media about her innocence. I should have done so many things, even if it meant being shut up in the closet earlier. And yet...Gianna hasn't been there for me either. Not for a very long time. We've both failed each other, and badly. "I'm sorry," I tell her. "I didn't know what to do." It's not what she wants to hear, but it's the truth.

She gives a condescending sniff. "You're done now, Sienna. You and your entire miserable family. You'll be lucky if you can avoid being committed to an asylum. And you have no one to blame but yourself." With that, she marches away, heels clacking and nose in the air.

Tomas doesn't say a word, just takes my arm and leads me out of the courthouse. I almost object to the casual touching, but Gianna is right. I'm ruined. It no longer matters what I do or don't do.

The world will find fault with me regardless.

CHAPTER 28

The tide of sentiment turns against Father, and when Burke is found innocent of all charges, Neopolitan sends an official request for Father's extradition. His political career in shambles, he'll be tried at home for first-degree murder and high treason. Zio Roberto is being painted as a saint, and Gianna is his angel of a daughter, now widely credited with her discovery that I'd been masquerading as a boy. Never mind that revealing my secret had nothing to do with the truth of her father's murder coming out. In Neopolitan, facts will only take you so far.

If there's anyone Neopolitan is united in hating, it's me. Maybe Father took backstabbing a few steps too far, but cutthroat politics aren't unknown in Neopolitan's history. People might be shocked by Father's actions, but it is surprise tinged with admiration. He was willing to do whatever it took to get what he wanted. His methods were to be deplored, yes, but his motives were pure. They want to punish him, but they also understand.

But me? I am anathema. I am the cautionary tale shoved into daughters' faces all over the country. They hate me for everything I stand for, but more importantly, for everything I am not.

I only hope some of those daughters ignore their distraught

parents and realize what I've accomplished. That I didn't marry the boor Father chose for me. That I didn't let an innocent person take the fall for a crime he didn't commit. That we all have it within us to resist, even when we are young and female.

I have changed the course of history in Neopolitan. The history books will not be kind to me, the media is already eviscerating me, and the Satori were right about the death threats, which I am not allowed to see. But still. I did it.

At least that's what I keep telling myself.

Burke comes to see me at the flat once he's released. When he bursts through the door, he's so happy he doesn't notice the bare walls, the clinical furniture, the symphony of clashing beiges. As soon as he sees me, he rushes to fling his arms around me, even though I'm still sitting down. "You did it!" His voice is too loud in my ear. "As far as I'm concerned, you, Sienna Tascioni, are a genuine first-class hero." He kisses my forehead, both cheeks, the tip of my nose, before leaning in to kiss my lips. I melt under the onslaught.

He takes my hand and his voice becomes serious. "I heard about the death threats. How are you holding up?"

It's hard to believe people care enough about me to wish I were dead. But there's something even more important for us to discuss. "Never mind that. I want to apologize. I'm so sorry, Burke." It's such a relief to say the words.

He furrows his forehead. "What for? You saved my life. You have nothing to apologize for."

"Yes, but it was my father who framed you and made you go through all this. I'm partly responsible."

"Have you been worrying about that?" I look down, unable to meet his eyes. "Sienna. You can't be expected to control anyone's actions but your own. You didn't know what your father had planned. And you did everything you could to stop him once you found out. I don't blame you in the slightest."

I hesitate. "Then you don't...hate me?" After Gianna's reaction, I've been expecting the worst.

"Quite the opposite. I'll never forget what you've done for me." He surveys my face, then sighs. "I promise, Sienna. What your father did has nothing to do with you. It's not your fault."

I'd had so much time to regret everything while I'd been shut in that closet. I wished I'd warned Zio Roberto sooner. But I'd had no idea the stakes at play were life and death. Now Burke's words help to release the guilt I've been carrying.

"Have you given any thought to what you'll do now?" he asks.

"I have to go back to San Marco to testify in my father's trial. I leave tomorrow. Irisa has said I can stay at your residence while I'm there." I pause. "Will you be coming?"

Burke shakes his head. "No, the Mission Council wants me to stay here. It's important for me to stay out of the public eye until we're able to leave the planet."

We have so little time left. Will I even get to see him again before he leaves Sanctum forever? "I see."

Burke reaches for my other hand. "I did ask the Mission Council about staying behind. We'll be leaving a small contingent to continue running the clinics and working with the more cooperative governments on Sanctum. But given everything that's happened, the Mission Council thinks it would be a strong detriment for me to stay."

He isn't telling me anything I hadn't already assumed, but the thought of him leaving for good physically hurts me. "Do you know where you're going?"

"A planet called Arbor. It will take us about twenty of your years to get there."

"Oh." He'd spend most of that time in cryosleep, so the twenty years for me would go by for him in the blink of an eye.

He leans forward to kiss me again. "Enough about me. I want to hear how you're doing. What will you do after the trial?"

I try to keep my voice light. "Oh, I don't know. I'll figure something out."

The truth is I have no idea what to do next. I've given up my future for the sake of my integrity. No one will marry me now, not with a murderous father, a disloyal temperament, and a penchant for dressing like a boy. And even if women of my class were allowed to get jobs, no one would be willing to hire damaged goods like me. Maybe in another country I'll be able to live down my reputation. It's my only hope.

"I have every faith in you," Burke says. "You're the most impressive person I've ever met, do you know that?"

I shrug and stare down at our entwined fingers. His hands are so much bigger than mine. He has no idea what I'm up against, and I have no intention of telling him. This is my battle, not his.

CHAPTER 29

ather is sentenced to life in prison. The judges are being lenient, the articles scream. They are weighing their appointments and other past favors more highly than they ought. But it doesn't matter what the media says. Justice has spoken.

No sentence will bring Zio Roberto back. But I won't carry the weight of my own father's death hanging around my neck. And without that worry, I can bear to see Leo again.

I use the servants' entrance and meet Lizabetta on the narrow back staircase. She stops a few steps above me, narrows her eyes, and gives me her classic look of disapproval. "Well, you've certainly caused a lot of trouble, haven't you?" She shakes her head. "Too much spirit for this family, and that's the truth."

"How are they?"

She shrugs. "Your mother is devastated. Stays in her bedroom all day long, complaining of being ill. None of her friends will invite her into their homes. She's talking about moving back to the country."

I decide to press her further. "You know Mother's not really ill, don't you?"

She shrugs again. "Rich folks. What can you do?" She gives me a pitying look. "They pay me not to ask questions."

That's exactly what I'd done with her too, wasn't it? Offering her money to help with my charade? I swallow. "And Leo? How is he?"

"I haven't seen him recently. Your mother, she's too wrapped up in her own misery to care about anyone else's."

Poor Leo. "Thanks for looking after her, Lizabetta."

"I'll stay on until she moves to the country, and then it will be time to start my nursing program." She flashes her teeth in a proud smile. "Thanks to you, Signorina, I'm going to become a true professional."

"The medical profession will be lucky to have you," I tell her. "I hope it goes well for you, Lizabetta. And thank you. For everything."

Her face softens. "Good luck to you too. You're going to need it, what with the mess you've made."

I go in search of Leo and eventually find him in my old bedroom, lying on my bed, staring up at my collection of masks. "Leo."

He sits up slowly and blinks. "I was afraid you'd never come."

We look so much alike, and yet we are so completely different. I used to think it was because I was a girl, but now I know better. "I wasn't sure if you'd want me to come," I confess.

"*Coglione*. Twin pact. Of course I want to see you." His voice is gruff, as if he's close to tears, and he's the one who comes to me and enfolds me in a tight hug. We hold each other for a long time.

"How are you doing?" I finally ask. "You have everything you need?"

"Our funds weren't frozen or seized, if that's what you mean. They're too worried about setting a precedent. The whole fortune's been transferred into a trust. I'll gain control over it on our eighteenth birthday." Only a few months to wait.

"Good, I'm glad." I look around my old room, a picture of idyllic girlhood. Everything is exactly as I left it: my cosmetics in neat stacks on my dressing table, my favorite shawl draped over one of the matched armchairs, a forever unfinished floral needlework project on top of one of the cabinets. It all looks so small and circumscribed. I'm no longer the girl was who used to live here. "Mother plotting for you to marry the family back into everyone's good graces?"

Leo rubs his forehead. "It's her favorite topic of conversation, believe me. But I think our family might be beyond redemption."

I snort. "Give it a few years. You might be surprised how much people will forgive you for your money."

He leads me to one of the armchairs and sits in the one across from me. "Are you ready to come home for good? Your room is still here waiting for you."

The offer carries an unexpected sting. "Mother would never allow it."

"Mother does what's in her own best interest. She always has. And she knows who's about to hold the purse strings." His jaw is set, and suddenly I can imagine what he'll look like when he's much older. These last few months have hardened us both.

I look around my old perfect room and my heart cracks. I don't want to be here. Not anymore. I let his hands drop. "I don't know how to be this person." My voice quivers a little at the vast loneliness I feel.

"You don't have to be someone you're not." He says the words with conviction. "I'm serious, Sienna. I'll have control of the money, and everything will be different for both of us. Signor Gipetti has already accepted me as his apprentice. I'll be working with him every day on Paraval Island."

It's what he's always wanted, and I am thrilled beyond words for him. "That's wonderful, Leo."

"Maybe we can hire a tutor for you," he continues excitedly. "Wouldn't you like that? You've always been dying to get an education."

"Maybe." But what good is an education if I'm not allowed to use it? "I guess I'll have the time to spare, now that we're social pariahs."

Leo grimaces. "Good riddance. Which reminds me. Enoch Royse is still around. I thought the new Doge would insist on his father's resignation, but instead they seem remarkably cozy together."

More Neopolitan intrigue. I make a face. "It figures the Royses aren't suffering any consequences."

Leo looks uncomfortable. "Not only that, I've heard Enoch

intends to court Gianna. She's managed to regain her popularity, you know."

"No." I flash on Enoch grabbing me in our foyer. I can still feel his hand squeezing my arm. "She can't marry that *testa di cazzo*. She doesn't know how terrible he can be."

"I know." Leo slumps disconsolately in his chair. "I wish there were something we could do."

We sit in the deepening twilight, contemplating the injustice of the situation. It's a welcome respite from considering my own dim prospects. I've been a bad friend to Gianna, and I've had plenty of time to think about how I let her down. I don't want to fail her again.

And then I have the glimmerings of an idea. The more I think about it, the better I like it. "Leo." He gives me a questioning look. "I know how we can teach Enoch a lesson and make sure Gianna is safe. And I'm going to need your help to pull it off."

"Twin pact," he says without hesitation. "Whatever you need me to do, I'm here for you."

CHAPTER 30

My plan is simple: Leo will challenge Enoch to an illegal street race in the middle of the night in San Marco. If Leo wins, Enoch will agree to never race again. Enoch will be unable to resist such an easy challenge, and all the amateur racers will turn out to watch.

But once everyone's gathered, I'll demand to race instead. Enoch will be unable to refuse the challenge without looking like a coward for not being willing to race a girl. And I'll be able to show what I'm really made of. When I beat him, not only will he be unable to race again, he'll be a laughingstock and Gianna won't allow him to court her.

If everyone wants it to be shameful to lose to a girl, well then, I'm going to use that against them. Given my complete disgrace, it's the best plan I can devise.

Enoch falls for the trap with an ease that makes me nervous. He wants Leo barred from racing if he loses, a price Leo is happy to pay. They agree on several checkpoints the bikes will have to pass in the correct sequence in order to successfully complete the race.

I move back into the house, and Mother remains in her rooms, refusing to see me. I don't belong here, but I have nowhere else to go.

I spend all my time studying the race route, figuring out shortcuts and potential problems. Because the race is so much longer than a track race and we've agreed to use a lighter class of bike with less range, efficient energy usage is critical to a successful strategy. If I miscalculate, my bike could go dead before I reach the finish line. If, on the other hand, I can force Enoch to bleed excessive energy himself, that could win me the race.

This shift in strategy gives me an edge. I know San Marco better than Enoch, and I've been riding longer than him. His skill with curves is less important on the streets.

But I also know Enoch is ruthless, and he'll be furious at being forced into racing a girl. And there won't be any force fields to cushion a crash. I'll be putting my body and my life on the line for this race, and I'm going to need every iota of wit and bravery I possess to win.

It will be worth it. It has to be worth it. I have to win so no other girl in Neopolitan ever has to be as afraid of Enoch as I once was.

I'm studying in the playroom the day before the race when Leo interrupts me. "You have a visitor."

I don't look up from my qualpad. "Put them off, will you? Whoever it is, they won't be disappointed to miss me."

"Actually, I'd be very disappointed."

I almost drop my qualpad at Burke's voice. He grins at me from the doorway while Leo looks on smugly. Burke is so tall. I forgot how tall he is. My heart contracts strangely at his sudden presence, and I scramble to my feet. "I thought you were still in Fidelium."

"I came to see you." The look he gives me with his big gray eyes makes my heart beat faster. "Ereni told me you're about to do something foolhardy and brave. Again."

"She doesn't miss a beat, does she?"

"Not where anyone would notice."

Leo is watching our conversation with too much interest. I give him a pointed look until he sighs in capitulation. "All right, all right, I'll give you two a minute." I sharpen my look. "Or ten. But both of you, behave yourselves! Sienna's got way more important things to think about than your chiseled jaw, do I make myself clear?"

Burke looks like he's keeping himself from laughing with difficulty. "Imminently."

Leo gives me one last warning look before hustling off to his workroom. I wait until the door closes before flinging myself into Burke's arms. "I didn't think I'd ever see you again."

He buries his face in my hair. My real hair. I haven't been bothering with a wig, not inside the house. "Oh, Sienna, I was always going to come say goodbye."

The words rush from me in a torrent. "I'm happy you get to leave, I really am, but at the same time I hate it so much. I just, I don't want you to go."

He groans and squeezes me tighter. "I know. Believe me, I know."

I look up at him, at the whorls of different shades of gray that give depth to his eyes, at the slightly uplifted corners of his mouth, at the single eyelash that has fallen and stuck to his cheek. There's so much more I want to know about him, and I can already feel myself missing him. There will never be enough time.

But I have a race to prepare for. "The race is tomorrow," I say. "It's not that I'm not excited to see you, but I have to focus if I want to win."

Most boys would have pouted at this statement before trying to convince me otherwise. But not Burke. "If it's all right with you, I'll be there tomorrow to watch you ride to victory." His belief in me steadies me, makes me breathe a tiny bit easier. I nod my permission. He leans down and gives me a single kiss that burns against my lips. "Good luck, Sienna," he says softly. "Till tomorrow."

He leaves then, just as I've told him to do, and it takes all my willpower not to call out after him. But I'll have plenty of time to miss Burke after the race is over.

LEO and I leave the house the next night after midnight, stopping at the racetrack for my chosen bike, along with the agreed-upon size of battery, fully charged, that we'll slot into place right before the race. I change into Leo's flashy golden suit, and Leo gets on the bike behind me, letting me drive. We haven't ridden two on a bike since we lived in the country. So much has changed, but being here with Leo still feels completely natural.

Before we leave, he squeezes me and places his mouth next to my helmet. "Are you sure about this? Because you don't have to go through with it. I can show up by myself and hope Enoch accidentally steers into a canal."

"I've made up my mind," I say, kicking off the ground.

We arrive a few minutes late to the designated meeting place, a deserted plaza towards the outskirts of the city. Mist floats drowsily across the square, obscuring the features of a statue of Neopolitan's first Doge. I wonder how much of the city is covered by fog right now and how that might affect my tactics.

Enoch lurks to one side with a brand new bike, while a group of the usual racers from Leo's set cluster at the far corner of the plaza. I know a few of them have already left to take their places along the route. The rest will move to the finish line and watch the race together on their qualpads from the cameras built into our bikes for just such a purpose.

Leo hops off the bike first while I remain gripping the handlebars. No one's going to be happy with the switch we're about to pull. Leo pulls off his helmet and begins body checking his fellow racers, who give him good-natured insults. The Tascionis might no longer be welcome in their family's drawing rooms, but Leo still has a place among them as a racer. But no one thinks Leo can beat Enoch, who stands off to the side, arms folded in sullen silence.

It's now or never. I leave the safety of the bike and take off my own helmet. Everyone stares, but their judgments don't matter. I walk up to Enoch, refusing to show any signs of the fear I feel whenever I see his face. "You won't be racing Leo tonight," I say loud enough for the whole group to hear. "You'll be racing me."

Enoch laughs. "You've got to be kidding. I can't believe you're showing your face in public after everything you've done."

"I can't believe you're showing *your* face now you know you were knocked out of the last race of the season by a girl."

Blood rushes into his cheeks, and his upper lip curls, showing me a glimpse of white tooth. "Anyone can get lucky once."

"Well, we're about to find out how much of that was luck." I raise an eyebrow. "Unless you're afraid?"

"Don't be ridiculous," he scoffs. "I could beat you without trying. But I can't let you get back on that bike. It's an abomination, a girl pretending to be a man."

His words hurt, not because they come from him but because I know our audience agrees with him. "I'm not pretending anything," I say. "But if you're too scared to race me, I'll understand." I give him my best cocky smile.

"This isn't what I agreed to." He's blustering now, and I know I've gotten to him. The other racers sense it as well, drawing closer around us.

"She right? You scared, Royse?" one of them calls out.

"She's such a little thing," another one shouts. "But we all saw her take you out."

Leo swaggers up beside me. "Sienna beats me all the time," he says. "You really think you can do better?" I know how much the words cost him, but he says them with fondness instead of shame, and I love him so much in that moment, my chest hurts.

That does it for Enoch. "Well, she's not going to beat me," he says, and the boys roar their approval. This race has just gotten way more interesting for everyone.

Enoch turns his back on me as if I'm not worth another second of his time, but I don't care. I'm not going to let him rattle me. I don't want to talk to him either. I want to beat him.

No, that's not right either. I want to decimate him. I'll stop at nothing for victory.

Leo gives me a last hug. "Be careful," he whispers in my ear. He can tell how reckless my mood has swung, but I won't back down, not even for him.

"Love you," I tell him. I remove the old battery from the bike and insert the full one with care. I'll need every bit of power this thing can deliver. One last check-over, and I mount my bike and drive it into position. Let the race begin.

CHAPTER 31

*E*noch revs his engine as we wait for the go sign. He'll do anything to shake my nerves, but a strange calm falls over me. I take in my surroundings with a crisp clarity: the gentle rumble of my bike between my legs, the tense lines in Leo's face, the smell of the blackened sausage a few of the boys are eating. I check my displays, energy at 100%, and look down the alley that begins the optimal route to the first checkpoint. Nothing bars my way.

Dante holds his qualpad in the air. A bright light pulses three times before turning green. Enoch and I both surge forward. He's faster and barrels down the alley in front of me, but he paid an energy premium for that lead. It's my job to make sure it's a cost he can't afford.

At the end of the alley Enoch breaks left. My own navi-computer is telling me to turn right, not that I need prompting. I've memorized the optimal route plus a score of variations. With Enoch going left, I'll be able to do some clean driving and save a lot of fuel through this section of the race. The apartment buildings pass by in a blur as I maneuver my way through the twisting maze of alleyways and bridges over narrow canal offshoots. There is barely any wind, and the air blows crisp and cool in my face. It's the perfect night for racing.

Another pulsing light signals the first checkpoint. Enzo pulls in behind me from a different side alley. My route was better. His engine makes a burst of bright staccato sounds, loud as gunshots in the still night air, and I know I've made him angry.

The angrier he is, the more reckless he'll become. This is exactly what I'm counting on.

It's a good thing I've etched the route into my brain because now I have to focus on Enoch driving right behind me. I only take my eyes from my mirrors to check my energy status. 82%. Not as much leeway as I was hoping, but not terrible. In the blinding light of his headlight, Enoch looks like part of his bike's machinery. He's edging up on me, which means his bike probably has the advantage over mine. *Merda.*

He's weaving behind me now, up and down, back and forth, my head beginning to ache from the effort of following his bike's bright light and countering. And then, right when I'm wondering if I can keep this level of driving up, he makes his move.

His engine growls into higher gear as he shoots almost straight up and then right over me, the bottom of his speeder coming within thirty centimeters of my head. I have to abruptly change course to avoid being hit, almost careening into a cigar shop's plate glass window. He's ahead of me now, and my heart is fluttering in my throat. If I had reacted a second later, I could be dead.

This was always the gamble. I say I have nothing to lose, but the truth is, Enoch is willing to do anything to win, including kill me. And even though I'm angrier than I've ever been in a lifetime characterized by my simmering rage, I don't think I'm ready to go that far.

Does this mean I'm weaker after all?

The alley opens onto a larger street, and doubts assail me as I stay on Enoch's tail. The hollow space in my stomach expands as I consider the possibility of losing. We've staked everything on this gambit, and I don't have a backup plan.

We pass the second checkpoint, the light flaring in the darkness in time with my heartbeat. Power is at 59%. I've used more than I should to keep harrying Enoch.

We're close to the city center now, with wide avenues, large piazzas, and the multi-lane bridges at our disposal. Also more risk of our illegal race being detected by the police. Enoch keeps making loud noises to intimidate me, but he's also advertising our location to anyone who might be paying attention. We both know as a diplomat's son, he'll get off with a slap on the wrist. I won't be so lucky. This race is feeling more and more stacked against me.

I keep to the narrower alleys as much as I can. I've plotted a route that is almost as efficient as keeping to the great open stretches. But Enoch doesn't have to keep to the shadows. I start cutting the corners almost too close, drifting through them while finessing the brakes, pushing to make up the difference. My energy is down below 40% by the time I reach the third checkpoint. Enoch is already on the far size of the plaza. Only one more checkpoint and then the finish line.

At least we're moving back out of the heart of the city so Enoch has to contend with the same sharp turns and narrow spaces. I waste more energy on the longer stretches in order to catch up with him. By the time we reach the fourth checkpoint, I'm right behind him again, but my gauge has turned red: 16%. I just hope he's having similar troubles.

I have one more trick up my sleeve. As we speed into the next warren of narrow streets, I take a sudden left into the tightest alley yet. Enoch, with his bigger body size and commensurately bigger bike, couldn't hope to fit without slowing down, and maybe not even then. Leo and I used to speed through tight forest trails all the time back in the country. For once my small size makes me powerful. This is my chance to overtake Enoch once and for all.

I crouch down as low as I can, molding my body into my bike, the vibrations running from my jawbone through my ankles. I've spent the most time studying this sequence, and with so little fuel remaining, I'm going to have to perform it flawlessly in order to have a chance.

It's not an alley in a traditional sense: there are several places where I have to fly over barriers that would make this a dead-end for an amphicar. The walls are right up against my shins and I move too abruptly through one turn, brushing my elbow against a building. My skin burns through my suit, but I ignore it as I prepare for the next turn. My energy gauge flashes its warning.

I cut every turn, every lift, every brake as close as possible. I see every building and stair and bank with absolute clarity. My bike and I are an inseparable unit; riding feels more natural than walking. As I twist through the network of passageways, dark but for my own light, I know exactly what to do and how far to push.

I'm almost through, the triumph rising within me, along with a sense of belonging, of mastery, of being where I'm supposed to be. And that's when I turn a corner and ride straight into a white sheet hanging low on a laundry line. It comes loose from its pins with a snap, and for a few brief seconds before I can wrest it from my face, I'm driving completely blind. I bank up, not letting up on the accelerator, and I fling the sheet from my face just as I break out into the wide-open plaza below me, letting out a whoop of sheer euphoria.

I can see the finish line. Past this plaza, across a large bridge, down a wide boulevard, right where the next plaza opens up. I can see the cluster of boys waiting for me, and I know Leo is among them. I'm two thirds across the plaza, going at maximum speed, just enough power left to maintain speed until the end, when Enoch roars out of a different alley behind me.

His bike might be superior, but it isn't *that* much better. There's no way he can catch up. This race is mine.

I'm halfway down the boulevard when I look into my mirror and see him fling his helmet off and ride his bike off the side of the bridge, steering directly towards the side of the next, taller bridge down the canal. Is this some kind of trick? How can this help him beat me?

He hits the bridge with a large crash. His limp body falls into the water below, followed by the wrecked bike.

It takes a moment to hit me that he's no longer trying to beat me. The best he could do is making sure nobody wins.

~

LEO PULLS me away from the horrible aftermath. He doesn't let me look, and for once I'm grateful to be protected. I lean against him, helmet fallen forgotten on the ground. I am numb all over. I don't understand what's happened.

Burke rushes up, Ereni close behind him. He envelops me in his embrace, his rough cheek against mine. ""You're okay," he whispers. "You're okay, you're okay." He sounds like he's trying to convince himself.

My body begins to shake even though I don't feel cold. "She's in shock," Leo says. His voice comes as if from a great distance.

I pull back from the comfort of Burke's arms to see Ereni's scowl. "We have to get you out of here," she says. "Before the police come." I can already hear the sirens in the distance.

I shake my head, the numbness refusing to fall away. "Won't they want to talk to me? Won't they want to know what happened?"

Ereni grips my hands with so much force I wince. "Sienna, be smart. They'll blame you for what happened. This is the excuse they've been waiting for."

"Excuse?" I keep seeing Enoch's body falling like a sack of flour into the water. "I want to make sure Enoch's all right." I may hate Enoch, but I didn't expect the race to end like this.

Burke puts his arm around me and starts gently leading me away. "I don't think he survived that crash, sweetheart." He says the words as if I'm made of fragile porcelain.

Ereni isn't as patient. "Don't you see, Sienna? The country hates you, and now they can lock you away in an asylum for good. A flashy murder charge will do the trick."

I finally realize what she's trying to tell me, and the nausea I've been barely keeping at bay hits me full force. I'm too much of a threat. They're right: a murder charge would stick, regardless of the facts. And who's to say Leo's racing buddies will tell the truth about what they saw? I'm in deeper trouble than I thought possible. I have to give it to Enoch: even in death he's somehow managed to endanger me.

The thought fills me with confusion; this has all happened too quickly. I believe Burke's assessment of the accident, but the reality of Enoch's death seems impossible.

Burke escorts me to a nondescript black amphicar. "But what about the bike?" I ask.

They all ignore me. Leo is looking out the back window to see if anyone is following us, while Burke and Ereni are locked in some kind of incomprehensible staring contest. I don't know where we're going, and it's hard for me to bring myself to care. My body is still shaking, no matter how hard I try to hold still.

We drive off into the night.

CHAPTER 32

*E*reni and Burke take us back to the Satori embassy, but they park the amphicar a few minutes' walk away. We walk through the rose garden and enter the house through the glass doors in the sitting room. One of their security people who I recognize from Fidelium lets us in, and she and Ereni decamp further into the house to consult.

Leo slumps onto the closest overstuffed sofa, but I remain standing, staring vacantly at a particularly pretty lamp with a rose and gold glass shade. Burke stays so close to my side I can feel his arm brush against my own, which reminds me I'm still wearing Leo's racing suit. I don't know what's become of my helmet.

"We can't stay here long," he murmurs to me. I know I should be panicking or trying to figure out what to do next, but a wave of exhaustion washes over me.

Leo groans from the sofa. "Of all the possible outcomes of tonight's plan, I wouldn't have foreseen this one in a million years." He puts his head in his hands. "From now on I'm sticking to making art. My attempts at intrigue consistently backfire."

His words prick through my numbness. "We did what we set out to do. Gianna is safe now."

"For all the thanks we'll get from her. I doubt she'll come rushing to your defense when tonight's events become public."

I know Gianna will be angry about what we've done, but it doesn't mean we didn't do the right thing. Would I have gone through with our plan if I'd known it would result in Enoch's death? It makes me sick to realize I'm not sure. I don't think I would have tried to arrange his death on purpose, but now that it's happened…I shudder to think there might be even the smallest similarity between Father's morality and my own.

Burke slips his hand into mine. "We'll figure something out," he says. But his words ring hollow; I can't see any escape from the consequences of tonight. The Satori no longer have any influence here, and my family name no longer offers the possibility of protection.

I grasp Burke's hand more tightly. The authorities must have arrived at the race's finish line by now. They must have fished Enoch's waterlogged body from the canal. I can't seem to move past the shock of seeing him deliberately steering his bike into harm's way. It's hard to believe he'd choose to die rather than lose a race to me. It's hard to believe anything about tonight.

Time passes, and Ereni re-enters the room by herself. She looks at me and Burke holding hands and frowns slightly. "I've spoken with Irisa. We have approval for contingency C."

Burke goes suddenly still. Ereni gives me the slightest nod, and when he turns to me, there's a new light in his eyes. "We'd like to invite you to accompany us off-planet for our next mission."

I gape at him. This is not what I expected. "What?"

"We leave in a few days, and the mission team has agreed we feel partially responsible for the precarity of your position here." He squeezes my hand. "*I* feel responsible. I know how harsh the consequences have been for your testimony on my behalf."

I blink at him. Never once have I considered the possibility of leaving Sanctum with the Satori, and I'm having trouble keeping up.

"We know it's a big step to take, and frankly, we wouldn't have made the offer if you weren't in such dire straits," Ereni says. "But Irisa is afraid your government will wish to make an example of you, which is why we discussed this possibility. If you come with us, I've agreed to take charge of your diplomatic training. We can spend enough time out of cryosleep on the voyage to prepare you for a junior position at our next stop."

I look from her to Burke and back again. "You want me to leave Sanctum…forever?"

Ereni nods. "I'm afraid it's all we can offer."

I consider what they're telling me. I'd finally receive an education and become a diplomat in my own right. I wouldn't have to live the small life I'd been trying to convince myself to accept here. I'd be traveling further than I could imagine, and I'd be a part of the Satori mission—something bigger than myself.

"I know it isn't what you were thinking," Burke says. He offers a tentative smile. "But I think the diplomatic life might suit you." He doesn't speak of love, and I'm glad he isn't using any feelings I might have for him to persuade me. Whatever lies between us is too new and fragile to be a part of such a life-changing decision.

Leo is sitting upright now, his face gone carefully blank. Ereni and Burke are offering me everything I've ever wanted. But I can't leave my brother behind. "Leo?"

He doesn't meet my eyes. "If you stay, you'll be charged with murder. And Mother has already been doing everything she can to get you committed into an asylum."

I struggle to handle this new blow. "You didn't tell me that."

"Yes, because I was working to contain it. But with this fresh ammunition, I don't think I can win." He runs his hand through his hair. "I hate to admit it, Si, but you'll be safer if you leave."

"Can Leo come too?" I ask Ereni.

But Leo starts shaking his head before she can answer. "I belong here."

I can't bear to lose him. I sit beside him on the ridiculous sofa, taking both his hands in mine. "We belong together."

But I see in his face that he's going to be stubborn. "We both deserve a chance to follow our dreams," he whispers. "Yours are out there." He gestures up towards the ceiling and the stars beyond. "But mine are still here."

Tears begin to slide down my cheeks. "But how can I go without you?"

"You can't turn down this chance because of me, Sienna. You have to go. We'll always be connected, now matter how far you travel. Right here." He places his hand over my heart.

I reach out and place my own hand on his chest. "Right here," I echo. But I know how space travel works. I know by the time I reach Arbor, he'll be almost forty years old. I know with Satori medical technology at my disposal, I'm likely to outlive him by many decades. I know I'll never see him again.

"I hate to interrupt this deeply touching moment," Ereni says, "but we need to get as far away from San Marco as possible if you want to leave the planet with us. The Mission Council is *not* going to be happy about this. As if this mission hasn't been enough of a disaster as it is." She looked as close to harried as I'd ever seen her. "I'm afraid you need to decide what you want to do, Sienna. If you aren't coming with us, we can't be seen as being involved."

I take a deep breath, my eyes never leaving Leo's face. I have to look at him enough to last a lifetime. But I know I can't delay any longer. "Yes," I say. "I'll come."

I hug my brother for the last time. We've always been so close, I can't comprehend what my life will be like without him. "Twin pact," I whisper. "I'll never stop missing you."

"Twin pact," he replies. Both our eyes are wet as we say goodbye and my life changes forever.

CHAPTER 33

*E*reni and I stand in front of one of the Satori starships. I stare up at the alien monstrosity, the smooth surface of its curving body gleaming black with strange silver accents. "We've buffed it up for the big day," Ereni says with a laugh. I can't tell if she's joking.

I ask her the question that's been on my mind during the whole trip to Fidelium. "Do you—the Satori, I mean—do you think you ever manage to change things? Will your clinics will make any difference? Will you even manage to keep them open?"

"Fourteen clinics across the planet so far, and yes, we'll keep at least some of them open. I may have cut a few deals in Neopolitan to make sure of that." She winks at me. "We're starting a training program for medical personnel in Fidelium that will help, and we have plenty of funds." She pauses. "But that's the thing about incremental change, Sienna. We don't see our job as forcing unwanted change; if we were interested in that, we'd bring in a military force. Our goal is to facilitate change that's already ripening from within a given society. And that is a long, slow, and mostly thankless task. Three steps forward, then several steps back, then try again. It's creeping change on the scale of generations, not months or years.

Just because you can't always see it doesn't mean it isn't happening."

"But how do you know? What if nothing you're doing matters at all?"

I expect some vague tripe about hope or morality, but I should know Ereni better. "Case studies," she says crisply. "And statistics. The Satori have been involved in these kinds of projects for a long time, and we record everything. Part of your education will be reading a huge pile of case studies."

Her answer is so unexpectedly concrete, it makes me smile. She has a solution for everything. And even if the change she's describing isn't sweeping and dramatic, I want to be a part of it. I want to make a difference however I can.

Burke comes strolling over from the main terminal. He slips his hand in mine. I know he means it to be reassuring, but for an unmarried couple to hold hands in public? He doesn't even have gloves on. I take a breath, then let it out again. Things are different now.

I'm different now.

"Let me be the first one to welcome you to your new home." Burke nods up at the ship. "A real beauty, isn't it? I think you'll really like it."

I hope he's right. I'm taking the biggest gamble of my life boarding this ship with them. "Thank you for giving me this opportunity."

Ereni smirks. "I'd say you earned it, but we'll see how you feel about it after you've spent a few months studying with me."

She doesn't know—she can't know, coming from where she does —what a miracle it seems that anyone would be willing to teach me. That anyone would be willing to take a chance on my potential. She can't imagine the mixture of joy and terror I feel at the trust they're putting in me.

I never expected my life to look like this.

Burke squeezes my hand. "You ready?"

This is it. My last time with my feet on my own planet. "I need a minute."

"Take your time. We'll meet you right inside." They start up the ramp together, not even waiting until they're out of view to start bickering. I wonder what they'll decide to look like on the next planet. I wonder if I'll make some changes myself. I reach up and touch my hair, my face. I don't know if I'm ready for that, but there's time to decide.

I look back at the cluster of bland maintenance buildings behind me, my final glimpse of home. In the distance the fragile spires of Fidelium shimmer in the sunlight. I remember when all I wanted was to travel here. And now I'm going so much further.

I take one last deep breath. Then I peel off both my gloves and stuff them into the pockets of my new Satori pants. This is it. This ship is my home now.

It's time to fly.

THANK YOU!

Thank you for reading *My Stars Shine Darkly*!

If you enjoyed reading this book, I hope you'll consider telling a friend about it or leaving a review. And if you want to stay in touch and find out when the next book in The Satori Chronicles comes out, you can subscribe to my newsletter at www.amysundberg.com.

Until then, happy reading!

ACKNOWLEDGMENTS

No novel is written in a vacuum, and I am very grateful for all the support I've received in creating this one.

First, thank you to my marvelous beta readers Barbara Webb, Les Howle, and Beth Dawkins for your critical feedback. And thank you to David Anthony Durham for your steadfast encouragement.

As always, I want to thank my mom, who encouraged my love of writing from a young age. I know if she were still alive, she'd be my biggest fan.

Thanks to my sister Heather, for being present and understanding as only a fellow Sundberg could.

In terms of influences for this particular novel, I have much gratitude for the work of Sylvia Engdahl and Ursula K. Le Guin.

Finally, thanks to my readers for exploring this new world and these new characters with me.

ABOUT THE AUTHOR

Whether Amy Sundberg is writing romping YA science fiction of self discovery or clever historical fantasy steeped in political intrigue, her novels feature intrepid heroines, refined prose, and questions of agency and power.

When she's not plotting how to someday have her very own library ladder or elaborate indoor reading tent, Amy is drooling over grand pianos and singing her heart out. She indulges her sweet tooth with some abandon (her favorite treat is pie, followed closely by ice cream). Driven by an insatiable curiosity, she has been lucky enough to travel to six continents. She can be easily coaxed into playing board games or going for a walk at a local park. She has a passion for theater, and she enjoys cooking a variety of delicious soups. She lives in Seattle with her adorable little dog.

For more information visit her website amysundberg.com or follow her on Twitter @amysundberg and Bluesky @amysundberg.bsky.social.